Water,

Wasted

RARE BIRD

LOS ANGELES, CALIF.

Water,

A Novel

Alex
Branson

Wasted

THIS IS A GENUINE RARE BIRD BOOK

Rare Bird Books
453 South Spring Street, Suite 302
Los Angeles, CA 90013
rarebirdlit.com

Set in Dante
Printed in the United States

10 9 8 7 6 5 4 3 2 1

Publisher's Cataloging-in-Publication Data

Names: Branson, Alex, author.
Title: Water, wasted / by Alex Branson.
Description: First Trade Paperback Original Edition. | A Genuine Rare Bird
Book | New York, NY; Los Angeles, CA: Rare Bird Books, 2020.
Identifiers: ISBN: 9781644281697 (pbk.) | 9781644281864 (ebook)
Subjects: LCSH Death—Fiction. | Family—Fiction. | Marriage—Fiction. |
Divorce—Fiction. | Floods—Fiction. | BISAC FICTION / General
Classification: LCC PS3602.R36498 W38 2020 | DDC 813.6—dc23

To Alana

2019

THERE WAS A DEAD armadillo covered in yellow paint in the middle of the state highway. It was about seven feet away from an armadillo-sized gap in the otherwise continuous yellow traffic lines. The armadillo was decaying steadily minus its thick, leathery back.

From the bridge leading south over the Missouri River into Armin to the civilization of the interstate a couple dozen miles north, State Highway 333 was dotted with dead armadillos. The soft parts of them inside decayed much quicker than their thick, leathery backs. After a while, their corpses looked like deflated footballs and time burned that armadillo blood black on the road.

The armadillos had come up to Missouri from the south in recent years because that was the weather of the world now.

1

THE ROOM EVERYONE SEES

1984

BARRETT CALLED IT A building. Not a home, not a house. A building.

His cousin was a fireman. Through him, he enlisted the help of seven other firemen to begin construction on this building. In the county, being a fireman was a volunteer gig, something you got paid miniscule wages for, if any. It was more like a fraternity. It was basically an Elks Lodge type of deal, minus the pool and all the ceremony.

Barrett told them of his vision of a square house full of square rooms, with no hallways, with the kitchen opening up into the living room which led into the bedroom which led into the combined bathroom/laundry room. He told them of simple, white walls, with no shelves or artwork, cleanly designed and without pomp or circumstance. As he told them his imagined blueprint, they all nodded, gathered around beers, and the oldest of the firemen drew out a rough draft on a sheet of graph paper.

Barrett measured the facial expressions of the firemen and could not decipher if they were impressed or not. The firemen seemed legion, singular. They all seemed to laugh at the same time and always innately knew if they should or shouldn't make eye contact.

The firemen didn't have any fires to worry about. They built houses.

Barrett enjoyed the time he spent with them. He considered volunteering for the fire department after this was over. Anything to break the monotony. All he did was go to work as one of the on-site mechanics at the Chrysler dealership in Osage, in that little town by the new interstate. He was still single despite trying. At the age of twenty-five, in the country, that felt worrisome. Most of the women that were single out here at twenty-five were divorcées.

They built the house slowly over the course of four months. Barrett was sleeping in a crumbling farmhouse on his dead uncle's property about five miles south. Barrett had been lucky enough to buy a couple acres on a little set of hills above the floodplains flanking the Missouri river. It was good, open territory. He bought a bright red mailbox and made himself a nice gravel road.

Half the house sported linoleum and the other sported carpet. The walls went up quickly and then they got it winter-proofed. The wiring and plumbing went in without incident. Barrett kept drawing things out, finding things to complain about, making last-minute requests. He needed another outlet. The kitchen should have a ceiling fan. What about a bay window in the living room? The firemen thought him reasonable overall and always obliged, but as they celebrated at the end of a day of work, Barrett would cross his arms and stare at the home, lost to himself.

The firemen were not psychologists. They were firemen. That meant that they built houses.

So this is it, then? This is what I got myself into. I can live my life out here alone and have some dignity about it, for once, Barrett thought.

When there was nothing left to sand, sweep, or wire, Barrett moved in furniture. A small, iron kitchen table with two chairs. Optimism. It was like something you would find in the mess hall of a battleship. Square, invulnerable, and shiny. What pots and pans he had sat in a brown box for weeks. He took most of his meals by microwave.

In the living room he bought a futon and a recliner. One to sleep on, one to watch television on. He went large for the recliner, getting a premium La-Z-Boy. It had wide arms and reclined perfectly horizontally and was wrapped in dark green leather. It was the most expensive item in the house. He bought no little trinkets to decorate his home with.

In his bedroom, he had a twin-sized bed and a bookshelf for all his paperbacks. Barrett digested Louis L'Amour books. He went on binges where he could read two a day, but could also go weeks without reading at all, either wandering around the fringes of his property or soaking in television during his off hours.

In the first night he slept in the new home, he wrapped his fingers around the corner of his small bed and thought a little but not too much because he had to work in the morning, which he thought a blessing.

Loneliness suits some people, I guess. More than others, at least. I just think love and companionship and stuff, that's for other people. It just is and there ain't no use beating myself up over it, he thought to himself.

Within the year, he was married.

2019

AMELIA HAD SPENT TWO thousand dollars during the last year putting various decorations and doodads into the windows of empty, closed storefronts for her "Armin Main Street Beautification Project," something she had been attempting to pitch to the various city bureaucrats since the first businesses began to close in 2008. She would gather wicker, arrange plastic flowers, paint small advertisements for the businesses that were still open on small, polished oak signs, and arrange all of them pleasantly on white linen.

She didn't have permission to do this. Most of the lots that the failed businesses were on were owned by out-of-town banks or property-grabbing LLCs that came in to scoop up cheap riverfront property in order to resell for a profit whenever the economy skewed north again. The city politicians she knew she called, and they just shrugged. Didn't have the authority. Best they could do was make a phone call on her behalf. It was all pointless. The individuals or business entities that actually owned the buildings didn't want any kind of liability for things going wrong on their property. Insurance-wise, it made everything real complicated. The safest option, financially, was the blanket no to all requests.

It was safer to ask for forgiveness than it was permission. The actual owners were hundreds of miles away. She used what social capital she could to get her way. Frankly, Amelia had to bully the locksmith into opening up the first abandoned store.

"This isn't in any way legal, ma'am," he told her.

"C'mon, Curtis. You known me for years. You think I'm asking you to do a bank heist?"

"If it ain't your property, I ain't popping the lock."

"Nobody will even notice. You know my friend, Mary Ann? She teaches at the school. Before Rose went and closed up shop and moved up to, what was it, DeSoto, I think? You know, up where her son teaches at the college? English, I think? Anyways, she, Mary Ann, used to come see Rose after her classes got out. Have you ever met her?"

"Who? Mary Ann?"

"Yeah."

"No," Curtis said.

"Real pretty number. About your age, I think? Single, too. Moved back here after she got that divorce a couple years ago. Now she was up in Columbia, with the high school. Her husband was supposed to be doing something with the business school, you know, but he did her wrong. You know how it is. Anyway, you should meet her. Ya'll would look cute together," Amelia said.

"I know what you're doing, Amelia," Curtis said.

"Oh, shut up. You know how us old ladies are. Can't stop talking. Anyway, Mary Ann is at school now, but she said she thinks she left her old engagement ring in the little cubby hole in the back wall by where she used to keep the register. Now her husband, or ex-husband, he said something bitter and asked for it back, and she wants to record herself throwing it into the river. Well, I suggested it, to be honest, but I think it's there. Curtis. Please."

"I don't know, Amelia. I want to."

"It's a powerful metaphor to be the guy who brings her old ring back. Shit, you'll probably have a white shining outline around you as you walk through that door. We should bring it back together. That'd be cute."

Eventually, they took a short drive down to the back door and popped the lock open.

"All right, go on back home, Curt. I'll call you later. Don't want you getting mixed up in all this."

Amelia went into more and more of these closed businesses. Over the course of six months, she had renovated the storefronts of seven businesses. All buildings on the riverfront had six foot by six foot display cases on both sides of the front door that were meant to display various goods or trinkets. A holdover from the fifties. She covered the windows in white linen so that you couldn't see the dilapidated interiors. She decorated the display cases with wicker chairs, novelty signs about wine, stuffed animals, and antique televisions. She would take spools of yarn, pile them by color into a pyramid, and place two decorative sweaters down next to them. She would place a large teddy bear onto a wooden rocking horse and put plastic cowboy hats on both of them. Amelia did this in broad daylight.

She used to date the Sheriff in high school. The only repercussions were social. She got called old, nosy, a busybody, and it was said that she needed a husband. Never within earshot, of course.

Small, old-fashioned towns do not accept change well. A building becoming more and more dilapidated year after year never evokes the focus that a proposed department store might.

People reflect on the ivy and the big oaks over cobblestone streets and do not consider that the sons and daughters that they send to college won't return. They don't figure that the rich donors who move out here from St. Louis will ever stop supporting the town's local traditional brass band or that they'll get bored of going to the wineries and overlooking the cliffs full of grapes leading down to the river. Once they realize that the locals are fiercely protective of the culture of their town and won't even let them get a seat on the hospital board, that care for the well-being of the town ends. They'll buy up some property and treat it just like anywhere else. They'll open up a property speculating limited liability corporation during the height of an economic downturn and buy up 1.3 million dollars' worth of property in Duden County.

Visitors might come to the riverfront drive in Armin and, thanks to Amelia, not even be able to tell that business after business was falling over and sliding into the Missouri River.

Amelia had lived an idle life. She had left her husband a few years back—a towering, passive man—after their daughter had passed, and she moved back to her hometown to be closer to her sister, and things were slow. The days seemed to be without a wavelength. An even-keeled thing, calm. Time seemed like a placid body of water. She didn't feel much, had no real sexual pleasure. Like bored people tend to do, she developed habits. Coffee well into the day, stopping at lunch. Lots of wheat bread, cream cheese. She walked to the library to get on the internet and send emails to old, faraway friends. She would show up at her sister Marie's home and bullshit around with her. She had fun, killed time, did things appropriately.

But it was always when she was alone that she felt the stillness and dead complacency not within her but within the air around her, and while she knew she didn't want to meet any other men (the idea embarrassed her too much to even begin to accept it), she could not figure out how to approach it.

She would daydream about catastrophic events happening. Meteors, floods. Invasions. Sexual assaults, home invasions, robberies. She did not approach them with fear in her head. They were tests, almost. She thought about them a lot. What she would do, how she would behave. She tried to not let herself give herself any easy answers.

She would be okay dying in an earthquake or a fire, but not in an assault. She would be able to easily get over a flood as long as she was able to keep her stuff dry (she had a large collection of crafts and books and other miscellaneous objects). She would rather have her stuff completely destroyed than damaged.

As she began thinking about these things, she noticed other things. A large tree branch over her home that, if struck by lightning, would collapse onto the roof above her kitchen table. While it did not have the mass to crush the entirety of the roof in, she wondered if it could spear her, in a way. She didn't share these thoughts. They were hers, and she would chuckle to herself about the glibness of it all.

She had had a long, uneasy life, and knew that she deserved the luxury of fantasizing about a violent death.

While flattening the corners of the white linen and rubbing out all air pockets, Amelia thought about a drunk driver veering off the road, ramping up on the curb, and smashing her against the glass and wicker of the display.

I wonder if the old wiring back there could just spark up and burst into flames, burning almost immediately through the thin metal holding up the big system of fluorescent lights and sealing the door off and making it unopenable. I think I would be able to throw myself through the glass. I'm not what I used to be but I could do that. I mean, I know it isn't sugar glass. If I went through it shoulder first the glass shards could cut me up. I could get an artery in my leg cut, it wouldn't even have to be at my head or throat. I might live for a couple days even, only to have it get infected.

I might live, still. Definitely if I was younger.

Amelia thought about youth constantly. She had always intended to marry young, right out of high school, but it didn't turn out that way. The idea of marriage sounded incredibly romantic to her. She essentially drifted through school, under the radar, slightly pretty, but bony and wispy. She didn't draw much attention from boys. There was a vague, understated element about her that seemed to cast an aura to teenage boys that somehow, someway, they would be punished for trying to have sex with her. She seemed downtrodden and serious. She seemed unconcerned about men.

After graduation, she stuck around town. In a town that small, new people didn't arrive much. There were weekenders, but they were mainly concerned with each other. They ran through the town, got what they needed from the wineries or the bars, and rifled away on Sunday. The idea of a local didn't mean shit to them. If anything, it was negative. A definite yokel vibe is cultivated in a folksy bubble.

She had romantic visions of men that would arrive, but they were never emotional or grandiose or metaphorical. Someone dressed nice, someone pleasant. Someone with a mustache. The fantasies were almost analytical. Young Amelia described minute details of fake dates with fake men to herself.

The locals she knew meandered in and out of relationships with each other and there was a general vibe that sooner or later everyone would settle down with someone by their mid-twenties. If you didn't get married the first time around, the high school sweethearts that married after high school would divorce and you could catch one on the second go-around.

She felt like a spinster at twenty-five and laughed about it. In her future husband daydreams, he started looking more and more like a lump.

She was married in a year. And she left the town and immediately felt superior to it. It definitely hurt when she swallowed her pride to return south years later, after everything had gone so terribly wrong. She let Barrett keep the furniture because he wouldn't have got any if she didn't.

Because of her mindset prior to marriage, and because of how it burned down and withered gray so steadily and predictably, Amelia didn't feel like a fully realized individual until her divorce. That, despite her being close to fifty at this point in her life, she was destined to have that failed marriage, and that because of who she was and the type of man she had sought out, the marriage was bound to last a long period of time, and that it all had to have happened how it happened because that was her worldview at the time, and now that it is over, she didn't have to have any hang-ups about it.

She felt no hostility toward Barrett, but almost something worse. No malice, but her emotions all reflected the crystallizing thought she held about him, that *you had me then. You had to have had me then because you were what I wanted but I am not that anymore and you cannot have me and I know this better than I know anything else in the world.*

Now, ironing out white linen in an abandoned storefront, the adolescent daydreams returned. Barrett, tall, face casting some kind of whiny brooding, stood over her. They began having sex, and he came inside of her. And time passed, but it didn't, and she had her daughter.

And their daughter grew up and it was not exactly memory, but definitely memory's kin, because everything happened as it did in reality except their daughter had not died at twenty-three and in this fantasy she did not imagine them hugging, crying, talking about anything, nothing was addressed or swallowed or dealt with, she fantasized about her and her daughter shopping for clothes at that nice mall in Chesterfield, and when one credit card was rejected, they laughed and used another.

And she was not crying or smiling but ironing out the white sheet to wrap around the composite board display, which she would line with small pictures, advertisements, and a rocking chair.

The reality was she was ready to be alive, and she was thinking, and was good at being alive for once, but she felt too old to try anything new, so she tried to bide her time well and have fun.

Amelia began to think about plane crashes.

1836

Philadelphia Germans! Do you see your brothers and sisters of the city of Philadelphia losing their essence? The pride of their ethnicity? For too long have our sons and daughters abandoned the purity and pride of living a German life, and have begun to abandon their lineage, betray their ancestors, to forget the language that is their birthright, and become nothing more than the non-people that are the American mutt? Can you imagine your daughter, your son, begetting with the Irish? With the Italians? Or even a Jew?

Be proud, Germans! We offer a different idea! A new weltanschauung for the modern German-American!

The new Rhineland awaits! Field leader Koeper has marked a fertile land on the banks of the Missouri River, and planning for a new township has already begun! With the strife and starvation in our homeland, this may be the only way to ensure the German way of life. I will hope that the reader of this pamphlet understands the holy cause that this undertaking truly is. While our forebearers are in turmoil, and our kin on the dangerous brink of assimilation, this may be the best chance to guarantee German purity moving forward.

The Armin township will be named for the Germanic hero Arminius, a brave warrior and general who defeated the Romans eons ago. This town, named for the man that guaranteed that the German way of life would not be tainted by outsiders, will seek the same goal he did.

Cultural independence for Germans!

10,350 acres have been purchased and are available for those who pledge to join this township. The fertile valley has been called a veritable Eden by Friedrich Koeper, who has written at length about the German potential of the Duden River Valley.

Come to register at the Philadelphia Settlement Society for Proud Germans at 130 Hursch Street in Philadelphia, PA.

MARCH 2019

So when the rain came down in sheets so quickly that it obfuscated all vision in front of him, a teenager pulled his truck off of a dirt road and meandered through a short patch of gravel toward a small carport underneath a short bridge elevating yet another country road. And since the truck itself was weathered and tended to groan, he had tentatively decided to wait out the worst of the rain and make the last stretch toward the paved state highway after a brief respite in this little enclosed cover.

He had just gotten some pussy and had about a three-hour deadline to get back home, at around 8 a.m., when his parents would wake up and notice him missing or wouldn't.

He had decided to head out the night before at about one in the morning, and didn't really get any high-quality sleep, just nervous postcoital naps as the girl dug her head onto his shoulder, and he felt tense and nervous and content. Her name was Harper and she had a tendency to roll around in her sleep. He felt happy, but tense. Like the happiness was a thread that could be snapped in a split second, so that he had to enjoy it while he could.

At five thirty he got nervous about his parents waking up and seeing the truck missing and calling him and chastising him so he told Harper this and she pouted but then she heard the automated coffee pot click on and, thinking it was one of her parents, spurred him into leaving. He slunk out the front door as the sun oozed into the living room, and he climbed into his truck, tired but smiling meekly.

So he was very tired, very pleased with himself, and in this mindset of temporarily successful peskiness he slid his car underneath the country bridge on a gravel road and waited for the torrents of rain to let up so that he could at least see the road in front of him.

And alternative rock music was playing lightly on the radio.

And he put it into park.

And he thought about the curvature of Harper's legs and fell asleep.

And the engine ran idly and the gasoline was broken down and the car emitted carbon dioxide and other, unimportant chemicals, and in the unventilated solace of the space beneath the bridge it built up enough that it was poisonous to the human body, and his sleeping nose wafted in the poison and put it into his bloodstream, and he died wordlessly in a quietly purring pick-up truck underneath a bridge in rural Missouri.

⫶⫶⫶

AMELIA RARELY DROVE. THE mid-size sedan seemed to churn on gravel roads, and she didn't know if that was bad or not, so she would suck her teeth the whole time she clutched the steering wheel.

"Whoever thought that gravel made a good road? I swear," she said.

She often talked to herself when she was anxious and alone. Amelia thought about Barrett. She imagined him in the car, responding to her question, saying something like "gravel seems fine to me." Amelia scoffed, again, to herself.

Amelia usually visited Barrett after coming back into town from Columbia or Washington, usually for some shopping trip, or to visit old friends. This meant she would be coming in south on highway 333 and could just swing right off the highway into his driveway. She tried coming in from the east this time, going over the bridge in McMaren, and winding through some back roads in the hills. She didn't know the way.

The sedan grinded to a stop on the gravel, and she pretended to touch up her makeup in the mirror so that people would think that was why she stopped. She contemplated calling Barrett, but she didn't want to owe him anything. She decided to take a twenty-minute detour to loop around to highway 333 and go in toward Barrett's house from the south.

　　　　　　　　　　　　　　　WATER, WASTED

He didn't know she was coming, so she wouldn't be late. She imagined how he would come out of the trailer as she stepped out of her car, still drinking coffee at three in the afternoon, waiting for her to talk first, and she smiled.

"Oh, Lord," Amelia said to herself. "If I didn't check up on that man, God knows what he would be living like."

Amelia put it in reverse and started heading back the long way. It was a calmer drive. No mystery involved. She turned left and headed north on the other backroad.

The car clambered into drive. The gravel appeared near-black when wet after the morning's storm. Small, shallow pools of water lay uselessly strewn in the ditches framing the slightly (albeit strategically) elevated country roads.

The countryside did seem to evoke something. She liked how the henbit weed made all the empty farm plots burst into purple before they tilled it all up. It didn't seem appropriate. It seemed almost profane in how neat it was. She remembered the first spring she had been living with Barrett, how she asked him later in the afternoon why all of a sudden the winter farm plots turned purple with that stubbled foliage, how he said, "Yep, they get purple."

That wasn't a good enough answer. And how he got tired with her when she said that he had lived out here for his entire life and he didn't know what the weed was called that turned everything purple. That is what he did. He never got angry with her, not even once. Just tired. She made him tired, and he would get quiet, but she would never let him rest. She got him to call it henbit a few months after she dug the answer up in some agricultural pamphlet.

She liked driving past the henbit. She liked the lack of traffic, so she didn't feel bad about how she stared out the window for just a few lingering moments too long, probably driving too fast, oozing into all the other lanes of traffic or off the road.

The gravel road crested a hill.

Moments later she saw an odd, splotchy blend of brown and red out of the side of her eye, gyrating slowly as she scanned the muddy purple farmland, and whipped back, and her eyes got wide, and she slowed down the car as she processed the scene.

There was what appeared to be a well-groomed golden retriever (no leash, no collar) slowly, casually eating a roadside deer corpse, with its neck driven into the ground and bent back into itself like a parabola, its eyes cast upward, past the dog into the overcast sky.

The dog did not regard her as the car slowed. The dog was in a low trench by the side of the road slowly chewing on what appeared to be the low, fleshy part of the deer's chest. She wanted to stop the car, but couldn't make it her place to do so. The scene confused her. There was a casual primality to it that was confusing. She wished Barrett was here. He would immediately say to "run it off" or "ignore it" or tell her it was common or tell her that the dog would get sick. Something.

After a minute of driving past she circled back and found the dog still casually chewing on the road kill. The dog glanced up when she honked her horn and looked for a few moments before dipping its head back down. She honked again. The dog did not regard her.

As she stepped out of the car the dog looked peaceful. His golden snout was wet with with wwthin blood. He panted and looked at her. She was afraid it would attack her, but it immediately stepped away from the dead animal and sauntered toward her in a happy trot, and she retreated quickly toward one of the backside doors and emerged with a towel to wipe the blood off.

The dog was more concerned with sniffing, and tried to work its nose around the towel toward her, and left smudges of blood on her white khaki shorts. It had no tags, no collar, but she decided that it was lost because of the fact that it didn't appear mangy or unkempt.

She scanned for nearby homes and saw none. She considered what was nearby and where she could drive to ask, but was scared away by the presence of "no trespassing" signs and rusted piles of junk.

The dog needed little convincing to get into the car. She imagined Barrett becoming very tired with her. She considered naming the dog Henbit, in order to rub it in. An imaginary petty victory over an imaginary transgression.

The gravel road crested another short hill to reveal, seemingly, a way out. She saw a bridge in the distance, a road running beneath it and looping back around, and a pickup truck idling underneath it blocking the path.

She paused a moment, waiting for the truck to move. Just a red truck, idling. It was too narrow a passageway to even open your door in. There was no way someone just started that car and left. She waited a few moments, then sighed, and pressed on the horn gently just to alert the driver of her presence.

Nothing happened. She honked with more force. Nothing stirred.

Amelia put her car in park and unlocked the door, but as she reached for the handle she hesitated. The dog was sniffing a bag of modeling clay she kept in the backseat. She could feel the force of his tail hitting the back of her driver's seat.

Carol posted that thing online about how there were people who would go to Wal-Mart and take pictures of a lot of people and pick the ones that they wanted to kidnap later. They'd block in their cars when they were in the parking lot and would abduct them, throw them into vans, bind and gag them and stuff. Like how in the one cannibal movie the buffalo guy always asked women for help loading stuff into the van.

Does this scene seem just as innocuous? What if, the second I get out of the car, someone pops out from under the bridge or jumps down and grabs me? What then?

But what would people want with an old woman anyway? I mean, I'm not that old, and I was very pretty once, so I can imagine. But isn't there easier ways to do this? I mean, if I had to bet, I'd say someone drives on this gravel road under this bridge twenty to thirty times a week, tops. And even then, most of the people driving this road are probably drunk teenagers or closeted gay guys who have to hide out away from their wives or weird hermits or oh God what am I even talking about.

Amelia opened the door, grabbed a flashlight for defense from the glovebox, and took a few tentative steps toward the truck.

If it comes to ransom I think my family, my sisters for sure, would definitely pay a lot for me. Barrett, God bless his soul, would scrounge up whatever crumbs he has to help. He'd sell everything he owns, I think. Maybe I should go get him to figure this out. He's only a few miles away. He'd just drive right by I bet. Good lord.

I'd play it smart as a hostage. I think I'd handle it way better than most people. I'd never give them the satisfaction, even if they did the—oh God—the sex stuff. I'd bide my time, and I'd make sure they go down. I'd get through it better than most people, but I think, dealing with it after, I'd deal with it way worse than most people. It'd break me. But they couldn't break me, I don't think. Not during it. No way.

She approached the red truck. It was only a single cabin truck, and she could see the back of the man's head. Light, slightly curly brown hair, short. Head cocked to the side, loped slightly.

Oh God, a fucking drunk. Good lord.

She tapped the flashlight on the driver's side window as she came around to look at the man's face. Her lips curled tight and her nosed pressed out and she looked like she wanted to give him an earful.

"Excuse me. Excuse me," she said loudly.

She got a good look at the face. Eyes closed, a nice roman nose, chin scruff, and pockmarked face. Young.

Good lord, he's not even a man. It's a god damn kid.

"Oh my God, kid, wake up, I cannot fucking wait to figure out who your mother is."

Amelia tapped on the window authoritatively. It was relatively early now, around nine in the morning, and the downpour from last night made the air heavy with water. She saw lots of fog sweeping off the river this morning.

Amelia kept tapping.

All of a sudden, the anger that she felt morphed. The red, righteous anger flipped upside down in her stomach into a kind of intense, narrow panic.

Wake up, kid. Wake up. WAKE UP. WHY AREN'T YOU WAKING UP.

In one fluid motion she ripped at the door handle and, once it gave, grasped his wrist wrathfully, and, feeling how cold it was, shrunk backward, pale, and screamed a tiny, muted scream, and, in one last moment of hope, shoved his shoulder sternly, and finding him slumped, screamed and backed against the cool, rigid concrete supporting wall of the underpass and fumbled for her cell phone.

The lady asked her to check for a pulse, she did. None. She told Amelia to wait. Stay on the line, she said.

She waited.

Oh, God, I can't go just sit in my car and wait. I can't just leave him there who is he what happened how does this happen here where are they where are they

I can't just go in my car and leave him there. What if I know his mother or one of his aunts and what if they found out I just sat in my car oh my God.

Amelia sat on a damp patch of grass on the side of the gravel road right outside the mouth of the underpass. She made sure she was in eyesight of the boy. She stared at the back of his head.

Light brown, slightly curly hair. Nobody with hair like that should die.

There were still birds chirping. It was late winter now, but she swore she could smell honeysuckle growing nearby. She could see the tree line in the distance through a small film of mist.

I can't believe the birds are fucking chirping I cannot fucking believe it I cannot believe no one is here yet I can't believe this. I can't believe this! What the fuck is anyone supposed to do about the worst things. I wish all these fucking birds would just die. I really do.

The dog had snaked its way out of the back seat and through the open front door of the car and trotted slowly toward her. The golden retriever looked like it was smiling. Amelia extended her hand toward the dog to pet him as she sat in the wet grass. The dog weaved around the outreached hand to try and start licking her face. Amelia's cold facial expression did not change as she palmed the dog's face and pushed him back. The dog started licking her hand. After a few moments, it got bored, and started sniffing at the back tires of the truck.

Oh, God, I remember Edi's funeral. Barrett shaking everyone's hands. What the fuck was he doing that for? Oh, God.

The dog started heading to the driver's side door.

"Hey!" Amelia yelled.

The dog looked backward. It paused a moment, then took another step toward the door.

"HEY," she yelled louder, "Get the fuck back over here right fucking now. Not the time."

The dog turned around lazily and made his way back to her as she heard sirens coming down a gravel road to the south.

What the fuck? That's all I can say about anything. Just what the fuck.

Amelia stood up and crossed her arms. The dog sat next to her.

Oh, my God, Amelia thought, looking at the dog, *I can't keep this dog now. Oh, my God. I got to get rid of it. Who was I kidding? I'm such a bad person.*

Tears started welling up in Amelia's eyes as she looked at the truck, then the dog, then toward the sirens, then toward the dog, and then toward the truck again.

Oh, God, maybe if I was stronger. I'm so sick of trying to be strong. Just let me be.

THE GAS STATION ATTENDANT stood behind the counter in his gas station with his hands on the sides of the cash register. The gas station was empty. The Gas Station Attendant was fairly tall and a little overweight. He wore wide, brown-framed glasses and had long brown hair, just about to his shoulders. His face was covered in stubble but was otherwise pretty round and featureless. He was wearing a yellow and red polo shirt with the company's logo on it tucked into high and tight jeans. The way he held his hands on the register gave him the visage of a gargoyle. His posture was rigid.

People can buy anything at a gas station in Missouri. At the Gas Station Attendant's gas station, one could buy alcohol, cigarettes, GPS navigation systems, T-shirts, paper towels, toilet paper, coffee, chips, or books. There was a milkshake machine in the gas station in case you wanted to have a milkshake that was from the gas station. Soft or hard pretzels. There are slowly rotating cylindrical meats of various regional styles that one can eat on a freshly steamed bun. The Gas Station Attendant even knew of a gas station up near the Ozarks that you could even get a haircut at. Really, the only thing you couldn't get at the gas station is a gun.

The area near the hot food had two tables. The Gas Station Attendant knew a myriad of old men on a first-name basis who liked to buy a coffee and a newspaper and post up in this area, talking to each other as their morning ritual, greeting everyone that came in.

"I hold the door here so much that you guys should pay me!" is what all of their joke was to the Gas Station Attendant.

When he heard the joke he would smile normally.

The Gas Station Attendant knows that the Gas Station is an important cultural gathering place out here in isolated communities. It has almost nothing to do with gasoline. This is why the Gas Station Attendant does not complain about his job.

At this moment, the gas station was uncharacteristically empty. The Gas Station Attendant had a moment to himself. He headed to the front door and propped it open with a garbage can. The gas station was just above the floodplain north of the river, right where highway 333 and Supplemental Road Q met. The ground was still low enough that if the Gas Station Attendant looked out of the front door, to the south, he could just make out the river and see the low fog. The weather was just warm enough to leave it open for a minute. The Gas Station Attendant liked the smell of the rain and of the river.

The Gas Station Attendant saw the sirens before he heard them. Heading on the bridge over the river he saw two police cars and an EMS vehicle heading north. His posture didn't change, and he watched the vehicles intently to see where they turned. The Gas Station Attendant took a cigarette out of a pack in his front pocket and ripped the filter off and lit it.

The Gas Station Attendant watched intently as the vehicles zoomed right past Supplemental Road Q and turned left onto a gravel road a half minute later. The Gas Station Attendant grunted.

An old man waved to the Gas Station Attendant as he stepped out of his car and approached.

"Man, what was that about?" he asked, pointing toward the sirens.

The Gas Station Attendant shrugged.

"Well, guess we'll know soon enough. You know how this town is," he said, walking inside.

The Gas Station Attendant put his cigarette out carefully on the sidewalk and placed it in his shirt pocket. The Gas Station Attendant walked inside.

ᛞᛞᛞ

Harper fretted over what to wear. They couldn't afford to buy anything, and a sixteen-year old girl rarely had funeral-ready outfits in her wardrobe. She settled on a gray sweater and khakis. It took her over an hour to get ready.

Some funerals are sadder than others. There's no exact formula for the contest. When a high school kid dies, it ripples. Parents in the town, even if they never met the kid or knew his parents or ever even heard his name, imagine what it would be like if it was their own kids who died and take the death to heart. Ruminate. Acquaintances of the kid were now their friend. Friends are now close friends. Close friends become brothers. Girlfriends become wives.

It's usually a car. If it's not a car, it's usually drugs. Opiates, mostly. Very rarely heroin. People wanted to know how he died immediately.

In the car? Was he drunk?

They don't know yet. Toxicology didn't come in yet. But why would he be out at that hour?

Harper showed up to the funeral with her mother. She begged her mother to come. There weren't many sophomores there. Derek was a senior.

The man started talking. The religious man. Whatever the Lutheran one was called. The religious man said his name. She choked up a little. Derek was his name.

When I think of him I just think of the name him like of course its him who else would him be. And now hes gone and he was just here and now im here. And im alone with all these people who loved him and I just have to sit here staring around crying because I don't know who knows.

But I was there.

In a small town a young death is expected sooner or later. The mourning ritual is understood and inevitable. Gestures will be made. The basketball team will dedicate the season to Derek. The valedictorian will mention his name during their speech and everyone will clap. Things have to be done. Facebook posts will be made in his honor over the next three years with less and less frequency. However, things will proceed more or less as usual. They, the children, will feel more adult. They will gradually understand that adulthood is not independence or emotional stability or self-discovery. Adulthood is concrete, not prone to metaphor. It is filled with duty, first to yourself, then to others.

Harper fiddled with her hands. The twin doors opened and people formed a line to view Derek. Harper grabbed her mother by the elbow and got in line. Harper was staring at the floor. Then there was his face, still, almost polished looking, animatronic. This Derek had no acne. It wasn't Derek.

A few older girls raised their eyebrows when she hurried out the front door of the funeral home crying.

She pulled at the locked car door of her mother's station wagon. Her mother followed behind and unlocked it. Harper sat down. She turned to her mother.

"Mom, I have to tell you something."

Her mother just looked at her.

"Mom," she continued.

"I'm listening. What?"

"…"

"What is it?"

"I just. I just want to go home, please. Please."

"What is it though?"

"Can I just fucking go home? PLEASE."

They drove home with the silence vibrating all around them.

BARRETT HAD HEARD ABOUT the death at the grocery store, at the gas station, and at the bar. It dominated conversation and any conversation not related to the boy's death always seemed to steer itself back to it. Everyone either knew him or knew someone who knew him. It wasn't a big town and he played football. It was only yesterday.

The news was still with him when he went home. He tried to watch a replay of a St. Louis Cardinals baseball game on Fox Sports Midwest at three in the morning. He couldn't shake the feeling. He struggled to not think about the boy. When he thought about the boy, he thought about his daughter. In order to shake the feelings of his daughter, he tried to think about the boy. But death is death, it is a universal black line that consumes equally, and his death was the same as her death, and it's like she died all over again, at least a little bit.

There is a gnawing little thing in our guts that chews harder when it is looked at.

Barrett knew that no matter how the rest of his life turned out it would always carry that gnawing thing for better or worse. Barrett is old. He is sixty years old. His dad died at forty-two. Heart attack. Barrett stays up all night and gives up trying to sleep at six. He makes a pot of coffee and turns on the television. His back hurts.

By noon he worked up the courage to drive to Amelia's house to ask if he could look through Edi's things. Barrett paused as he says her name out loud. Edi. It had been a long time since he had said her name out loud.

Barrett eased into his truck and took a deep breath. He felt comfortable driving and when he found himself feeling restless, he often would aimlessly drive around the countryside listening to the radio. He pulled out of his driveway onto State Highway 333 and headed south past the gas station over the bridge into Armin. He went straight past the fire station onto Main Street and took a left after the old folks' home and followed that road down a hill into the wooded hollow where Amelia lived.

The road Barrett followed was one of the only freshly paved roads in the region. A new slate of houses had been built down here a couple years ago and they were nice enough to merit the road getting redone. He drove down here pretty regularly. He told himself it was because of the new road and the nice, cool feel of the low valley but it also just so happened to have a four-way stop close to Amelia's house and gave Barrett a view of Amelia's driveway without his truck being seen from the window.

Barrett lingered at the four-way when he saw Amelia's driveway. It was empty. He sighed and turned away from her home, back into the woods.

Need a minute to gather my thoughts, he told himself.

An hour later, Barrett was thirty miles north sitting in a fast-food parking lot eating hamburgers wordlessly, listening to sports radio. He kept his head down, careful not to make eye contact with anyone doing the same.

He thought about Edi. He sighed. He put down a hamburger and put his truck into reverse.

"Welp," he said to no one, "Guess if I'm going to do it, I'm going to do it."

He pulled back onto State Highway 333 and crossed the interstate, heading south, driving with one hand and eating with the other.

The road south into Armin was rough. In the winter, you had to be careful because the road snaked abruptly back and forth, making it an absolute nightmare in the snow. This was the spot where the flat farmlands of Northern Missouri give way to the creeping hills and overgrowth of the Ozarks. Hills burst out of the ground in nonsense patterns, the roads shear through cut limestone growths, and sudden valleys put the road into free fall. There is about one inch of buffer between the road and the forest. Deer fearfully scramble all over the asphalt. Barrett had driven these roads thousands of times, and idly slid back and forth for mile after mile, juggling the gas and the brake.

About ten miles in, Barrett saw a man standing in the middle of the road. There were no cars nearby. He was wearing a black suit jacket with a white shirt underneath and a black tie. His hair was neat and parted. He was squatting near the road overlooking the remains of a deer that had been hit by a car. Barrett applied the brakes as his truck approached the man, who seemed unconcerned. Barrett eventually came to a complete stop. The man did not turn around to regard him. After a moment, Barrett lowered his window to speak.

"You all right, bud?" Barrett called out.

The man turned slowly. The man had a blank facial expression. He didn't seem to convey any relief or pain or confusion—he just looked. Barrett waited for the man's response. He lingered and turned his attention back toward the dead deer. Barrett could have sworn his face was twitching.

"Do you—do you need a hand, bud?" Barrett asked.

"A hand?" the man repeated, monotonically.

"Yeah. You got a car around here?" Barrett asked.

"I need hand, bud," the man stated, uneasily. His words mimicked Barrett's drawl. He seemed to be evaluating each word as he said it.

Barrett frowned as he stepped out of the car. This wasn't uncommon. It was the right thing to do to drag the deer off the road so nobody would hit it again. He'd done it before.

"I'm Barrett. What's your name?"

Barrett stuck out his hand. The man looked at it for a brief moment before shaking it.

"Yes," the man said, "yes."

"Your name?"

"Yes, my name. I'm just a man," the man said.

"All right, Mr. Mann, wanna grab this leg and I'll grab the other?" Barrett said, already moving to pull at the dead deer.

"Mr. Mann, that's right," the man said.

"What's up, buddy? You helping or what?" Barrett said, a little frustrated.

"Who did this?" the man said, pointing at the deer.

"Some car. Out of towner, probably. Didn't think to move it, just kept going. Who knows," Barrett said.

He looked up from the deer to find the man close to him, staring, wide-eyed, lips taught but not smiling. Barrett was larger than him by a few inches, but the man seemed completely unafraid. Barrett dropped the leg and backed up.

"The fuck are you doing?" Barrett yelped.

"I know you," the man said.

There were just the two men and the car. Barrett's truck idled nearby. The dead deer lay at their feet. All through the forest, the gray trees of winter had started to live. It always smelled like rain, no matter the weather.

The man kept staring at Barrett, unmoving.

"You don't know me," Barrett said, tensely.

"You are a witness," the man stated.

"What the fuck are you talking about?" Barrett said.

"You get to see," the man stated.

"See what? Give me one fucking reason I don't kick your little ass," Barrett yelled.

"Little ass," the man repeated, staring back down at the deer.

"What you doing out here? Where's your car? Are you some kind of little freak? How'd you get here?" Barrett demanded.

"I don't get to decide where I go," the man said.

The deer had an open wound from the impact of the car that had hit it. The man lowered his hand and placed it inside of the deer's carcass. His face was tense and kept twitching. Barrett backed up and looked around. He started walking alongside the gravel that flanked the road, trying not to lose his footing, and moving back to his truck.

"I didn't expect to see you this quickly," the man said.

"Excuse me?"

"I see it around you. You stink of it. You are going to see, do you understand? You are more like my Little Ass than them."

"Fuck you," Barrett said, jumping into his truck.

The man pulled his hand out of the deer. It was covered in blood. He pulled a handkerchief out of his breast pocket and began wiping his hands. Barrett cast one last look at him before putting the truck into drive, but when he looked back up to pull away, the man was standing in front of his truck. His face was not twitching.

"You have to remember," the man said, "to not take it personally."

Barrett put the car in reverse and abruptly swung around the man. He gunned the gas, frantically looking back into the rearview mirror. The man was standing there, facing the departing truck, not moving. Barrett turned a corner, and the man and the dead deer were out of sight. Barrett scrambled for his cell phone. He pulled up Amelia's number. He called it and immediately hung up. He put the cell phone down and picked up one of his remaining hamburgers.

"Fuck, fuck, fuck," Barrett said, "I can't, I, fuck, she'll think I'm drunk or fucking nuts, fuck, fuck. Fucking tourists! Fuck! I'm too old for—shit!"

Barrett rubbed his hands on his face. He breathed steadily as he drove down the road.

It was just a guy, it was just a guy, maybe he needed help, maybe he was crazy, concussed... And someone could easily fuck up their car if they slid into that deer... Fuck. Goddamn it. I'm acting like a pussy. Fuck. I'm being ridiculous, Barrett thought.

He turned the car back around and began to head back to the man and the dead deer. He used the car around the corner and saw the dead deer in the distance, alone. He pulled to the narrow gravel strip flanking the road and got out of his car.

"Hello? You out here? Do you—you need help, right? You need help, mentally or medically? I'll help," Barrett said.

There was no answer. Nothing to indicate that a man had been here. Just a deer with a hole in its side. Barrett yelled a few more times but nothing changed. No man emerged from the wood seeking aid.

Barrett took a step forward toward the deer to drag it into the woods. A car slowly passed him as he grabbed it. He waved at the driver and drug the deer off the asphalt and rolled it down the gravel into the woods below.

He got back in his car and drove to Amelia's home.

◈◈◈

AMELIA DROVE TO THE spot she found the dog at. The deer corpse was gone. People were always picking these up and butchering them. Usually, they would pretend that they shot them. Maybe make jerky out of the venison. She opened the back door of her car and the dog came trotting out.

The police and the paramedics had told her to just let the dog go.

"Country dogs roam all over, but they always go back home. Besides, we got bigger things to worry about right now," one cop said.

The process was awful. She answered questions at the scene and they drove her back to the tiny little police station way up north in Howe City, thirty minutes away, because the body was found in Howe County. She didn't even know any of the cops who lived up here. Her lip curled the whole ride as she looked out the window in the squad car as it drove north on State Highway 333.

After, they drove her back to her car. The dog was still there. She sighed and pushed it into her backseat. Then, when she got home the Armin Police were waiting for her. She pushed the dog into her laundry room and they drove her to the Armin Police Station, which was just the annex building next to the City Hall. Everyone in the department knew her and was very apologetic. They asked all the same questions the Howe cops did, and Amelia sat there, gray faced, thinking about how rude it was none of these young men in uniform offered her anything to drink. Amelia frowned the whole day, from start to finish. After getting back home for the second time, she got the dog back into her car and left again.

"Go home," she said to the dog.

The dog stared at her, tail wagging. The whole ride up it had been trying to jump into the front seat and lick Amelia's face.

"Go home," she said, "Get out, okay. I can't keep you. Not now. I'm sorry. Go."

The dog cocked its head to the side. It looked at her, and then got a little apprehensive about making eye contact and started peering side to side. Amelia opened her mouth to tell it to go away again, but suddenly, from the woods behind her, she heard a slow and low rumbling groan. It was strung out and seemed to have a deep vibrato to it. She immediately thought it was a bear and grabbed her front door handle. Before she even had the chance to open it, however, the dog darted off straight in the direction of the bellow.

"Hey! No! Don't!"

Amelia climbed into the car quickly as she saw the sleek golden tail wind its way into the brown, rocky woods. She locked the doors and rolled the windows down and listened in the direction it had gone. Ten seconds later, another groan, but not like the first. Amelia couldn't describe it, but…it seemed sad. Powerful and pitiful. Like in movies when a great beast gets a thorn in its paw.

"It's all in my head. I'm in my own head. Dog ran off, which is what I said I wanted, I suppose," she said.

In times of stress, Amelia imagined her daughter watching her. Not in a religious or spiritual way, but like a hypothetical. Amelia liked to imagine what her daughter would think of her at any given moment. In the imagination, just like reality, Amelia never actually verbalized to her what she thought, just flashed a facial expression.

It was impossible not to think about her. Always studious, always mumbling, always with her little black leather idea book.

The big writer, Amelia thought.

Amelia calmed herself while thinking about her daughter as she stared off into the overgrown brown and gray woods and tried to locate either a dog or a weird, groaning bear.

Edi wrote because she told herself she was a writer. Growing up, in college, she said she wrote. She was a writer. That's what she told people. So the writing itself was a defense mechanism toward protecting that identity. She had said it enough that she had to write something, anything, in order to prove that she was, in fact, who she said she was. After writing enough, Edi, in the fake-it-until-you-make-it mindset, finally learned to make a truth out of the lie. She wrote. So, she was a writer.

She didn't turn out to be the writer she wanted to be, however. She loved literary fiction, finely-tuned, spindly tales like Yates and Fitzgerald, and she wanted to evoke some kind of dissection of a town or era or feeling, but her writing never went that way. She mostly wrote fantasy stories about lost people who never quite became great, but became close, became essential cogs for something very important, but were never quite rewarded for their valor. Her stories typically featured mushrooms as big as trees as a key calling card. She purposefully wrote those into every novel and story.

She finished her first book when she was twenty-one. No one knew. She edited it, formatted it, set it up as an eBook for sale for three dollars on a website, and advertised it only to a small part of a fantasy-based web forum and made about forty dollars off of it. She cringed at every notification of a purchase. She didn't process it. She described the book as 'fine.' It was called *The Trees of Iron County*. She had decided to disown the book by the time she wrote her next one, and didn't want to talk about it or acknowledge it. It was about a girl plucked from obscurity from a suburban neighborhood by a hairy, cloaked man-creature and, suddenly waking up in a swamp, tracks what brought her there, and, unwillingly, becomes the force who unites a village with some sentient tree men who are, thusly, able to fight off an encroaching dark cult. At the end it is revealed that the dark, hairy figure who brought her there was some kind of Bigfoot-esque figure, unnamed, who, during the battle, she sees strangling out the leader of the cult in some wooded glen, and, after he falls, turns onto her, and she wakes up in her bed again. And that would all be good, but Edi added an epilogue that seems to say more than the whole book did. She lived her life normally, telling no one what had happened, but still had this hunger within her, the discontentment, this bland grayness that she had to carry silently for the rest of her life, and she struggled with having feelings of simultaneous hate and love for the hairy, Bigfoot-like creature.

Edi had not let either of her parents read the book.

The second book was called *The Riverside Ascetic*. She had thought of the title before she had written the book. She wrote it almost as a direct response to what she saw as the faults in her first book; the generic nature of a young girl plucked from obscurity, her being an obvious (to her) Mary Sue character, caused a reactionary response to make her main character entirely inhuman, a slender, genderless monk from an order whose purpose was to go out and catalog all possible tragedies. They lived in a cave on the hills of a river and ate only bread and drank only water. Edi maintained the fantasy setting; she gravitated toward it naturally, and she felt she could accomplish certain themes within it. The main character goes out into the world, into various fantasy kingdoms, following the trail of one particularly evil mercenary, detailing his exploits for the audience, before the main character themself is captured by the mercenary and forced to write about their own torture and death. Soon after doing their duty and dying, a Bigfoot-esque creature (who is alluded to throughout the book) emerges from the foliage to face off with the mercenary.

Edi had not allowed her parents to read the book. She said it would be "too depressing" for them, and she didn't want them to worry.

The third book was the last. She rushed to finish it because she was going to die. It was called Pig Iron, and it was about a group of mercenaries who take a contract out to go to a magical Orcish kingdom and steal a cache of diamonds for an archaeologist. By doing so, they insert themselves into a battle between native and invading gods fighting over the very fabric of the world. She had rushed to finish the book because her blood was filled with cancer.

Neither Barrett nor Amelia had been able to bring themselves to read it.

Amelia shook herself back to the present. She did not like to think about the books. The woods were quiet. There was no sign of life and no sounds emanating from them. She drove home with nothing on her mind.

ılıılıılı

THE GAS STATION ATTENDANT's shift ended. He grabbed a few bags of garbage from a back room filled with mops and sawdust and headed to the dumpster out back.

At least a mile of flat, empty fields were in front of him. The weather had been consistently warm enough to till the fields without them being frozen but not quite ready to plant seeds yet. The Gas Station Attendant loved the look of the barren fields. They were uniform, structured, and simple. The Gas Station Attendant always hated it when some high school kid in a big truck sprayed mud everywhere by driving through it like a lunatic. It always looked so messy until the rain came to fix it. The Gas Station Attendant took a deep breath at the field as the sun started to set.

Simple things, The Gas Station Attendant thought, *that's the only thing you can really trust reliably to take pleasure in. Without particulars, without context, without ending up dripping in metaphor. Simple things you can just look at and say "nice" at.*

The Gas Station Attendant chucked the garbage and turned to walk toward his car. It was parked way to the side so that it would take up none of the good spots for the customers. As he walked, The Gas Station Attendant saw a well-done-up man in a black suit, black tie, and white button-up come walking down the ramp from State Highway 333. While walking on that highway was illegal, it wasn't unheard of. There were always a few stubborn types that thought they were invulnerable to cars.

But none of them were ever dressed this nice.

"Car break down, bud?" The Gas Station Attendant shouted out.

"Yes, car broke down," the man said.

The man maintained eye contact and began to approach The Gas Station Attendant. The Gas Station Attendant held his car keys but didn't put them in his car door for fear of being rude.

"Bad luck," The Gas Station Attendant said, "It's getting dark, too."

"Yes, it is bad luck. And it is getting dark. Do you know of an inn, or a motel, or a hotel close to here?" The man asked.

"You don't want a tow service for your car? We got a phone inside."

"No. That is not necessary."

"You'll get it towed in the morning?" The Gas Station Attendant asked.

The man leaned in toward the Gas Station Attendant and squinted his eyes a bit. He was a remarkably average-looking white man. Short brown hair, maybe slightly balding, brown eyes, medium build, about five foot nine with a clean suit. The only thing that seemed out of place was the sleek briefcase he carried with him. It was a gleaming, pockmarked leather that seemed so black it almost looked green.

"Yes," the man said.

"Tired, I suppose," The Gas Station Attendant said.

"Yes, tired," he said. "Do you know of an inn, or a motel, or a hotel close to here?"

"Across the bridge. There's a hotel way down Main Street about a mile or two. On the river. But there's tons of bed and breakfasts and little hotels in Armin. Just go over the bridge, take a left, and then the first right and follow that road. There's a place called the Calm Sea Guest Haus. A woman that comes in here often runs it."

"Thank you," the man said.

He turned around and walked back up the ramp to State Highway 333. He walked south.

The Gas Station Attendant sighed as he got into the car. He turned south as he headed home and saw the man walking. He waved as he passed. The man looked but didn't wave back as The Gas Station Attendant turned right onto a gravel road that ran alongside the river.

"Not good," The Gas Station Attendant said. "Doesn't seem good at all."

The Gas Station Attendant thought, *I bet if I drive north on 333 I wouldn't see a single broken-down car. Not for forty miles. I know. I know in my gut there ain't no broken-down car up north. But, shit, I'm not gonna look. The only thing I know about whatever that is about is that it is not any of my problem. Not my problem.*

The Gas Station Attendant went home and read a book about Suleiman the Magnificent until he fell asleep on his couch.

❖❖❖

ONCE A WEEK, AMELIA drove forty-five miles for grief therapy. It was a facilitated group discussion run by a therapist, consisting of a fluctuating group of around five to ten people. Plenty of people only showed up for one week and never came again. Amelia had been a staple for about a year. About three other people could be counted on to be at every meeting. One was a woman dealing with her husband's death from a heroin overdose. The event propelled her to get clean. One was a quiet man who almost never said anything, but who appeared to struggle with his son's suicide on an ideological level. One was a middle-aged woman whose small dog got ran over by an eighteen-wheeler after it escaped from the house. She cried the loudest. She was not mocked.

Amelia talked about Edi.

There were about seven people at the meeting. Only one completely new person. Amelia recognized her, vaguely. Armin held about three thousand people, but if you were a socially active person, most people who lived there would be somewhat aware of who you were. Amelia knew this woman's son had died from carbon monoxide poisoning about a week prior. She knew her last name was Bundren. She was the one who found the son. Amelia didn't know if the woman knew that or if she knew who she was.

"We have a new face today. Would you like to introduce yourself? It's okay if you just want to listen," the therapist said.

The woman nodded.

"Hi, my name is Debbie."

"To make you more comfortable, Debbie, I'm going to ask everyone who has already been here before to introduce themselves, and they will tell us their reason for being here, and then you can tell us yours."

People spoke briskly. Their tragedy was summarized, without emotion, and was easy for everyone to say. Things moved around the circle quickly. Debbie paid close attention, and it got back around to her, and the individuals present were curious but respectful, and doubted they would be surprised, and they weren't, and they knew it was her son found under that bridge, and they knew that she knew they knew that already, and, in a way, that made it easier.

They discussed things for an hour. Helpful tips, self-thought coaching, approaches that made her scenario easier in practical ways. Nothing dramatic. No syrupy emotionality today. People tended to distrust progress when it was dramatic. People put on shows for themselves.

When it was time to leave, people tended to linger in their cars in the parking lot.

Amelia headed home. By the time she was closing her front door, she saw Barrett turning off the road onto her driveway. She shut the door, unsure if Barrett had seen her yet.

It's always something.

Barrett realized he made the right decision to come over only when he reached Amelia's front door. He did not call beforehand to announce he was coming simply because he himself didn't know if he would be able to follow through with it. He anticipated himself turning around before he got here. The type of sureness he carried surprised himself. He hadn't been sure about anything in decades.

Her house was nicer than his. A fancy brass door knocker was the only color present on the front of a bleach-white linoleum house. The windows were covered with curtains. There wasn't anything in the house visible from the outside. It was a fortress, impenetrable, sitting atop a small hill overlooking Armin, protected in the back by the woods.

Barrett did not understand the terror in her eyes when she peeked past the curtains and saw him. He had been awake for thirty-six hours.

"Barrett? What are you doing here? Is everything all right?"

She answered the door by opening the door as little as possible and slipping out to join him on the front concrete steps. Barrett sighed. He took off his baseball hat and scratched his hip. He wondered who she had in that house before deciding that that, like many things, didn't concern him.

"Hey, Amelia, how you doing? How you been?"

"I'm...I'm fine. What are you doing here?"

"Good, I, uh. Listen. I ain't ever been good at this, and I'd rather not be...talking to you about this. I was hoping that you kept onto some of Edi's things."

"Oh."

"Did you hear about that boy?"

"I...I was the one who found him."

"Jesus Christ. Shit. Like in the thing?"

"..."

"Look, I'm sorry, I ain't been...sleeping or thinking straight. Maybe now is a bad time, it seems like a bad time. I didn't mean to impose."

"Just...what is it? Tell me."

"Can I come inside?"

"No. Just tell me."

"Why not?"

"Barrett."

"Fine. Okay. Can I look through Edi's things?"

"For what?"

"She was my daughter too."

"Just tell me what you want."

"You don't have the right."

"You can't come inside."

"The fucking book, Amelia, give me the fucking book. The last one. You know which one. The pig one."

He had never cursed at her before. She looked ashamed, all of a sudden. The whole time she had not let go of the front door handle. Barrett looked at her for the first time since he stepped outside. She was still pretty, still delicate, thin and bony. Her eyes were still hard. First and last love. He knew it and didn't kid himself. Some people's hearts just don't shift, even when they should. It was the harshness of it that exhausted him. He felt ready to sleep.

"I don't know about that."

"Why not?"

"You are going to read it?"

"Yeah. I need to. Please. Have you read it?"

Amelia shook her head and frowned.

"I always wanted to, though," she continued.

"Why haven't you?"

"After that...that's it."

Barrett put his hands on his hips. He wanted to console her but feared the repercussions.

"We really messed everything up," he said.

"It's not like there's a right way to do it," she said, sighing.

A car passed below on the highway. The driver waved to them and they waved back, despite not seeing exactly who it was. Barrett put his ball cap back on his head.

"I'm sorry. I always been sorry. Can I have the book?"

"Yeah, but not now."

"When?"

"I'll bring it by later. Go sleep. You look like shit."

"I'm sorry, you know, for looking like shit," he said.

"Jesus Christ."

AMELIA COULDN'T STOP HYPERVENTILATING for minutes after Barrett had left. She read the suspicion on his face easily. He was a man, so of course he thought she was hiding another man. That's all that lizard brain would fixate on. Better he think that than know the truth.

She slowed her breathing eventually while placing her back firmly against the inside of her front door, periodically checking the driveway to make sure Barrett had left. Eventually, she eased her way past the stacked boxes in her front hallway and followed the path to her kitchen sink, in which she poured herself a glass of water and desperately drank the entire thing, dribbling it on her chin. She cleared a space on her counter by moving two stacks of magazines to a milk crate in the garage in preparation of going through Edi's things. She kept them upstairs, in the guest bedroom. It would take her at least an hour to get to it.

The floorboards of each room were lined with twelve-inch cubed boxes that were clearly labeled and taped shut. Most rooms had boxes stacked two to three high. They were labeled things like kitchen utensils, yearbooks, summer clothes, winter clothes, CDs and movies, electronics, pictures 1995–1996, Christmas Lights (white), office equipment, Mom's ceramics, jewelry kit, workout clothes, coffee cups, tools, remotes/knives, textbooks, Edi's clothes, sports memorabilia, and western novels.

Strategic paths were carved in each room so that Amelia could still access what she needed to on a daily basis. The couch was cleared for one spot, with the rest hoisting old romance novels she hadn't sorted and packed yet. In the garage, she had dozens of flat boxes ready to be filled. It was a brutal operation, and Amelia felt like she was a few weeks away from being back in control. She always told herself that she would eventually rent a storage space for all of these boxes, but eventually "always" seemed to get further and further away. Plus, the idea gave her enough anxiety, having all this stuff somewhere else. More so than the anxiety she got from having her house filled with it. The idea of eventually moving it was like a negotiation that her brain had with itself, to ease the anxiety of the present by placing some of it on the future.

Amelia sat on the couch to try and relax. The emotional weight of Barrett's request combined with the intense fear of her peculiarities being discovered caused her to enter a defensive mode where she didn't even inquire about what Barrett's potential emotional state could be. Everything he asked...It was out of character. She always told him that he never really processed their daughter's death, and now that he seemed to approach it, it made her feel scared, almost resentful of him.

Amelia exhaled and turned on the television. On the television, a woman up the road in Howe County was being interviewed about her goat that sounded like a man. The reporter was trying to get the goat to say something but it wouldn't.

Amelia leaned back and rested her head. She closed her eyes and imagined a home invasion. The burglars didn't expect her to be there and weren't wearing masks, so they had to kill her. This thought calmed her. Eventually, she stood up and walked to the guest bedroom. After moving a few heavy boxes around, she picked up the box labeled Edi's Work. She calmly walked it downstairs and placed it on the counter without opening it. She put some water in a kettle and began to heat it up. She cut a lemon into wedges and placed one into a mug with a teabag. The mug said Mark Twain National Park on it and depicted a family walking through the trees. She gripped the edge of the sink as she waited for the water to boil and thought about how she would bring this up in group therapy later that week.

Barrett had mentioned the boy. The boy who died. She remembered being so angry seeing that car idling with the boy in it. She got so angry thinking about kids these days, about boys of all ages, just going around, fucking things up, making the world the hay they flounder and shit on, like animals, brutal, unkempt things who can't keep their own problems in their own house. She was going to yell at him when she swung that door open and felt how impossibly cold he was. The slight, unnatural order. Stagnation. She saw the body lurch downward without any evidence of thought or sentience. Dead. Dead as a fucking doorknob. Just…sitting there. Then she retreated back, called the police…just her and that dog. She had been planning on keeping it before that, but now?

She peered out the kitchen window for a moment, looking for the dog. The woods ran deep and long, and she saw nothing but the tangled gray and brown of the late winter to early spring woods.

She had the vague feeling Barrett was trying to ruin her life again, and she suppressed that feeling immediately. Amelia opened the box. There was a myriad of notebooks. One bound book, a project Edi did by herself in college on a machine in the library, *The Riverside Ascetic*. Then there was a copy of *The Trees of Iron County* bound in computer paper. Under that, three spiral notebooks full of notes and concepts. At the very bottom, clumsily stapled by her daughter's weak hands into a chunk of computer paper as thick as a toilet seat, was what Barrett wanted. The title was *Pig Iron*. She had drawn a concept for the cover on the front. A large, looming Bigfoot-esque creature covered in soot, washing himself idly in a placid river.

BARRETT FELL ASLEEP AT home, leaning back in his recliner, to some college basketball game featuring two colleges he had never heard of before. When he woke up there was a copy of *Pig Iron* on his coffee table. One-hundred and seventy-two pages of computer paper, front and back. Attached to the front was a pink Post-it note.

if you ever tell me anything about it I will ruin your life

—A

I still love her, Barrett thought.

I'm so fucking stupid for that, Barrett thought.

❖❖❖

HARPER HAD FIGURED SOMEONE would ask her something about it sooner or later. Whether it was her friends, kids at school, or the police. She made the decision not to lie about anything but was too afraid to say anything about it unless prompted. She stayed in her room and cried a lot. Most people knew it. They let her stay home from school on Monday, and she stayed in her room. She ignored all messages or texts and stayed under her covers shaking. *This was the last place he was alive,* she thought, *here, with me. He had me here, and it's my fault he died. I'm a slut, a whore, a killer. That's what they will say. That's what I would have said if this happened to someone else. I would have and I would have meant it. I would have texted everyone about it.*

I'll be hated. People will look forward to seeing me so they can hate me in public.

No one knew he was here no one even really knew we were seeing each other like that but I thought he had told his friends don't all of them tell their friends I never asked if he did I never told anyone. If we were dating only he and I knew that and I can't believe he is dead.

I thought we were dating or we were going to go on dates I guess

No one knew he was here and no one has asked me what I knew or where he was.

If I told he was here who would I tell first and what would they think of me. If I told what would it change anyway. Would they blame me. If I hadn't asked him he would be alive I didn't want him to leave I wished he could stay but that's not true I got him to leave but it was his idea it wasn't just my idea

If I say that they would just hate me more

A whole town thinking I'm some kind of slut

I can just say he came over to talk and we didn't do anything but who would believe that but maybe it is the best I can do people will say everything I imagine even if it is not to my face but it is always possible and people like to know the worst possible thing to say to a person even if they never say it because it is always a holstered weapon to get at people and if they think they have to they will tell me I killed him and this will define my entire life

And I wish he was alive and I was dead and it's a pretty simple feeling

They had found his phone in his pocket. A friend knew how to unlock it so the police were able to take a look at it. They went to the school looking to talk to her, but she wasn't there. Eventually, they found their way to her front door. And when her father answered, he brought them into the living room, made them coffee, and knocked on his daughter's door. He apologized to the officers for the delay, saying that she has been taking this really hard.

Harper emerged from the room with a wet face. She knew her father had been knocking for a few minutes, and she figured he was trying to feed her. She came out only to grab some water. She turned into the living room to see the pointy hats of the county cops drinking out of coffee cups and immediately began bawling while everyone in the room frowned and offered no condolences.

The Sheriff read the texts messages on Derek's phone. He had a thick accent and exhaled hard when he spoke.

"'Come over. Come over. I need you to come over right now. Tongue emoji. Monkey hiding face emoji.' Now, miss, was that you?"

Harper said nothing.

"How old are you, miss?"

"Sixteen," Harper said.

"Sixteen," the sheriff repeated.

Harper's mother, Rose, tapped her feet. She kept staring out the window, staring at all the sheriff's car in the driveway.

The sheriff held Derek's phone and kept reading.

"'Idc,' guess that means 'I don't care,' 'what time it is. Come over or I'll let all those senior girls know you are messing around with a sophomore. Skull emoji. Jk. I'll make it worth your while.' And then there is a picture."

"A picture?" Rose repeated.

"It is sexual in nature," the sheriff stated.

"Harper," Rose said.

"Then there are more texts—you asking him to come over, I don't need to read them. This is you, correct?"

Harper said nothing.

"Why didn't you notify anyone? This is serious. The picture alone, as you are underage, is—"

"We don't need to talk about that right now," Rose stated.

"We need your statement, miss," the sheriff said.

"I sent those texts," Harper said. "I was just flirting, I didn't know—"

"Why don't you go ahead and come with us?"

Harper looked at her mother. She was looking out the window from behind the blinds seeing if any cars were passing by.

⍔⍔⍔

BARRETT DRANK A BEER and stared at the ceiling while lying down on his couch. It was dark. The room was cast in a pale blue light emanating from the television that he wasn't watching.

There's this feeling that's like loneliness but isn't. When I was lonely and I was younger all I cared about was drinking, and so I drank a bunch. Then I saw Amelia, and then I just cared about Amelia. And even though I always knew nothing I did seemed to really impress her, I felt comforted by the act of loving her, of caring for her, of trying to make her like me. There was still a void that I felt between her, but I had direction, passion. I loved her and the love itself shot me toward her. There was a logic to my emotions, I wasn't just flailing around in the dark, reaching for anything to draw meaning from. It was something I could locate and understand within myself, and even if I never directly acknowledged it, I understood it. I told myself one person is always chasing another in relationships, and I just thought one day she would give in.

I think having Edi changed things for both of us. For her, it must have been something like surrender, her life turning to concrete around her feet, but for me, I found someone more dependable to love. Amelia was a wispy thing, either pushing or pulling, never content. I loved Edi so much, and I loved Amelia for giving her to me. I never said it enough, of course. I mean, I said it every day to both of them, but not in that rich, syrupy way I felt it. I couldn't ever really melt down and buckle down and cry in front of Amelia, telling her how bad I needed her. I think it would have made her guilty if I did that. I think she loved me too, in her way. The best she could. The best a person like me deserved, anyway.

I won't get into it all but when Amelia left and Edi died I felt like there wasn't anything to build to, in regards to my life. It was just waning now. Just watching the leaves fall. I said that at a bar once and a guy I know said now was the time to do whatever I wanted, but I didn't want to do what I wanted. I just wanted to feel at home somewhere. I didn't say any of that, I just said yeah, I figure. But when you don't want something out of yourself, when you ain't got a direction to point, that's when you just… that feeling is worse than loneliness. It's sharper, more specific. It's like getting gutted but not feeling a tinge of pain.

At this point in my life when I feel restless I drive down to the river in the night and stare at it. It just flows. It just keeps going east.

◈◈◈

It is hard to suffer in dignity in a small town. After Edi died, Amelia was careful to not buy wine at the local grocery. She never went out of the house until after seven or eight, simply to avoid the amount of people who would approach her, ask her how she was doing, and tell her how sorry they were. To even brush off these people would be considered crass, and despite her daughter's death, people would have difficulty empathizing with her. Everyone offered endless condolences because they wanted to imagine themselves as good people and wanted to make Amelia feel better. Even if they didn't, their intentions were pure, and that's what mattered.

There really is nothing to say, I'm so sorry, but here I am, saying it.

Amelia drove thirty miles out to a gas station off highway 70 in order to buy her wine. She never drank more than one or two glasses, but she knew how gossip works. One person sees her buy wine, one bottle becomes two, someone flashes back to seeing her in the grocery store and imagines another bottle, and next thing she knows there is a breakfast discussion about her in a house she is unfamiliar with where people discuss her name with raised eyebrows. Social bloodshed.

She had to consider Barrett. In her own defensiveness she hadn't considered much of his motives or feelings. She always had the vague idea that Barrett was a man that had to be protected. She stared at the number of objects stretching from her front door to her kitchen, leaving only a thin, narrow path. All this stuff. She sighed. She felt guilty about giving him the book. *It's his life. It's not like he's doing well. You can't save anyone, anyway. People always find what they are looking for.*

Barrett did not begin reading *Pig Iron* until the third day that he had it. The first two days involved orbiting around it, glancing at it on his coffee table, and feeling a heavy, crushing sensation in his forehead. At nights he would drive around slowly, maybe going to bars, maybe getting fast food, trying to think of things to do just for the sake of doing them.

The town still spoke of the boy who died. Of the girl he had been returning home from after sleeping with. The discussion made Barrett frown. When people asked for his opinion in the wood decor bars with the plastic furniture, he simply shook his head and raised his eyebrows and said nothing. There was nothing to say about it. People did things, and things happened.

"It's just these kids these days. Girls weren't like that back when I was a kid. Didn't need that extra level of temptation going around. Boys are going to take what they're given. And then someone died. Girls weren't sneaky like this back in the day. But that's how it looks to me."

He thought of Edi, either to distract or punish himself.

Edi had never liked the country. There were plenty of kids like that out here, more since the internet. She didn't want to fit in. Barrett thought his daughter was a genius, but that she was unsettling. She nitpicked at things, vocalized complaints that seemed pointless (why do you only wear plaid), and was constantly asking (her mother, mind you, never him) if she could dye her hair. It was, on a fundamental level, difficult to relate to his own daughter. She inherited none of his interests. She was on the computer a lot, in her room, reading, writing, watching cartoons. As an adult, mind you, or close enough to one. Edi had made a conscious decision to not fit in. It made Barrett a nervous wreck. He worried that she had no friends and then would try to give her money so she could go out with some people. Amelia always wondered why he was giving her so much money. He never verbalized his concerns.

Barrett would have killed for teenage moodiness. He got teenage aloofness.

In his tiny house on a hill overlooking the Missouri river, alone, Barrett looked through the brush in his backyard that ran to a small cliffside. He thought that it might be a good place for teenagers to sneak off to together to drink or kiss or look at the river at night. He tapped his fingers on his coffee cup and stared into the backyard. He narrowed his eyes. He saw what looked like a seven-foot-tall bipedal forest ape stumble through the foliage before ducking behind a thick plot of honeysuckle.

He craned his head to the side, trying to get a different angle on it. The enormous, shadowy figure remained. Something had to be up with his eyes. He opened the door and smelled the air wafted in from the river replace the stagnant domestic smell of bachelor living. He took a few steps toward the figure suspiciously. As he reached the beginning of the brush, the figure dissipated into the form of the thick plot of honeysuckle. He frowned. He didn't like the way it stunk up the yard once it got hot.

Honeysuckle is an invasive species to America. It comes from Japan and chokes out the local fauna. Barrett decided that he would clear it tomorrow, and maybe build a small chicken-wire fence by the cliff so that if anyone drank there, they would be safe.

2

THE ROOM ONLY YOU SEE

FROM THE COMFORT OF a decade-strong leather recliner, Emery rested. The small house built by a cadre of pear-shaped cousins sat all lonesome on a hundred-acre property flanking Supplemental Road Q a dozen choice miles out of Armin. Emery was an Imperial boy, a son of Jefferson County through and through, and it had taken forty years of adult living, a divorce, an impish daughter moving to New York, two back surgeries, a drinking problem temporarily mastered multiple times, and one unceremonious retirement to make him want to leave it, and when he did, he only shuffled a few counties down. Howe County was isolated. Not particularly more isolated than Jefferson County in the grand scheme of things, but it was isolated in the fact that none of his family lived around here, so if they wanted him to come visit, he always had a built-in excuse.

Hours always slipped for Emery. It was the kind of existence that was only sustainable by college students in summer and single, retired men. It was March, and in the morning the sun blasted in and made the small rooms swelter. The only respite Emery had was his living room window air conditioner. The window unit was aimed directly at the position of his face and belly while seated in the recliner. He rarely slept in his bed. The only difference between being awake and being asleep is that right before he went to "bed," he draped a small blanket his ex-wife had made for him (post-divorce, they were on good terms) over his outstretched legs and drifted asleep to baseball highlights. He would return to the bedroom in October, most likely, as the season chilled. The bedroom was the smallest room and contained the fewest windows, so it held heat much better. The television was exchanged for western novels at this juncture. His daughter had set up a computer for him in there as well, and this was usually the only time of year he would get set on tinkering on it, usually playing free cell.

Retirement had come easy for Emery. He got it relatively young, having worked for General Motors since he hopped out of high school, and they had cut a deal for a few of their employees as looming pensions began to scare the company. Emery got to retire early as long as they took a sizeable chunk out of his set pension. Emery had never needed much, and looking at what he had already saved, made the decision to quit working for the first time since he was thirteen. Retirement was as easy as work was. There is a special kind of laziness that can also drive people to be reliable employees. It was a social laziness. Emery, after all that had happened in his life, desired simplicity above all else. He understood what was required of him to maintain his level of comfort in society and did what he had to do to make that work. He worked so that when he got home he could sit down on a couch and not worry. He accepted the inevitability of work and vowed to do no more than he had to, but did what he did have to do unflinchingly.

It was one o'clock in the morning, on the cusp of daylight-saving time. It was the free hour. Past the final tick of one fifty-nine the hour would purge itself and be reset. Emery was only aware of it because a late-night talk show host had brushed on it as a joke setup during the monologue. The extra hour made Emery feel nothing but a slight justification to stay up even later.

In New York City, Emery's daughter Carrie sat on a wooden floor at a coffee table in a semicircle around a television with her boyfriend and other friends. It was two in the morning, and everyone in the room was experiencing a waning drunk, where every additional beer became a decision. She sat in between her boyfriend's legs, who sat on the couch.

The extra hour had been the reason for all of them to go to the bar, come back, drink more, in the way that any event, no matter how mundane, can be used as a structure for makeshift celebrations. The extra hour was buffer armor toward the next day.

Carrie was the only Midwest transplant to the group, most being native New Yorkers (to at least the state if not the city), with the other exception being a girl from Boston. Missour-uh had become somewhat of a punch line to the group, as Carrie had used this pronunciation when she differentiated her two perceived realms of Missouri. She often defended her college town, Columbia, parts of St. Louis, and Kansas City. These were the civilized lands, in her mind, where people didn't call soda "pop," where people didn't wear overalls. When a state legislator was mentioned on NPR for trying to put the Garden of Eden into history textbooks, that was Missour-uh. Missour-uh was the drunk, cross-eyed guy at the bar who claimed he beat up three future NBA players at the same time while in college.

She had always had the desire to leave Missouri. There was a condition in small towns. Kids who wanted to go to college would do so and rarely return. What they coveted in other locations they often saw as the downfall of their own rural upbringing, whether it be class or intellectualism or exploration, and in this way their home was viewed as something they had escaped from. In their own criticism of their homes they validated the criticisms of others who had never been there with their own preconceived notions of where those people were from (whether it be the country, small towns, suburbs, whatever). If you listen to most criticisms of small towns, whatever people call those people is what they themselves think they are not and are affirming that loudly. Call them dumb to look smart. Call them ignorant to look enlightened.

Carrie had been talking to her boyfriend about the so-called "dog incident."

"It was this thing with my dad and my mom. You know how my dad is. My mom, Deb, kind of steamrolls people and my dad, Emery, doesn't offer resistance to anything. They both mean well. Things kind of just happen. They both do the best they can.

"Anyway, my mom and dad split about ten years back and about six years ago she remarried. Rodney. A whole thing, I won't get into it. Jesus, when I went back for Christmas and I saw that gun cabinet in the living room, I thought it was a second fridge. Anyway. Okay. Dog incident. Rodney had a dog and my mom had had a dog. Both mutts, mostly labs. Neither had been fixed because they had both got their dogs the same way, some dog has puppies, they ask people if they want them, they scoop one up. I mean, they took them to the vet. They weren't monsters. Well, they have puppies. By this point Mom and Rodney are living in an apartment closer to St. Louis. They don't know what to do, Rodney's adamant about not keeping any. He goes to get his dog fixed during the whole thing. But the other dog's still pregnant. My mom told me she called a bunch of people and no one wanted to deal with it. She said she waited until the dog was about to pop until she called Dad.

"But of course Dad don't answer. He loses his cell phone, turns it off, or just don't pay attention to it. If you call him he usually gets back to you within a day or two. Last time I tried to call him he called me back at one o'clock in the morning the next day. He just slips through time out there. It seems sad, but he seems okay. I don't know."

"That seems sad," someone chimed in.

"Anyway, my mom had been able to put her dog up with her cousin in their backyard for a few days on the condition that after she gave birth they would be gone. Like, my mom's primary concern was getting dog afterbirth on the carpet and not getting her security deposit back. By this time my dad still hadn't called back, and when they argued about this my mom made him feel guilty even though she was trying to ask for a favor. So when he did call back, the dog hadn't given birth yet but had been at the house for a day and a half, and my mom preemptively refuted the help my dad didn't offer. The call was short and callous. Basically, the dog gave birth, and my mom tried strong-arming her cousin for more time, which was refuted, as everyone in my family knew how to handle my mom except my dad. That's why he married her. Anyway. So now she's got ten puppies in her apartment along with the two dogs and her and Rodney start freaking out. They handle it for about one or two days before the apartment starts smelling like a kennel and neighbors complain about the noise. My mom picks up the phone again, starts rifling through the usual suspects. I swear, she's got like problem solvers on speed dial. I've been around my family members when my mom calls, and they all tense up when they answer it, expecting to be asked some kind of favor. It's sad."

"A lot of drama over some dogs," someone said.

Many started drifting off, having side conversations about music or television or other people's lives. Carrie looked around the room.

"Baby, go on," her boyfriend said.

"It's getting late. When are we leaving?"

"A bit. Go on."

"My mom calls my dad. Look, it's been long established he owes her nothing. Like, my dad has issues, but he internalizes them at least. My mom divorced my dad and then got mad when I told him that I didn't hear dad cry while I was staying with him. Like, that validated the divorce, or something. Like he owed her tears. He didn't divorce her. I don't know. I was older then, at least I felt older, and I knew how to handle my parents, so I kept quiet. So he calls, no answer, my dad calls back later that night, around midnight. My mom stays up late too but when she told me the story she said she was asleep when he called. I think she was lying and just threw that in there as some kind of petty power play. That's what I deal with. She starts crying on the phone, asking my dad to take the puppies for a bit. My dad says he can't afford to feed them all, to watch them all. She asks him if he wants to take any of them to own. He says no. Look, I knew at this point a dog would do my dad good but I kept neutral. If I would have given any endorsement to my mother she would have swung it around until it was in tatters. It starts getting really shitty because my dad agrees to watch two of the puppies while she looks for people to adopt them, and when my mom and Rodney drive down, they got all the puppies in the car."

"Ouch."

"So she is crying, says some story about the other people who were going to take them, I never figured out who, can't because they got sick. She just steamrolls him. My dad, who had made a little fence out of chicken wire for one or two puppies, relents to take all ten of them. Rodney shakes his hand in the way that men with stuff to prove shake hands. Shakes his hand with his shoulders up and square, leering. Like he wasn't shaking my dad's hand but sizing up the entire prior relationship him and my mom had and the whole life they built together. He makes a gesture to help build a fence for the puppies, and drives off to some hardware store while my mom and dad get out all of the dog food and bowls she had brought and figure out how my dad was going to set it up. That's how it was. My dad couldn't even set it up himself, he had to get coached. I used to think that my dad was just weak and he let my mom get her way, but he just didn't care. He just was completely apathetic. So basically fifteen minutes after crying, my mom is mad at my dad again, 'cause he didn't invite her inside his house. Which was definitely weird, mind you, but I don't think my dad wanted this to last longer than it had to. They sat on the porch with all the dogs. Rodney comes back and him and my dad build a fence off to the side of the big, metal garage my dad has. Now, my dad worked for a dealership forever after the factory closed, working as a mechanic, and had a good collection of classic cars. Now, he always keeps this locked, so that ain't a problem. He tells Rodney what cars he has but doesn't open it. But behind the garage my dad has a completely trashed, broken-down pickup truck alongside piles upon piles of scrap metal, and Rodney gets super excited about it, talking about all the money he could sell this for, that he would haul it off for him, he has a truck, etc. My dad wasn't interested, whether out of pride or complacency, I don't know. But Rodney tries to convince my dad to let him take it for days following this."

"Are you ready to go? It's late. But I still want to hear the story. Keep telling it to me."

"I'm sorry it's long. I thought it was a short story when I first started it."

"It's okay. I like it. Are you ready to go home?"

"Yeah, I'll finish it on the walk."

"Okay."

"Did I tell you the big spiel my mother told me? After I came home from college for the first time? And I was tired, but she thought I was mad at her?"

"No," he said.

"Listen," she said, "When I first met your father he was considered a joke. I know you think I am bossy, or that I'm a bitch, or whatever, but I liked your father, he was a good person, and his friends treated him like a mule they fed wine to. He'd do it. They would all get drunk, all older guys too, all knowing better, past their thirties, all single or married to passive women who let them roam wild, all shooting guns and guffawing and riding four wheelers and fishing. All in a state of arrested development. Country boys are told they are men at thirteen and that's when they stop growing up too.

I don't even know why I was there. I was older too. You start to feel a certain way, in a place like that, growing older. You don't know now, honey, or you might. I don't know what it's like being a girl your age. I can imagine it's less different than I imagine. I remember how I felt looking at my sister. She's ten years older than me, remember? Well, people get married so young out here, she didn't, and later on had to resort to taking a married man away from his wife. I had all that paranoia. All that anxiety. So Gail dated Jim, Jim was friends with your father, and on the weekends I would sit around your father and his friends and whatever women they had tricked into coming or liking them or loving them, and I would be very quiet and polite and stay as far away from the men who would roll around or wrestle or drink until they fell.

Your father was really sweet. I started showing up really early so I could talk to him before he got drunk. It's hard to say that a man that got that drunk was shy but he was. I think he would drink to get the nerve to make a move on me, but by the time he was drunk I would do whatever I could to avoid him. Gail would tell me that he would drink even more after I left. Like he was holding back. But I couldn't talk to the man with his eyes lolling and his head craned toward me in fake interest and aggressive posturing with his very plans for me visible in the back of his eyes.

His buddies were awful, too. Gail once told me that Emery fought someone over something they said about me, her eyes all beaming like that was exactly what I wanted. I didn't want that. I hated the brutality of it.

So when he finally did ask me out (sober, mind you) I accepted, thrilled. And I do not regret anything I did after that. I just wanted it to be me and him, I didn't want those awful people around, I didn't want the bonfires and the four wheelers and dip spit cups, the beer cans pitched into fires. I was only there 'cause I had to be. His friends may hate me, but that's because they lost their mascot. Gail told me they had a game they played. If they saw a bug, they would all try to catch it. Whoever caught the bug would bring it to your father, and he would eat it. They talked to him like he was shit. He let them do it. He liked it. You wouldn't guess it now, but your father just wanted to be liked. He got drunk, he fought, he drove drunk even, with a childlike innocence. So I took him, I made him a better man. I made him a man good enough to be with me. He never fell asleep in a lawn again. And you know what? He wanted it. He wanted me to tell him what to do. If you don't believe that, honey, I don't care. If you ask your dad about it, I don't care what his answer is either. He's always been the last one to know what he wants."

"This isn't what this is about. This is about the dogs," Carrie said.

"About what? The dogs? I don't want to talk about the dogs," her mom said.

✤✤✤

At one thirty, in the free hour, Emery stirred from his recliner in half-sleep to the barking of dogs. It was the steady, consistent, deep bark, the alarm bark, of a dog that thought he was a hero. Emery lumbered out of his house without displaying emotion, slipping into some sandals by the door, shuffling toward the pen he kept his dogs in at night (a formality, really, it's where he kept their food and a small constructed doghouse his brother-in-law had made, but the dogs had long since displayed the ability to jump the fence at their leisure).

Free time, Emery thought.

If this hour was a fish I'd throw it back.

There were things that Emery considered about himself that he never really had the gravitas to bring up to other people. He thought he was a somber, introspective man, that he wasn't sad because sadness was irrelevant, it wasn't something that could be held in your hand, so, it wasn't real, and with that happiness too was a casualty, irrelevant, trite. This is what he thought when his daughter would express concern for him, down in Missouri, all alone, living the simplest existence possible, avoiding everyone he could, in his small house, watching television but never even really watching it, never really paying attention to anything, slipping in and out of time, almost ethereal, shuffling along, never questioning what he was doing.

"I'm fine. I like it," he would say.

You know how unhappy I would be if I worried about being happy, he thought.

Emery was aware that his daughter could see through his bullshit, but he was also aware enough that as long as he told her he was fine she wouldn't bother him about it as much. One time his daughter had outlined this grand plan. She was going to land this job at some internet company just outside of New York and move there with Brian, her boyfriend (whom Emery had met once, and Carrie had been amazed that Emery had displayed an effort to be gracious and welcoming, and Brian regarded Emery with a sheepish sorry-I'm-fucking-your-daughter smile and weak handshake), and with the new money Brian and Carrie would settle down, buy a house, probably get engaged, and then Carrie told her father that he should move to New York too, at least upstate, on some property just as isolated, but somewhere where Carrie could take care of him, as she considered her mother to be a chiding, almost predatory influence (this mostly projection on her part) on her father, too concerned with herself to help him when his inevitable back surgeries finally came and he found himself bedridden for weeks, in which his sisters would bicker over who got to keep him on their couch, only for him to last two days before returning to the old recliner, bearing his problems on himself.

"If I piss myself, I piss myself," he had told his sisters.

After Carrie detailed her elaborate plan to her father, one that hung on so many variables of jobs and relationships and money, she paused, waiting for a response. Emery sighed.

He said that country "well" that is almost musically strung out for three seconds, the kind of "well" that always means "nah, but thanks," and then followed it with an "I don't know about all that."

The request made him smile, though. It was sweet. It was about the most youthful thing he had ever heard. His daughter was twenty-five now but the request might as well have been drawn with a crayon.

Emery finished thinking about his daughter as he approached his dogs. Lulu was sitting on top of the doghouse. This was a source of amusement for Emery. Smoky jumped the fence as he approached, head-butting Emery's thigh.

The dogs had been good for Emery. It was a simple thing. They were detached from his personality of detachment. Emery had been long accustomed to having a sense of duty, something that he was much better at providing for others than he was for himself. The dogs required something, and he could attend to it without complaint. It was simple. It was discipline long lost.

Lulu was barking at something around the corner of the metal garage. Emery shushed her. They were overactive dogs, desperate for any kind of stimulus, and often invented interlopers in order to warn them off. Emery turned the corner expecting critters, and as his eyes focused in the dark for something, anything, to justify his dog, Lulu shot past him into the dark, and Emery began yelling. He saw the flood light reflected in the dull yellow eyes of a polecat as it squared itself up to Lulu's happy barks. Pfft. The spray seemed almost mechanical, like it was a nozzle to be flicked. Lulu sneezed and loped back with her teeth bared, nipping forward one last time to get caught with a final spray, until she retreated to a sensible distance and began to look at Emery for guidance. Emery was yelling "Lulu!" repeatedly, for what reason he wasn't quite sure, because he knew he didn't want the dog to approach him. The stench was invading him already, making him gag, so he meandered back to the fence and after a few moments Lulu appeared behind, sneezing repeatedly, rubbing her face into the grass.

Smokey began rubbing his head into his leg only to collapse ungracefully begging for a belly rub. Emery obliged and tried to decide if he wanted to wash the dog or not.

He waited for the hour to reset in the metaphorical hope it would take this with it.

"I'll wash her tomorrow," he said, staring at the empty pile of dirt that his truck used to sit on, recollecting, remembering, but definitely not thinking, if there is such a thing. He stared and remembered and petted Smokey and processed no new information about his life.

╬╬╬

CARRIE CLOSED HER EYES as she leaned on her boyfriend in the subway train.

"So when was this?"

"What?"

"The story with your mom and dad and the dogs," he said.

"It was while I was still in Missouri. During my last year of college. We were talking a lot more at this point so my mom would fill me all in about it and then when I would come home I would hear all about those dogs. She tried to get me to take one. A year before she had said I wasn't emotionally ready enough to take care of a dog."

"You're kind of hard on your mom sometimes."

"I'm really not. You know how they say you reach a certain age where you start to realize that your parents are actual people? Like your mom and dad are just some girl and some guy. Well, it's true but it also kind of isn't. Because they may be some girl or some guy but that's how I feel right now, like they are just some dude and some woman, except that that dude and that woman are my parents."

"I don't get it."

"It's impossible to divorce the concept of 'my parents' from the people that are your parents."

"What happened after the dogs were at your dad's place?"

"The deal was that my mom would stop by at least once a week to resupply dog food and make sure the dogs weren't sick or anything. That's one thing my dad worried a lot about. He didn't want to have to be responsible for having a dog get sick and die on him. It worked like this, with my mom swinging by occasionally and my dad doing the bulk of the work until my dad messed up his back again. They scheduled him for surgery. This is about three weeks after the dogs arrived. They kept Dad in the hospital for about a week and some change, then he spent a couple days at my aunt's until he couldn't take it anymore and he headed home. He had a walker now and scars all on his neck. It was gruesome. They had to shave his beard too, so my dad looked really different in a really short amount of time. I was home from college for the vacation, staying with my mom, and it was her job to go check on the dogs every day. I volunteered to go stay at my dad's place for a week and take care of the dogs while they were in the hospital but my dad didn't go for it. He said it was locked and that he didn't have a key with him. I just don't think he wanted anyone in that house, like foreign contaminants could ruin it. Baby, you should have seen his face. You saw he had the beard when you visited, right?"

"Yeah."

"He looked so young without the beard. With all the gray hair gone, with a smooth face, my dad actually looked a lot younger despite having to use a walker. It was weird. His facial expressions had changed though. He was really muted, never laughed out loud, only let out thin little smiles occasionally or microscopic frowns. I think he was thinking a lot at this point. He said stuff like, 'Oh, I don't know how much time I'll have left.' It was cryptic."

"He really said that?"

"Yeah. My aunt was talking to him about what the doctor said about walking without a walker again. He told my uncle that it would be about two years physical therapy. He refused it and said that about not having that much time left. He was only sixty-three."

"Morbid."

"Baby, it's a lot of stuff like that. I thought about Missouri a lot when I read Faulkner novels. Except instead of everything being haunted and bad, everything was just boring and bad. Like bad stuff happened and people didn't even put down the remote. The same muted tragedy everywhere but without all of the confederate ghosts."

"How were the dogs when he got back? That's where this is leading to, right?"

"What? Oh, the dogs were fine. My mom had given one away to a woman she worked with, so they were down to ten now. That wasn't the problem. When my dad came home he found that that rusty truck he had parked out back was gone, along with his big pile of parts and scrap metal."

"Oh, shit, was it Rodney?"

"I don't know. Seems like he would be involved. I worked up a theory that he told one of his buddies about it while drinking and the guy low-key did it a few days later. Rodney seems okay but the guys he brings around sometimes are shysters. Or he just nabbed it with the hope that he would give Emery some of the cash later, but by the time Rodney heard about it he was so upset that Rodney didn't want to tell Emery, like, I don't know, like my mom was still a competition and that by coming clean Rodney would go down in points to Emery. My dad wasn't even mad at Rodney, too, it's stupid. He's such a sad sack. He told me he was mad at himself for letting people into his home to bother him, that he was mad at himself for letting mom steamroll him, that he was mad that he told anyone where he lived, because once people know where you live, they come and fuck up your life. Either way, it didn't matter. The truck was gone and the scrap metal was gone. I don't think my dad cared about those. It was the principle of it. It's a bad idea to give a loner curmudgeon justified reasons to hate the world."

"Was it worth anything, anyway?"

"A good car can get you three hundred dollars or so worth of cash from scrapping it. It depends on what was in the piles, but you can make good, quick money from scrapping stuff. That's why a lot of people steal it."

"People steal scrap?"

"Yeah. It's why people bust into air conditioners, rip out copper wire. All that stuff."

"So what did your dad do?"

"Nothing. He didn't even tell Mom. He told me when I called him on the phone. Mom didn't even know. I told Mom. I think she suspected Rodney, but she never let me know if she did."

"Well, what then?"

"Three of the dogs ran away."

❖❖❖

IT WAS MY DAUGHTER *that got to me the most, I was already working all the time, I was already stressed out after moving in with Rodney, after all of the dogs. I don't think she was really upset about the dogs. I don't think Carrie was really honest with herself about me and her dad splitting up. So she would try to waylay into me on some moral high ground stuff, defending her completely blank, absent father, the father whom she had called me to complain about when he forgot her birthday (which he told me he did not forget, but simply forgot to call) but she herself never brought it up to her father, she, who gave her father a pass, for what reason I don't know. Probably because I was the one who left.*

And then she told me about the missing car and the missing scrap metal, and I almost screamed. I'm not sure at what, even. Emery had his pension, his retirement, and here I was still working, still at the hospital all of the time, having to pay for most of the things around the apartment because Rodney had dried up on contracting gigs (whereas when we first dated, he sought every opportunity possible to flash money in my face, which, although I couldn't be bought, I didn't mind the gesture), not including busting my ass trying to do the right thing with those dogs.

I had thought about bringing them in to an animal shelter to get put up for adoption but I had read a book where someone did that and they put the dogs to sleep.

And they were so cute, Christ, they were so cute, all of them running around our apartment, pissing, shitting, stinking up everything, eating everything, Rodney going red from it all, me flustered as all get out. I called everybody because I knew that if I called Emery my daughter would have more ammo against me. That was my little girl. Got what she wanted. We paid for her to go to college, she finished, she took some graduation money and ran. Because she wasn't tied down by the world yet. Not like me or Emery, actual adults with actual responsibilities, who get drawn and quartered to the land, held hostage by their own hometowns.

And then she brings that New York boyfriend down here, her affect changed, her presentation different. She didn't say ain't or y'all once. That used to be a staple of her vernacular, even if it was ironic. The boy she brought down wide-eyed and overly polite, either too afraid to tell jokes or he had decided that we weren't worth the effort to impress. And her introducing her boyfriend to Rodney like he was a convict I let sleep on the couch.

By the next time she brought up the truck I had spent the prior few days rehearsing what I would say back to her in debate. I had spoken with Rodney at this time, who assured me that it wasn't him, that he used to be a highway patrolman and that people would drive around those winding country roads looking for sheds or scraps that people had left unattended on their lawns to swipe up. He did concede that it was almost always friends or family. He told me he had asked a few friends he knew that actively scrapped how much you could get for a truck nowadays. I had all this prepared. But my pièce de résistance was this power point, that if your father cared so much, why didn't he file a police report? Then I would tell her how she always scapegoated me.

Of course, then the dogs ran away, and your father couldn't care less about the scrap. All of a sudden he went from wanting the dogs to *go away as soon as possible to having his heart broken that some of the dogs had gotten out. He mounted his four-wheeler and traversed all over his property looking for them, drove all the local roads, made inquiries with neighbors. He even contacted the police and tried to file a report for missing dogs, which they said they did not do. While describing what happened he mentioned his broken-down truck got stolen and they offered to take a report on that, but he declined. That's when he named them, too. The seven that were left after the first three ran. He didn't even name the dogs until then.*

❦❦❦

EMERY DECIDED THAT HE wasn't going to sleep tonight so he began the process of washing the skunk spray off of Lulu. He wasn't quite sure where to begin. Although he knew that he had been told what to do, he couldn't quite remember what the folklore remedy was, or if it worked. He believed that he had been told either tomato sauce or peanut butter, so he got out both. All he had was dandruff shampoo, so that would have to suffice for the dogs. And since it was too cold outside to bathe Lulu, he decided that he would bring her into the house and do it in his bathtub.

At this point, Emery's back felt like it was on fire, so he reverted to grabbing the walker to shuffle back and forth and took himself a painkiller.

Lulu and Smokey were ecstatic to come inside. They burst into the house like a sharp wind, sprinting into every room, jumping up and down on top of Emery, going in and out and under his walker. He coaxed Lulu into the tub only for Smokey to immediately follow. They hadn't been inside this house since they were puppies.

Back then it was Lulu, Smokey, Buddy, Ozzie, Lankford, Louie, and Copper. He kept the majority of them in the pen with their doghouse. They got big too quick, so he had a small barn that he kept his truck and ATVs in next to his garage that he closed up and got a space heater in there for them. He left the door open for them to wander about.

Emery closed the door on Lulu and Smokey to keep them in the house, and wandered back to the barn. He opened it and peaked over to the pen by the truck and saw the other five dogs lying in the hay. He closed the barn door and locked them in for the night.

He shuffled back to his house and thought about the three dogs who ran away from him. It was only a few months ago, before the surgery. He had forgotten to close the makeshift door of the chicken wire fence. They just left. He looked and looked. Nothing. Always that guilt.

Halfway back to the house, piercing in the middle of the night, a howling drone sounded off in the distance. He saw Lulu jumping up and down at the screen door to his house, looking at him. She was using her paw to hit the handle of the screen door to open it. The dark sky tinged a sickly yellow green and the clouds seemed close. The wind seemed to be getting slowly sucked out of his lungs, dragging low along the ground to a nexus in the distance. The horns blared. A tornado was coming.

Lulu and Smokey burst out of the house toward him and galloped into a circle around him. The door to the house was left wide open. Emery stared at the sky.

"Ah, well," Emery said, "nuts."

He had made up his mind to trek out to the pen in the barn and drag them all into the house. The air began to look bleak outside. When he opened the gate, Lulu and Smokey groped at his thighs with their wet faces and Buddy circled around them all with his ears down. Copper, stirred suddenly awake, was barking at something indiscriminate. He jimmied the fence sideways so that they could all come out and Copper came leaping over the other dogs out of the front door of the barn hauling ass toward some invisible varmint, completely undeterred by the tired yells of Emery, Emery's back and belly lolling toward the mutt at dangerous speeds, all the while Emery aware of his own body's limits, hoping to bend them slightly. He used a walker with little tennis balls on the end of the legs, which never remained, as the dogs would rip them off and run away, bringing them back to Emery not out of compassion but hoping that he would throw them. Ozzie, Lankford, and Louie stared at Emery from the barn doorway, not moving.

So he heard the wind pick up as he circled around his large metal shed looking for Copper as he held Smokey and Buddy by the scruffs of their necks both for balance and to simply account for them. Lulu he wasn't worried about, as she was either loyal or needy enough to rarely ever take her eyes off of Emery when he was in the room. Emery kept turning around to Ozzie, Lankford, and Louie, yelling at them to come here, come here, and they simply watched, occasionally licking at their paws and looking around skittishly.

Emery hit a rut and took an old man fall, the kind of fall that seemed like it was almost preserved in amber, beginning with a few inevitable steps, unpreventable, falls that took fifteen seconds from start to finish, like dominos getting tipped over. So after stumbling and scratching his hands and knees on gravel, Emery sat there breathing for a few seconds, getting up far earlier than he should have got up as to avoid the breathy waxing of dog tongue on his, both immediately deciding that he had to go inside and immediately regretting his decision but doing nothing to change it, pulling the dogs into the house, leaving Copper, Ozzie, and Lankford outside and hoping for the best.

It was tornado sirens then, the loping sirens heard in the distance, the closest ones in Armin he believed, being carried down the highway, barely audible past the whip and whir of the green and purple winds invisible in the night air, and Emery stared at the moon. He thought about feeling helpless, about his whole life, about how good the dogs are, that in a world that no one has control over everyone is helpless, and that if everyone is helpless then every action is a cry for help, and he wished there was a god, there was anyone, and all he wanted was the dogs, the dogs he just had gotten enough balls to actually name.

Emery laid there in the gravel, breathing, feeling the wind whip the nape of his neck.

And because everything seemed biblical, Emery was stunned when the winds came down with seemingly no climax, and, since he figured this forebode ill news, like the universe was a sentient being bracing him for the fall, he was absolutely positive he would emerge from his house to find Copper and them dead among the uprooted trees and eviscerated branches, his tongue hanging, the dogs all trying to console him, licking his hands as he stared lifeless at the dog, but no, Emery emerged and he walked, wearing only thin house shoes on his feet, miles in circles around his property, not even calling the dogs' names, either not wise enough to do so or too fatalistic to allow himself optimism, sure at any moment he would see Copper dead, but because people's metaphorical impositions on the world are nearly always wrong, Emery circled the property a few times finding nothing but branches and dents in his shed.

It was worse. Emery couldn't find any of the dogs. The front door of his house, open, the barn door open, nothing damaged.

The void of the dogs hung like fallout. It had a humidity to it that strangled Emery. He stood there, on the gravel he fell on, tennis balls clinging to his walker. The dark night was even devoid of the chatter of insects. The silence sounded like doom. He felt the silence in every fiber of his body.

"COPPER!"

"LOUIE!"

"SMOKEY!"

"LANKFORD!"

"OZZIE!"

"BUDDY!"

"LULU! LULU, COME HERE GIRL! LULU! LULU, PLEASE, COME HERE."

As he gained hope, he then thought that surely Copper and the rest would return home, that the disaster was averted, and he was a fool to assume the worst, but since the stories we tell ourselves are never the x and y, the black and the white, the good and the bad, the dogs never appeared, either alive or in corpse form, and Emery didn't know how to process it, the lack of totality, other than to look away from his television set to the blankness of the wall, biding his time for a few moments, chewing on his thoughts, only rarely allowing himself the decadence of hope to stare out of the window through the bent blinds toward the woods and prairies behind him, looking for those dogs.

"Well, I can look in the morning. I can't…I can't see nothing out here. And if something happened… They'll come home. Eventually."

The weight of the dogs' lives put a guilt on Emery that was hard to pin down, complicated, these dogs thrust upon him despite objections, who, despite his feelings toward them, he grew to love, only to eventually fail them in a variety of dramatic ways, not necessarily even failing them personally, but he began to believe that the dogs were targeted, doomed, and that he couldn't protect them from the frigidity of the world, and he began to think about putting microchips in their necks, but he watched television instead, and hoped.

◌◌◌

"ANYWAY," CARRIE SAID, "AFTER the tornado… Months passed. And anytime I call him, he only ever talks about the dogs. I'm sorry, I've been talking too long. How are your parents?"

"They're fine," the boyfriend said, "they actually—"

"He hasn't stopped looking even, by the way," Carrie said.

"What?"

"My dad. He still drives around, looking for them."

"Oh."

❖❖❖

"NOT MUCH WE CAN do," the Sheriff said.

"It strips the paint, you know. The eggs. They set. It's not like— they didn't wake us up. Aw, shit," said Harper's father.

Harper's father was a rigid man who always tucked his shirt in. He was ill-equipped for handling any sort of harassment. Harper stood by the front door of their house, looking down the street, trying to guess how they had done it and where they had come from.

She knew why.

Emblazoned in black spray paint, the word "SLUT" was written on the garage of her family's home. The two cars in the driveway— one for her father and one for her mother—were splattered in what appeared to be four dozen eggs.

Her father had his hands in his pockets talking to the sheriff and her mother was inside crying. She had positioned herself on the loveseat in full view of the front door as she was crying. Harper hung outside so that she wouldn't have to see her mom cry. Harper's facial expression was cold and vacant.

Slut.

There was a rumor going around on social media. Harper saw it, of course, but said nothing. She locked down her profile at this point. People were posting that Derek had tried to break up with

Harper but that she threatened to send a picture of his dick around if he did and she made him drive over that night to talk it out. One of Derek's friends stated that Derek said that he thought Harper was a crazy stalker. It took about a day until the threats started.

What would I have done if it was someone else in my situation? Would I get mad too?

"Well, this can't continue," her father said.

"We can't put a car out here all night, Bob."

"Hmm."

"To be honest with you, I don't see it dying down soon," the sheriff said.

"Hmm."

"And I don't figure them seeing her at school is going to help," the sheriff said.

"Them?" Bob asked.

"Them. The kids. All of them," the sheriff continued.

"Oh," Bob said.

"So, as far as it not continuing, it's kind of your decision on what to do, Bob."

"I see," Bob said.

"Any ideas?"

"Maybe, uh, maybe we find some family somewhere where she can stay. I kind of, uh, I'm not an expert on teen girls, but I think this is probably, uh, bad for them."

"Right."

"I'll find somewhere. We. Me and Rose."

"Sounds good, Bob," the sheriff said, putting on his hat and walking to his car, "Let me know if you need anything."

Harper walked inside. Her mother, Rose, stopped crying audibly for a split second as they made eye contact. Harper walked down the hallway and heard the crying resume. She walked into her bedroom, and she shut her door. She slid the lock over it. She looked at the bed. The last place Derek slept. She went into her walk-in closet, pulled the door shut, and fell asleep on the floor.

ılı ılı ılı

THE FACILITATOR AT THE grief counseling group told Amelia that when she had panic attacks, if she recognized she was having one, she should take deep breaths, and to focus on something tangible, something real, and to keep concentrating on it. Amelia's object was a deck of playing cards that depicted the 1994 St. Louis Cardinals.

Amelia shuffled through the cards, and her breathing slowly slowed. Ozzie Smith was all of the Aces. Amelia thought deeply about Ozzie Smith. He used to do backflips.

He used to do backflips. He used to do backflips.

Amelia's phone rang. After a few breaths, she forced a smile, and answered it.

"Hello?" Amelia said.

"Hi, Amelia, how you doing?"

"Oh, my God, Rose, I'm so sorry. I haven't called. We have lunch today, don't we?"

"Well, that's what I was hoping to talk to you about."

"How is Harper? Is she okay? I should have called, oh my God, Rose. I should have called. I'm so sorry. There's just been so much going on, you know? I'm so sorry," Amelia said.

Rose was a board member at Armin Area Hospital. She had inherited a lot of money from her father, a doctor in the area, and was well known to everyone in town. People in Rose's position, from a good family that was considered a cornerstone of the community, kept very busy. From Wine Trails, to various German Festivals, to Brass Band events, to the Garden Club, to fundraisers and dances, she was a woman that seemed continuously busy.

Amelia liked Rose, and had known her a long time. Both were locals from families with long roots in the community.

She always wants to talk about how busy she is but I never actually know what she gets done. And always, with the wine.

"It's been hard. Luckily, the detectives told us first before it got out in town. Harper's just shut down. I don't know what to tell her. I want to yell at her so bad, but for what, you know? She's already punishing herself so bad. But sex? At her age? Not in our day," Rose said.

Amelia repressed the urge to make a contradictory comment.

"What's she been doing?"

"Always in the room, you know? She won't talk, she won't eat. But the crazy thing is—she isn't crying either. She was crying at the funeral… but then that was it. When the Sheriff came her face was blank. In her room, I hear just silence. Is that normal?"

"Well, Rose, I've been to grief counseling, and they say everyone processes it different. What's the correct way to mourn, anyway?"

"Just a little crying, at least. So we know that she at least feels bad."

"Trust me, Rose, she feels bad."

"It's just kids today. They are so selfish."

"People everywhere are selfish. It is how it is."

"I suppose," Rose said.

Amelia sighed.

"I heard what happened to your house. For what it's worth, I'm sorry," Amelia said.

"Bob's just worried about fixing it. About the cars, about painting the garage. He ain't even going to talk to Harper about it. She saw it. She knows. Actually, this is why I called, Amelia. I wanted to ask you a favor."

"Oh, anything, Rose," Amelia said.

"I know you live a few miles away, up there in those woods, by yourself. And how we're right in the middle of town? Well, I was just, we need to get Harper away for a bit. For all this to die down. Bob's brother is going on a cruise and can't cancel it and his sister is just so busy in that new development they bought out in Ladue and my sister's all the way in St. Louis and she still has school and all that and I just don't want to—"

Amelia looked in the room and saw boxes stacked everywhere.

"I just, well, I don't know, Rose, I—"

"Amelia, I'm begging you. I did what I could to help you during that holding Beautification whatever, kept the Aldermen from bothering you, please Rose. Please. PLEASE."

"I need a day or two to clean. Is that okay?"

"I'm sure it's fine," Rose said.

"I need to clean. Not for her. Me," Amelia stated.

"Amelia—I owe you for life on this one. Thank you."

"It's nothing. It's—"

Rose started crying.

"It's just been so hard for me," Rose said.

"I'll start cleaning," Amelia said, and she turned to face the boxes.

BARRETT PARKED HIS TRUCK in the gravel parking lot. It was late, and dark as pitch. Relief spread across his face when he saw other cars. It meant they wouldn't close up for a minute.

Barrett had spent the day reading *Pig Iron*.

I know why she didn't want me reading the book. I get it now. I read it myself and I'm proud of her and know she must have worked on it real hard and I don't get most of it and it's not the type of thing I like usually, like Lord of the Rings *or* The Hobbit *stuff, I can get why she didn't*

　　　　　　　　　　　　　　　　　　　WATER, WASTED

talk about it much but I think she, well, I don't know, underestimated her mother and I, because, well, I just read it and I get so damn proud it makes me well up. It's a hard as hell thing to explain but good lord I am so proud of that girl.

I don't know if that makes it easier or harder or what. I can get why Amelia avoided it

I never really read books thinking about what to get out of 'em. I just like them when I read them. You sit back and you read and you like it but now I'm all thinking and stressing over everything when I read every line and just wondering and it's something else. It ain't enjoyment. I don't know if that's worse or better it is like being in school again I guess haha can you imagine that at my age.

The Tin Nickel was a roadside bar off Supplemental Road Q, across from the dirt strip that was the airport. It was a steel building about as big as a trailer with a large garage door in the front that they opened up in the summertime. It was a purely local establishment, avoiding all the tourists that came down to tour the wineries. The owner of the Tin Nickel was a man named Rick, who had actually fought to keep the bar off of pamphlets they had on display for arrivals at the Amtrak station.

Ah, great, Carol is bartending again. I was hoping it would be Rick. He talks less.

Barrett seated himself at the thinly veneered bar top and made a curt nod to Carol. She finished her conversion at the end of the bar and walked down.

"Hey Barrett," she said, "how you doing?"

"Good, I suppose."

"What you drinking?"

"Bud, I suppose."

Carol poured him a Budweiser, handed it to him, smiled, and went back down the bar to finish her conversation.

I hate it when she does that and she tries to add up all the beers I've drank at the end of the night and it's always embarrassing and always wrong and short. Makes me feel like she shorts it on purpose like so I owe her something or something.

Edi figured out she was gonna die from cancer while she was writing that book and I keep thinkin' I'll be able to tell during the book when she figured it out while writing it like at what part and I haven't yet.

I know she wasn't religious or nothing but theres all these gods in the book and theres all these churches and none of the churches seem that good in 'em and I wonder if she knew then.

There's so many characters too and they all got different stuff to them like different weapons or abilities and it's hard to keep track. Like I really got to focus when reading it. Like there's the two sisters and the elf and the big mushroom guy, which, that guy is my favorite, I got to admit. His name is O, easy to remember. I don't remember the Elf's name, something fancy I guess. But he ain't fancy like Elves in other stuff. He's kind of, well, he's a dumb shit from what I gather. But the mushroom man is funny. He's like if C-3PO was as big as Chewbacca. Because he kinda talks like a homosexual not that there's anything wrong with that but he's the biggest fella by far

I guess that Henbit is the character that's most like her. I mean, I don't think Edi would say Henbit is like her, but I think she is a little bit. She's a watcher, I always remember that about Edi. Just quiet, looking around, watching everyone, seeing what they are doing. Even as a little girl, I saw her in the kindergarten and all these kids with grubby little hands, grabbing stuff, moving around, almost in a fog. And Edi would be in the corner, nibbling on a blanket, and just watching whatever the adults in the room were doing. Just staring.

Henbit's got the crossbow and stuff and is a deadeye, which Edi wasn't, she had like, no motor skills, poor girl, no interest in it, but Henbit was a tracker, knew the wilds, never got lost, and Edi was like that. She *wasn't a boy scout or nothing but I would take her to those woods just over here, like a mile west, when I would go morel hunting and she took to them faster than I seen a kid. She loved asking me what all everything was, even if I never knew.*

"Want another beer, hon?"

"Yeah. Thank you, Carol."

When they get to the city of snow, full of Orcs and, I don't know, they're supposed to be like Eskimo people and smart orcs, and she starts talking about all four of them, the two sisters who are black apparently, and the red elf and the mushroom man and they all get treated lesser, that's when I start losing track of what she's trying to say. I know they're after diamonds, and they gotta be hush hush about it, because the Churches in the area all fight for diamonds because they are needed to resurrect people, I wonder if she knew she was going to die then. I never got her a diamond. I never did and I feel awful about it. I got Amelia one, too, when we got married. I wish I would have got her a diamond. So they get to the manor that the diamonds are supposed to be in, and they get the sister, Sugar, she pretends to be a prostitute or something and gets to the top floor and unlocks the door and lets them all in, they head to the basement, she keeps the Lord or whatever he is busy by singing a, hell, what was it. She sings a David Allen Coe song. "She Used to Love Me a Lot." That was, uh, jarring. All these gods and elves and shit and just some old country song I used to play. That freaked me out so much. I had to put the book down.

"Another?"

Barrett raised his finger and nodded.

It was the damndest thing because she was looking at the guy and there was some kind of thing she did that was magic and he was, well, enraptured I guess by the performance, and started crying. Meanwhile the other three went downstairs and knocked some guys out guarding a door. The big mushroom fella kicks the door down and there's these three holy men in robes and they just stare at each other. They tussle and the one guy,

the main holy man, he looks right at Henbit and says something like, you
take these diamonds, people ain't going to have a chance to live again. You
do this, you are the same as a murderer, he says. And Henbit freaks out,
panics, the elf and the mushroom man grab it and run, and she runs, and
she sees her sister in the lap of the Lord, and she, well, I don't know why,
she screams and shoots him in the head with her crossbow. And there's a
huge messy scene where she is crying and they are fleeing through the back
alleys of this snow city, dodging orcish patrols looking for them, and they
slip through the cracks of the city walls and make it to a nearby forest.

And she just cries. She cries and cries. And they all think it's about the guy she shot. And it's not. It's about the diamonds she stole and what the holy man said.

What the fuck does that mean?

I wish I was smarter.

"Another," Carol said.

"Yes," Barrett said. "Thank you, Carol."

Carol nodded.

What was she trying to say?

"You good?"

"I could do another."

"Can do."

Did she know she was dead at that point? Did she know?

"Closing up soon, Barrett."

"One more, please," Barrett said.

I would just, I want to, I just want to know what she thought. More
than anything. I want to know if she was mad when she went. I want to
know what it means. Was she mad she had to die? Was she scared? That'd
be normal, right? I never remember her being mad. She seemed sad, but she
was always sad. The scariest thing is that when she did the treatment, she
seemed more than tired sometimes. She seemed bored. What's that mean?
I don't—I don't know if a guy like me can even understand what that felt like.

It wasn't a long drive back. Q leads to 333. You only had to be careful there, highway patrol from Howe County liked to wait over the bridge from Armin to get drunk drivers for revenue.

Barrett looked at himself in the rearview mirror of his truck. He touched his finger to the bags of his eyes and breathed deeply. Barrett pulled out of the gravel parking lot and turned onto Supplemental Road Q. After about ten seconds, he realized it was dark, and turned his headlights on.

There was a lull. He felt the wheels rotate. The air was gray mist and he heard something. He stopped the car in the middle of the road. The David Allen Coe song, "She Used to Love Me a Lot," came on the radio. He felt it echo. Barrett went pale. There were no cars coming either way. Barrett saw no lights. The old fat guy kept singing about his ex-girlfriend. It wasn't a particularly good song.

What the what. What. Good lord. Holy smokes.

"She used to love with a love that wouldn't die!" The radio sang.

"Holy smokes!" Barrett said.

The lights illuminated the street as he sat there with a dumb look on his face. He rubbed his eyes with his outstretched fingers and coughed. He tasted iron in his mouth and he didn't know why. It felt like the world stood still for a few seconds. A pregnant pause. He tried to taste his mouth again. The back of his tongue tasted like hot beer. The beer didn't spring from his stomach. It was from his soul. The fat fucker kept singing in his radio. His daughter was somewhere.

Barrett started driving. He drove with wide eyes. He saw a blurb of something gray on the road in the corner of his eye before he felt his wheel thump upward and continue going forward. He looked in the rearview window, but it was dark.

It started to rain. It came all at once, from nothing. Barrett slowed the car down to a reasonable speed, and started trying to regulate his breathing. He kept driving. Two thumps, this time, he didn't see them, and the rain coming down in sheets, oscillating like waves on his windshield, and then, a crack of lightning.

Barrett reached the intersection of Q and 333. Thunder first, then lightning. Barrett could see everything for a split second. The gas station to the right, framing the mouth of the river, the endless empty fields to the left, and due ahead of him, Barrett sees the remains of five or six armadillos. Armadillos don't leave a lot of blood. When they are hit by cars, their leathery skin can usually contain the split guts and internal bleeding. There were contusions and split skin near the fat of the top of their legs. The blood trickled, not flowed, and the rain made quick work of it.

And Barrett stared. He placed his fingers in the corner of his eyelids and pulled. He wiped his dry eyes.

Not too far now.

Barrett took a right onto 333. No one else was on the road. He passed the dead armadillos on the side of the road, and the lightning cracked, and it lit up the highway, an elevated plane framed by two gravel ditches, and within the ditches and just reaching the road he spotted an army of things, a great mass of animals and critters, crawling toward his car, and he was speeding along now, eager to get home, dull-faced and blank with apprehension as he gripped the steering wheel, driving, and the cacophony of small beasts, raccoons, squirrels, rabbits, armadillos, snapping turtles, dozens and dozens of them, without end, began throwing their bodies under his wheels, resounding with thumps, one after another, with enough force to bounce him in his seat, unbelted, hitting his head softly on the top of his cabin, and he did not stop, as his truck crushed beast after beast, and he heard his windshield crack, and saw staring at him the lifeless face of a raccoon stuck in his wiper blades, and another, a turtle shell, and another, the torn ear of a rabbit caught in the middle of his blades, and he closed his eyes and kept driving, and he did not slow, and he heard the animals raining down onto his car from above, with the storm, part of it, and saw the dents in the top of his cabin as they came down, and he closed his eyes and he drove, not too long now, not too long, and the turn here is on the left, not too long, and the thuds stopped, shortly, and he heard the crack of thunder again, and it felt so close this time, and opened his eyes to track the light and caught a brief glimpse of larger creatures this time, of deer and bucks and fawns, coyotes, foxes, racing alongside his truck, trying to angle their heads into the relentless churn of his tires, and he swerved left and right to knock them away into the ditch, and he breathed, and turned his brights on, and saw nothing but his driveway in front of him, and he pulled himself inside too quickly, and sprayed gravel all over, knocking over his mailbox, and raced up the driveway.

The rain slowed to a drizzle. He parked the truck and looked around. His windshield was cracked in multiple places. He stared at the rabbit's ear caught in his windshield wipers as it went back and forth, back and forth. He opened the door and walked toward his house and he opened the door.

◆◆◆

Chapter 14 of *Pig Iron*
By Edi Markham

THERE WAS A SINGLE, soft crunch on the winds.

"Whatever you are," O said, in his slow, fungal drawl, "I can kill you."

There was no response but the cold wind coming in from the east. The only stirring was that of my sister, Sugar, making a childish whining sound as she rolled over in her sleep.

"Get up," Aisir seethed, through his teeth.

"Is it them?" Sugar said, wiping the spit from the side of her mouth.

"Something," Aisir said.

"I am easily the strongest being within a radius of forty miles. Nothing in this wilderness threatens me. It would be wise of you to turn away, or to present yourself to us in a friendly and nonthreatening manner. At that time, we will—" O rambled.

"Shut the fuck up, O," I said.

"Henbit," Aisir said.

I looked at him. He tossed me my crossbow. His eyes lingered a bit. But for what?

We stood in the dark, peering around us, for what seemed like an eternity. I'm sure merely minutes passed. O did not move, his elongated arms clutching a longsword and a tower shield, perpetually ready. Aisir kept both hands on his glaives and closed his eyes intently, listening. His crimson red skin flickered in the campfire ominously. I loaded my crossbow and pointed it at the ground. Sugar's tension grew to boredom pretty rapidly. She stared at O and Aisir, who ignored her. She stared at me and shrugged. She sheathed her shortsword and sat on a small log flanking the fire.

"I won't do this all night," she said.

"What? Don't do anything stupid," Aisir said.

Sugar took her lute off of her back and crossed her legs, resting the lute on her thigh. She extended a single finger to the air and muttered some small incantation. We all turned to her as a small light shot from her finger and splashed the camp in green light.

O and Aisir turned back to the foliage surrounding the camp as she began to play her lute and sing.

My lover comes to me with a rose on her bosom
The moon's dancing purple all through her black hair
And a ladies-in-waiting she stands 'neath my window

And the sun will rise soon on the false and the fair
Sing a tune, Lorelai, oh

Ten hounds emerged simultaneously from the tree line. They crept in low and slow. They made no sounds. They stood at the edge of the camp, bathed in green lights. They marched in perfect order, and all sat down at the exact same time.

"Sporting dogs, from the look of it," O said.

"Where are their masters?" Aisir said.

"These aren't the dogs the Orcs from Sedna use. What is this?"

She tells me she comes from my mother the mountain
Her skin fits her tightly and her lips do not lie
She silently slips from her throat a medallion
Slowly she twirls it in front of my eyes
Sing a tune, Lorelai, oh.

O and Aisir held their ground. Aisir was merely a soldier, and O was incapable of imagination. He sized enemies up by the weight of their hammers. I saw something in the dogs, and had to get closer.

"Henbit, get back here," Aisir said.

The dogs all turned their heads in unison toward me as I stepped forward. I approached the dog on the farthest right. Sugar steered the green light closer to me, over my head, and I was able to see the dogs more clearly. They were prim and proper, with shiny and clean chocolate-brown fur.

It was their eyes that made me realize the alien nature of these dogs. Wet, purple eyes, glossy like dinner plates. Big. Empathetic. I immediately wanted to touch one of them, to stroke its ribs and feel its coat against my skin, but I restrained myself. I felt almost as if the dogs were at work and shouldn't be disturbed. I pulled my hands back.

I watch her, I love her, I long for to touch her
The satin she's wearing is shimmering blue
Outside my window her ladies are sleeping

My dogs have gone hunting, the howling is through
Sing a tune, Lorelai, oh
So I reach for her hand and her eyes turn to poison
And her hair turns to splinters and her flesh turns to brine
She leaps cross the room, she stands in the window
And screams that my first born will surely be blind
Sing a tune, Lorelai, oh

I stared into the purple mist of the dog's eye. It did not stay still. I had heard tales of things like this. The village Sugar and I grew up in was outside of a Vetian military fort on the Veti river. The fort was at the edge of the Kingdom's territory, before the unclaimed swamplands to the east. My father was an armorer who, when military contracts dried up, traded with the River Orcs of the Strongholds who made their home in the swamps.

One evening my father was completing an order of wrought iron tools for a nearby Stronghold. Its chief came by to collect, and as is considered polite, my father sat with him for coffee as the chief inspected the tools. Plows, picks, scythes, mainly. The River Orcs were peaceful agrarians. Sugar and I were with the chief's daughter. She was showing us how to do math on an abacus.

"Have you ventured into the lowlands?" The chief asked my father.

"No. Figure if the Kingdom moves further in, I will too, to keep my contracts."

"Vetians won't move into the swamp."

"You figure?"

The chief turned a scythe in his hand.

"It's hard to explain to people who weren't born there. The same rules don't apply down there. Here, I see a tree, it's probably just a tree, you know? A tool is just a tool. You walk down paths in the lowlands…depending on what's in your heart, they take you different places."

"People do have a tendency to get lost down there."

"Lost. A good word for it," the chief said, "let me give you some advice. If you ever find yourself in the lowlands or the swamps, and you see anyone or anything, an animal, a person, anything. Look it in the eyes. If it has purple in the eyes, it is, well, we call them Anomalies. At that point, you're not in the realm of logic. It's pure metaphor, and you have to be very, very careful."

I swear, as I remembered that, I think the dogs all nodded at me. Like they knew that I knew. Sugar ignored O, and kept singing.

So walk these hills lightly, and watch who you're loving
By mother the mountain, I swear that it's true
Love not a woman with hair black as midnight
And her dress made of satin all shimmering blue
Sing a tune, Lorelai, oh
My lover comes to me with a rose on her bosom
The moon's dancing purple all through her black hair
And a ladies in waiting she stands 'neath my window
And the sun will rise soon on the false and the fair

The last note of the lute hung in the air. Sugar's eyes were closed and her chin was lifted high in the air. She finally exhaled. O sheathed his sword, and his eyestalks stared at Aisir.

"It seems illogical that they would reveal themselves when we had difficulty locating them. I think by deliberately revealing themselves, they are showing that they are not intending to attack us," O said to Aisir.

Aisir kept his hands on the weapon. I stared into the dog's eyes, and watched the purple shimmering in them dance from side to side.

"WE THOUGHT IT RUDE TO INTERRUPT THE SONG," the dogs said.

"Oh, what the fuck?" Sugar said.

"What the fuck are you?" Aisir said.

"Oh, damn," O mumbled, redrawing his sword again.

"THIS ONE KNOWS," the dogs all said, staring at me.

"Henbit?" Sugar said.

"The story," I said to Sugar, "that that Orc Chief told us that one time? As Dad sold him the tools when we were kids? The purple in the eyes. Look, you can see it. It's glittering in there. It's an Anomaly."

"PRETTY GOOD," the dogs said.

Aisir frowned. Sugar walked up behind me. O's mouth flap beneath his eyestalks made a slow, wet clapping noise.

"For those unfamiliar with my biology, that sound indicates nervousness, and I cannot control it, and if it is grating to you, I apologize. I am familiar with Anomalies. My colony said that Anomalies are half-killed Gods innately tied to this planet. I do not know what to do with this information."

"What do you want?" I asked the dogs.

"YOU SHOULD FOLLOW US IN THE MORNING," the dogs said.

"Why?"

"WE DON'T KNOW."

No one had a better plan.

None of us could sleep, and we told the dogs that we should leave at the first break of light. They yipped in unison, and when the first orange strand crept over the landscape, they trotted us southwest, toward the river.

It has been three days since then. The dogs led us along a sloping path that ended in a floodplain of tepid water dotted with dead fish. We jogged. O was obviously struggling, being the largest, and occasionally the dogs would stop and wait if they heard his guttural wheezing. We were all struggling at this time, hungry, dehydrated, pressed for time. The dogs did not let us wait.

We followed the dogs to an open area, a slightly elevated cropping of orange stone with sparse foliage on it. The sun was setting, and the dogs laid down, meaning that this was our camp for the night.

"We need food," Aisir said, looking at me. "Come on, huntress."

"I can try. I don't even know these lands," I said.

Sugar looked at me hopefully, smiling slightly. She was about to do something to piss me off.

"Aisir, go with her. Can't just bark orders."

"Fine," he said.

Sugar smiled and waited until Aisir's back was turned. She looked me in the eyes and mimicked a dick-sucking motion, and I shot her darts with my eyes.

"What symbol does this mean, Sugar?" O asked.

"Shut the fuck up, O," we said in unison.

"Are you done playing?" Aisir said.

I sighed, exasperated. I was too tired to be embarrassed.

We took off. A few minutes passed as we ventured into the brush. Aisir grunted. He seemed to have something to say, just on the edge of his lips. He paused, then got low, and pointed to a small bluff.

"There," he said.

There was a small goat standing on a rock. He seemed to be chewing on some weeds positioned there. He turned to face Aisir and me. He was chewing a dandelion.

"Take the shot," Aisir said.

I drew my crossbow out and took a bead on the goat. It looked so innocent and stupid. It was a white goat with a brown-red chest ridge and legs. It had a plume of hair extending from its chin that stretched down nearly a foot.

"Take the shot," Aisir said.

I shot. The bolt flew right where I was aiming, slightly above of the front leg and skewed to the chest, hoping to hit the heart of the goat. A good shot always seemed to travel in slow motion. I watched the bolt wobble through the air, striking the goat, and it immediately crumpled on the goat's body, falling useless down the bluff to the ground underneath, while the goat remained completely unharmed.

"FUUUUUUUCCK," the goat said.

I didn't believe my ears. I thought, for sure the goat just screamed, it didn't say fuck. It just screamed.

"YOOOOOOU," the goat said.

Aisir and I paused.

"FUUUUUUCK. YOOOOOU!" The goat screamed, looking at us.

Aisir pulled me up from behind, and we started running back to camp.

APRIL 2019, HOWE COUNTY

Next up on KUFA out of Jefferson City, MO, we have the latest on a viral sensation that has been sweeping the nation, all based out of the quiet little town outside of Armin in Howe County. Meet Elmer, a 2 year-old Boer goat on the Circe Family Farm that has a lot to say. Here's the clip.

(goat bleating) HEYYYYYYYY.

(Voice offscreen) Would ya listen to that?

(goat bleating) YOUUUUUU.

(Voice offscreen) Haha!

(goat bleating) HEYYYYYY. YOUUUUU.

(Newscaster laughing) Well, we got Elmer here in studio today. I'm here with Elmer and his owner, Danielle Circe. Care to say anything, Elmer?

(Elmer the goat is being held on a leash by his owner, Danielle. Danielle is smiling and remaining calm. Elmer the goat is slowly moving his head left to right, staring at the grass, ambling left and right a few steps before centering. He seems unconcerned with both the camera aimed at him and the microphone placed in front of his mouth. While the reporter hopes that Elmer the goat talks, she has a backup plan to try to get him to bite the foam of the microphone off. That would be worth a few hits

on YouTube at the very least. But the goat seems passive, uninterested, scarcely making any noise but short, dry breaths that slightly honk out of his nose. This lasts more time than any decent person thinks it should.)

(Danielle laughs nervously) He's shy today.

(The reporter feigns laughter) Come on, Elmer, don't be shy.

(The audience shudders slightly as the reporter lowers the microphone back to Elmer. It seems immediately obvious to everyone but her that the goat will not be speaking today. The goat does not respect her. Perhaps the goat does not regard her as a peer or colleague. Regardless, the reporter remains resolute. This segment is supposed to book exactly thirty seconds of time, and if the goat doesn't want to talk, fuck him.)

(Danielle feels her body temperature rise. She would love nothing more than for her goat, Elmer, to speak a few words to the news reporter.) You might want to come back when he's hungry. He's a big talker then.

(The goat seems to react to this. Elmer stares at Danielle. The emptiness in his eyes seems to be ill-matched to the slow lolling of the tongue spilling out of his mouth, resting on the side. It is unknown if he was offended by these remarks or if he even has the capability to be offended. The reporter withdraws the microphone from the goat and begins to speak.) Well, keep that camera rolling on him, Danielle, and hopefully he'll speak up again.

(Danielle brushes a strand of hair out of her face.) Thank you. We will.

(The reporter turns stiffly toward the camera.) Back to you in the studio.

(There is a six-second pause where no one moves.)

(The reporter drops the microphone and starts walking away. She makes a quick quarter turn toward Danielle and begins to speak.) Thanks so much. We are going to get a few shots of the farm before heading out. We'll run it again at noon.

(Danielle loosens the rope on Elmer and addresses the reporter.) No problem. Thanks so much for coming.

(The reporter curtly waves in lieu of responding verbally. Danielle turns to Elmer after taking his leash off. He stares absentmindedly up at her. *Danielle stares absentmindedly back. Danielle addresses the goat.*) I don't know what the fuck she expected.

(*Elmer stares at her without moving.*)

(*The reporter is cussing quietly under her breath while walking toward a white news van with the station's logo on it. The cameraman is pointing out the spots he thinks are best to shoot to get a layout of the Circe Family Farm. The reporter seems uninterested. She is twenty-four and monologuing her own life*) Four years of school for this, right? Jesus fucking Christ. Least the goat could do is fucking talk. I hate that little goat. Chuck told me to dip the mic in chicken broth or something to get him to bite it. I called him a retard. I feel like the retard now. This is my life, I guess. I thought I'd be on location in Syria right now. I'm talking to a goat. It beats writing lists online, I guess.

(*The cameraman, blissfully unconcerned*) We get the gravel road coming up right before we leave, too. Gives depth to the piece, makes it feel like a location. Like, connected. Not just some isolated little imaginary place, you know. Connects right to highway 333.

(*The reporter, annoyed, gives the thumbs up to the cameraman, who wasn't looking anyway*) "Come back when he's hungry" Okay, bitch. He should have been hungry when we got here. She knew what we were looking for. That could have been seven-digit YouTube hits if it went right. Everyone would have seen your caterpillar eyebrows.

(*The cameraman, looking elsewhere*) You want her to starve the goat for this?

(*The reporter, defensively*) Not starve. Just hungry, so he'd talk more.

(*The cameraman, shaking his head*) Cold-blooded. You'll do very well in this industry.

(*The reporter smiles at the cameraman. He is confused as to why she is smiling*).

(*A few hundred yards away, the goat, Elmer, breaks his gaze on Danielle to begin walking back toward the barn. Danielle lifts her cell phone out of her pocket, but pauses, and watches Elmer walk away. Elmer doesn't look back, but stares out toward to south. He lifts his nose into the air. When the wind comes up from the south you can smell both the interstate and the river, some dozens of miles south, permeating throughout the whole farm. Elmer pauses, then turns to Danielle.) FUUUUUUUUUUCK. AHHHH. FUUUUUUCK.*

END SCENE

1841

Dearest Minna,

I never thought I would say this, Minna, but I miss Philadelphia. Yes, I miss your soft brown hair and the walks we would take nightly. Your soft hand is the only thing I fear that can make me gentle. I could use your gentility now, as I believe our so-called "Missouri Rhineland" was a huckster's farce. I wish I was back in Philadelphia right now, looking at your handsome face, but I chose to venture west to forge a future for us and for the German way of life.

Friedrich Koeper painted a pretty picture of the "Eden" that is the "Missouri Rhineland." However, the disappointment in everyone's faces was apparent when the caravan came to rest. In the Settlement Society in Philadelphia, he told us of deep, rolling hills containing rich green fields of dark grass, but when we got here, we found the soil ridden with stones and the landscape ill-suited for construction. Why, Friedrich bragged that we would have a main street twice the size of Philadelphia, but we can't even find a stable, flat area for it to be on! And the river! The river he promised as perfect for commerce doesn't even flow the same route every year! Friedrich has essentially been ostracized by the community here. No one takes heed of his deeds or proclamations, and we are all working hard to establish our footholds so that we may send for our families within the year.

The only thing Friedrich got right, it turns out, is the beauty of this place. It is wild and unruly, sure, but the only location you would ever see deeper browns or more vibrant greens would be the Rhineland itself. I haven't seen it since I was small, but the very idea of this place fills me assuredly with nostalgia.

The lot I purchased for us turned out to be a good one, however. Most of the caravan has been stuck with what they have called "vertical acreage." Cliffs and rocks, I'm afraid. Why, Walther has spent his first month only busting rocks.

Most of the tradesman and craftsman have put their shops on hold until we have a means to support ourselves. I know you laughed when I said I was to be a farmer, and it turns out, well, we won't have to worry about that. The land is suited well enough for livestock, and I've already put in for pigs. Walther has gone mad, and is wrapped up in the idea of growing grapes for wine. Says the hills are perfect for it. It doesn't seem reasonable, but Otto reminded me that we can't all get pigs.

I get so wrapped up in all this, my dearest, I'm afraid I've neglected you! Are you ready to head west? Are you ready to feel at home with your people again? The summers are scorching and the winter is bitter. The framework is nearly built all over town, and it cries out for a feminine touch! Are your mother and father well? Have they reconsidered joining us? Tell your father I haven't seen a single Catholic since I have arrived!

Your absence is felt in the pangs of my heart daily. Oh, how optimistic I am for the future! Of basking in the summer sun during Maifest, dancing hand in hand! And when you arrive from Philadelphia, we will send old Friedrich Koeper on the same cart back! Otto has already joked to me that when we all die, we must bury Friedrich far away from us. He is not to be buried in the graveyard, because with him as our spirit guide, we would surely land in the worst plot in all of heaven! A joke.

Yours in heart,

Herbert

HOWE COUNTY

AT KURTIS GRASS FARMS, we strive to provide our customers and communities with the highest quality sod delivered straight to your home or business. With our unique blend of seeds, our high-quality soil, and our can't-be-beat prices, we trust that you will see that Kurtis Grass Farms is the absolute best in sod production and sales. Our sod boasts the strongest roots, making it the easiest to transport and transplant into its new home. It is local to the Missouri area, meaning that there is very little chance of soil incompatibility or disease killing the sod off. We aim for a sod that has high water retention as well, meaning that you have to do less work (and spend less money) watering it!

Better yet, our blend of turf grass doesn't just look good. It is perfect for ball parks or soccer fields as well. Nothing like the feel of real grass over that turf nonsense! That stuff will skin your knees! Our sod is priced per ten-square-foot roll. This larger size saves money, as we cut less and pass the savings onto you. Worried about transport? Don't be. We deliver in less than twenty-four hours from initial cut, and make sure our grass doesn't vary in moisture or temperature. Worried we are too far? Kurtis Grass Farms services most of the east-central Missouri area, running from St. Louis all the way to Columbia, stretching all the way down to Reynolds County!

▉▉▉

THERE WAS A MAN in a clean black suit sitting at a table and eating chili. His white-collared shirt was nicely starched, and he was staring blankly into the chili as he ate it.

He was a Company Man.

This man was thinking *the name chili comes from the chili powder that you use to make the soup.*

His waiter was an old, circular man in a white smock. He was watching Maury Povich and mumbling under his breath that it was unacceptable for a father to abandon his daughter, even if the mother is a big bitch.

"Any more coffee?" he yelled from across the room.

There was a woman there, eating alone. She had big sandy hair and was eating a grilled cheese sandwich. She had taken off her sandals and the Company Man could see her feet on the floor.

The Company Man had short brown hair. It was combed to the side, but casually, not rigidly. He was not acknowledging the man in the smock. He took a final bite of chili and walked out the door. He passed by an older woman on the way out. She was wearing a sweater with a cartoon character on it and stared hard at the Company Man's face.

The Company Man paused as he went outside. He could smell the river from here. He could smell the farmlands to the north, nothing but patches of mud and weeds in the early spring. He could hear the general hum of automobiles. He smelled the density in the air and began to walk to the eleven-room inn a quarter mile away that he had made his home base for the next few weeks.

"Who was that?" the woman asked the man in the smock.

"Not sure. Normal enough fella. Said he was in town on business."

"Business?" she said, "with who?"

"I don't know. None of my business."

"Business," she said, sitting down.

"The usual?"

"The usual," she confirmed.

The Company Man walked to the Calm Sea Guest Haus. It was a bed and breakfast with two competing themes, German and Nautical, and it was decorated with things like lighthouse wallpaper and signs that said that the current time was wine. Maybe reaching at overarching themes of the Hanseatic League. The entryway was a retrofit living room reformatted to handle both a little sign-in desk and long, horizontal tables for breakfast platters, served every morning at a purposefully early six a.m. to eight a.m., even on weekends. But the Company Man didn't mind. He would be there waiting.

It is a chore for a man without pleasure to figure out what to do with his time. The Company Man had exactly ten hours until he had to be at the six a.m. complimentary breakfast. He decided to go into his room, take off his nice black jacket, hang it up, take off his nice white collared shirt, hang it up, and to sit on the edge of his bed for the remaining nine hours and fifty-seven minutes.

It will be breakfast time soon, he thought.

I should practice my talking, for the morning, he thought.

Heard there was a famous goat in town?

Heard you guys had some kind of weird goat in town.

How about that goat I heard about?

People keep telling me about some kind of weird goat. It can talk. Is that true?

The thing about talking is that you can get perfect at it if you practice enough and if you also go out and talk to the people you are talking to.

They call it breakfast because you are "breaking" the "fast" of the night, because you cannot eat while you are sleeping.

At around three a.m. a light rain settled in. There was tranquility in the room that felt foreign to the Company Man. Earlier, he had seen a woman at the diner take off her shoes under the table while she ate. He tried to figure out if this was abhorrent human behavior or not. The feet had slipped out of the soft notches of white leather of her closed-toe sandals and they were resting on the cool linoleum of the mid-Missouri diner.

They always made these assignments quick because they didn't want people spending a lot of time here in places like this and the Company Man wondered if that was because of big, bad things happening or small, confusing things like this.

Three more hours until breakfast, he thought.

You can turn the dial on the lamp to determine the intensity of the light from the lamp, he thought.

The Company Man imagined eating chili for the next three hours and took his shoes off.

It is time for breakfast, so I am going to breakfast, he thought.

The Company Man got dressed and descended from the narrow stairs to the first floor on his way to the buffet area of the Calm Sea Guest Haus.

"Ah, Mr. Mann, you look well rested. Get a good night's sleep?"

"Yes," said the Company Man, looking at the buffet. Eggs again, and circular pieces of sausage. "Heard you guys had some kind of weird goat in town. That true?"

◦ ◦ ◦

An Excerpt from *The Riverside Ascetic*
By Edi Markham

THE MERCENARY I HAD been tracking has captured me. Despite the sheer distance that I am from my monastery and my homeland, he recognized the robes of my order. He immediately sheathed his weapon and turned from me. "You are my prisoner," he said. "Do you understand?"

I nodded.

"How long have you been tracking me?"

"I was dispatched to find you after you orchestrated the massacre at Gunli. That was fourteen months and a week ago."

"How did you know it was me?"

"Blunt weapons to the skull, followed by a bloodletting of the throat. Then you burned them. Same as Rorwick. A tribal leader gave you up to avoid torture at Rorwick."

"Why bother?"

"Records on individuals of intense cruelty are scarce."

The mercenary began laughing.

"There's no way that's fucking true," he said.

"The Order sent me to find you and record your deeds."

The mercenary wiped his mouth with the sleeve of his leather armor. He looked at me with his head craned to the side. Eventually, he just stared into the sky. It was dark now, and this far away from the cities, all of them were visible.

"Anyway, you will answer my questions, correct? Your order does that shit, right? How much do you know about me?"

"Can you be more specific?"

"What is your earliest record of me?"

"Your father, Lynal Torbil, was arrested in the year 121. Sole custody of you was given to your mother's father."

The mercenary was silent for a minute.

"So here is how it is going to go. I know that they train you to be impartial, unafraid. I know that they fuck up your dick and balls or pussy or whatever so you can't enjoy nothing. They drive you, endlessly, to be tools. And you're going to tell yourself it is your fate if something happens. And that's why you're going to let me kill you. Because you lose nothing if you die. But if you resist, you'll lose your code of life, your way of being. It's all that you know. Please walk forward and let me tie you up."

I walked forward.

"You have a purpose in being here. But I'm not going to tell you about me. I'm going to tell you about what I saw. The Anomaly. There are things in this world that shouldn't exist. Not like me. Not evil. Evil makes sense. This is something else. You copy?"

I nodded.

"You'll see some shit. It'll be something. You'll see some shit," Torbil said.

HOWE

THE GAS STATION ATTENDANT was standing over a bucket in his kitchen. *They weren't made to be opened easily,* he remembered, *no shit, shut the fuck up.* Living this close to the water, in the flood plain, made him feel constantly moist. He dried his hands off on a kitchen towel before trying to dig his nails into the unlocking mechanism of the food bucket again. It clicked, gave, and came off. The Gas Station Attendant had just cracked open twenty-five pounds of cheesy cauliflower and rice, and the smell made itself at home immediately.

The food buckets were his dead dad's impulse purchase. His father, in his last decade, became fixated on the end of the world, the coming apocalypse, and things of the like. The Blood Moon. Pedophilic oligarchs with goat heads. The family ignored most of it. The food buckets were his last hurrah. A large truck arrived two weeks before he died with twenty-six buckets that weighed twenty-five pounds each. All the food was dried and prepped for upward of thirty years shelf life in case of a global breakdown or cataclysmic event. The dried food was nutritionally designed to be a group of people's sole source of safe food. It was recommended that the food be stored in a cool and dry place, preferably a basement or emergency preparation bunker.

In the advertisements for the food buckets on the televangelist's TV show that the Gas Station Attendant's father had watched, he stirred the food in the food buckets with a military E-Tool entrenching shovel. The Gas Station Attendant put a large metal ladle in the room temperature cheese and broccoli and filled up a large cooking pot. As he heated up the large cooking pot full of cheese and broccoli, he covered the top of the food bucket in aluminum foil. He placed the lid back over the aluminum foil on the food bucket and hoisted it onto the bottom level of his refrigerator.

The broccoli pieces were no bigger than a dime. They were mostly stems without the florets. The cheese was a classic orange color. The Gas Station Attendant covered the pot, sat on the couch, and continued reading.

All food tastes the same, if you think about it, he thought.

The Gas Station Attendant was reading a book about Suleiman the Magnificent. He was a Sultan of the Ottoman Empire that oversaw what was considered the Golden Age of the Ottoman Empire. He was both a great patron of culture as well as an expansionist, annexing much of Europe and the Middle East.

The book, it seemed, pushed the idea that Suleiman was a rare person. A calm, logical, and educated leader, a man of fully realized potential, that seemed to be capable of doing nearly anything he wanted. He called himself "the true Caesar."

What's the point of being so "great," just to be proud to hold some guy's jockstrap from over one thousand years ago? And not to mention, all the people that died, all the wars...

The house was starting to stink. The Gas Station Attendant walked to the pot of cheese and broccoli and stirred. He scraped the bottom. This food tends to stick. He had been eating these buckets exclusively for over seven months now.

He stared out his window as he stirred. It was growing dark now. The sun crept down in the west and bounced orange light up and down the river. The house was his father's, a raised trailer on the floodplains, and he faced Armin to the south. He could throw a stone out his front door and hit the river. When it flooded, well, he had to stay inside. Wasn't usually a problem, though. Only two flood seasons on the river, typically. One was coming up. The snow would be melting in the Rocky Mountains soon.

He heard dogs barking. It wasn't too uncommon, and he didn't pay it any mind. He took out a couple of wooden spoonfuls of cheese and broccoli and placed them in a small plastic bowl and sat down on his plaid couch.

The couch was the only place to sit in the house. The Gas Station Attendant's trailer had one bedroom, a living room/kitchenette, a laundry/utility room, and a bathroom. There was a coffee table in front of the couch. He stacked his books on the floor. The bedroom had a twin mattress on the floor and his clothes were folded and stacked neatly along the wall. There was nothing on the walls.

The Gas Station Attendant did not think about the food while he ate. He thought about Suleiman the Magnificent.

Back then everyone wanted to be Caesar or Alexander the Great or call their country the new Rome. The Turks did it, the Russians did it, every Holy Roman Emperor did it. Bunch of dipshits and assholes.

"I am the new Caesar. This is my Rome," the Gas Station Attendant said out loud, alone.

Everybody's just chasing ghosts, showing them how hard they can jack off. Hehe.

The Gas Station Attendant rinsed out his bowl of cheese and broccoli in the sink. He placed the lid back on the cooking pot filled with cheese and broccoli and put it in the fridge next to the bucket. These were the only two items in the fridge. He filled a jar with tepid water from his sink and stared outside. The dogs were barking more. The orange light had faded from ground level and only reached him by refracting in the air down in the miles above him. He heard more than one dog, and stepped outside.

There were about eight wooden stairs and a safety rail that took him to ground level. The dogs were barking in the east. He put his hands in his pockets and stared at the water.

The book he had just read before the one on Suleiman was about water rights in America. He thought about it as he stared at the Missouri River as twilight set in.

The focus of it, narratively, was the Rio Grande. Farmers from Texas and New Mexico both survived on water collected from a dam. Well, both sides wanted more of the dam, so to survive, they tapped groundwater. Well, they got mad at tapping so much groundwater, too, and they fought. And it's sad because you can't really tell who is right. Can't tell. It's so far removed at that point, so entrenched in bureaucracy. When you read it, the only thing that matters is like, well, who's going to win. Because there ain't just enough water for everybody to be happy. And no one really has a right to it anyway.

I mean, look at that river right there. All that water. Bet someone would like to do some farming with it, even as muddy and ugly as it is.

The Gas Station Attendant's train of thought was broken by the jawing of dogs nearby. Sounded like it was coming right behind the trees. The woods were still traversable here, as late winter trembled into early spring. The overgrowth was still below-ground. The Gas Station Attendant kicked off his cheap tennis shoes to go barefoot and started walking toward the trees. He was a bit pensive at the barking, because it had started to sound like it was coming from a dozen or so dogs.

The Gas Station Attendant stepped over the brush and walked on the bulbous roots of the oak trees that lay adjacent to the river. He pushed through the relatively sparse woods and came through the greenery resting on a large, flat chunk of limestone that oversaw a small inlet of water on the banks. The Gas Station Attendant saw eleven dogs, all brown labs except for one golden retriever, trotting and splashing in about foot-deep water, surrounding an impossibly large creature, bigger than a bear even, that seemed to be prone in the water. The Gas Station Attendant watched the dogs circle it playfully. The Gas Station Attendant did not move.

The creature stretched its spine, reared back, and got on its feet. It was easily over eight feet tall, covered in matted, brown hair. Splotched with mud. It hunched its spine, and took one of its large, hairy hands, and began cleaning out its asshole in the middle of the river. It made guttural, deep sounds as the Gas Station Attendant saw it manipulate its finger into its own asshole, presumably cleaning it. It seemed to take no pleasure in it, and angled its face upward. The creature flicked something off of the aforementioned finger into the river and splashed some water on it. The creature then began to slowly scan the river, and, turning, found the Gas Station Attendant, thin-lipped, unmoving, watching him from the nearby tree line.

What it saw: a lanky, middle-aged man in his forties. He was barefoot wearing a white T-shirt and jeans. His face was patchy with blond facial hair. He was impossibly skinny, sinewy, gristly. His eyes betrayed his otherwise calm demeanor. The blue of his eyes was almost run over by his pupils.

What the Gas Station Attendant saw: a bipedal North American ape that resembled the depictions of the supposedly fictitious creature known colloquially as Bigfoot.

Their eyes met for the longest fifteen seconds of either creature's life. The dogs then barked and ran east, without regarding the man. The creature that looked like Bigfoot dropped his stare from the Gas Station Attendant, looked at the departing dogs, and begrudgingly followed. The Gas Station Attendant slowly walked backward to his home.

He stopped in front of his house and looked to see if he was followed. He wasn't. He looked at the river. In the dark, without the benefit of the light, the water looked purple. He thought about farmers eight hundred or something miles away. He thought about Bigfoot cleaning his own ass.

He locked his door and drank a jar of water.

◈◈◈

BARRETT WOKE UP ON the recliner. There was exactly one beer on the folding table to the right and the television was on a Midwestern themed sports channel. The beer was half empty. He groaned loudly with every movement. It was a luxury of living alone. The room was impossibly hot for the time of year. The light streamed through the window into the unventilated room. The doors were all closed and it festered with the smell of feet, light perspiration, and beer. By the time Barrett woke up, he was so sweaty he thought he had pissed himself.

Barrett clambered out of the recliner and pissed for three minutes.

"Time to go check the trap," he said to himself.

He washed his face in the sink and rubbed soap into his armpits. No need to clean when you're just going to get dirty again.

It had been about three weeks since Barrett was in the storm. The day after, he walked outside right after abruptly waking up and began to scan for evidence that it had happened. He saw the rabbit's ear stuck in the wiper blade of his truck and sat down on the front step of his small home. He held his left nostril shut and blew some snot out of the right nostril.

"Well," he said.

Barrett got up and walked around his truck. It was dinged everywhere, the top, the sides, the bed of the truck. The windshield was cracked. No traces of blood though. No fur in the grill.

Barrett walked down his gravel driveway toward highway 333. Some things added up to his memory—the dinged mailbox, the skid marks coming from his left turn off the highway onto his driveway—but there were no corpses. No roadkill.

"But there were dozens," Barrett said.

Someone honked at Barrett. An old, black Lincoln he didn't recognize. One of those with the long hoods. He waved back, as is customary.

Barrett looked north up 333. Nothing. Not a single remnant of any creature left. Nothing but the rabbit's ear in his wiper. He walked back up his driveway, took the rabbit ear out of the wiper and held it in both hands. The hair was soft, gray.

Why? I don't get it. Did they do it on purpose? Was it even real anyway? Maybe someone slipped me something. Maybe I just ate something bad. Maybe.

Barrett wrapped the rabbit's ear in a paper towel, put it in a large zip-up plastic bag, and placed it in his refrigerator.

For the next three weeks, Barrett tried to ignore what had happened. He took in his truck to get the windshield fixed. Didn't speak a word of it to anyone, especially not Amelia. If he wanted to talk to anyone, he read *Pig Iron*.

For two weeks straight, he read it. He took his meals at the gas station nearby, with the old foggy-eyed scraggly blond guy in glasses looking right through him every time he bought a twelve pack and a couple microwavable chicken sandwiches.

He was at the end now, but he didn't finish it. He hadn't touched it for a week. He had just read a part where everyone gets separated by a bandit attack and some magical guy named The Company Man appears to everyone individually and tells them to find each other in the west. The elf made some kind of deal with him for his soul because he said he was in love with Henbit. He heads west, but Henbit heads east because her sister and the large mushroom guy got kidnapped by slavers. The last part Barrett had read is a part where the Company Man takes the elf to the center of the earth, which is a large, flapping tongue for some reason.

Barrett put the book down after that. Since the night of the storm, Barrett had been reading *Pig Iron* religiously. He just walked around his house for a bit, pacing, wiping his nose, staring out the window.

I had tried to read Proust once because Amelia had called a guy that read Proust impressive and it felt like as I read it a weird smattering of flowery-ass words just smashing into me over and over and none of them stuck and if I tried to read it slower to understand and it just felt like I was watching slow-motion replays of me not understanding stuff and this isn't quite like that but instead of words it's like metaphors. This was the last thing she wrote. She knew she was dying. She knew here. So what the fuck? What's she saying?

Barrett spent the last week alone, rarely leaving the house. He ate hot dogs for at least one of his two meals a day. He watched spring training baseball games on television. It wasn't until the end of the week he was drinking at home. He, usually right after the sun set, enjoyed going out back into his yard and pacing around, making sure everything was in order. His house was on a small hill overlooking the Missouri River to the south. It ended in the south at a small cliff, about twenty feet tall that sat above a little river inlet. It was nothing but brown water and brown mud. Barrett walked toward a large branch, put his foot on the base of it, and snapped off all the smaller branches sticking off of it, grunting a bit, until he had a suitable walking stick, about three or four feet tall. He walked west. The earth was a bit muddy, as it was a wet season, and he stayed careful to walk only on the grass so he didn't have to rinse his boots off later. He circled the perimeter and picked up a few errant pieces of trash, rounding south, heading toward the ten feet or so of brush between his yard and the cliff.

Barrett paused as he heard rustling in the brush. It was early spring, so the vegetation wasn't thick. There wasn't much room to hide. Barrett had no flashlight, and there was scant light left in the air, just thin strands of twilight remaining from the sunset twenty minutes prior. He tilted his head and squinted at something dim by the cliff, leaning on the walking stick lightly.

The dim figure was a lump of shadow and hair. It emerged out of a low and purple dark standing up straight, and it kept straightening, and kept straightening, emerging like a blackhead from the earth, clarifying the air around it, revealing a large, hairy bipedal creature, that stepped back tentatively, heading toward the cliff.

Barrett turned and gasped, struggled backward, twisting his ankle and falling into the damp dirt and loose grass below him. The trash he had gathered spilled out of his jacket pocket. He turned back to look in the direction of what he had seen and saw nothing. He laid in silence for a moment, listening for footsteps, or grunts, anything really, and heard only the thin whistling of the wind coming off of the river into the hills. Barrett exhaled.

It wasn't until he tried to stand up that he realized the issue. Something was gravely wrong with his ankle. He couldn't move it or put any weight on it. Barrett rolled onto his back and breathed slowly, thinking, listening for that thing. There's no way it left. Barrett couldn't see it, but he could still smell something of it in the air. It was alien, mangy, and rank. It was like matted hair and mushrooms.

Barrett got on his stomach. He dragged himself back to his front door and crawled up the stairs. Mud streaked in. Barrett kicked his boots off as he came to the threshold of the front door, rolled up inside, and kicked the door closed. The pain shot from his ankle upward, and all he could think about was the mud streaking onto the white carpet. He took off his muddy shirt and his muddy jeans and lay down on his white carpet in his gas station boxer shorts grimacing at the ceiling.

Barrett heard the wind turn. He looked over his own gut to see the door creaking open. He kicked it shut in a panic and artlessly rotated himself to grab the lock. His fingers were caked in mud as he turned to lock his thin plywood door. The unfastened screen door clambered back and forth, slamming into the frame. Barrett drug himself to the sink and pulled himself up to look out the kitchen window. The blood rushed to his feet as he stood, and he blinked while staring out the window. The highway lights backlit the black woods in front of him. The silhouette stood unmoving, but Barrett could feel them breathing. He caught his breath, darting his head left and right to try to put eyes on what he had seen. The screen door still clattered rhythmically. The shadows swayed as Barrett's vision straightened.

"Fuck," Barrett said.

He felt his stomach sink to his ass as he remembered that Amelia took his guns in the divorce. He threw open the kitchen cabinet and grabbed a dull knife.

A low, barely perceptible groan started outside. Barrett leaned in to make sure he wasn't imagining it, his eyes wide and yellow. The wind stopped. The door no longer clattered into its frame. The slow groan grew in volume over the course of a few moments. Barrett didn't move. The animalistic rumble grew into a shrill whine within half a minute and all the while Barrett stood still, staring, gripping the knife over his kitchen sink. What started as sounding like the slow groan of a cow grew into the outward shriek of a banshee. Barrett stared into his sink. He saw the dirty silverware and glasses below vibrating. He backed away and positioned himself behind the front door.

The shrieking continued but he could tell it was moving toward him. He started to push his couch into the door. Barrett heard the deep crunch of a tree being sundered in half over and over and over as it moved closer. He considered calling Amelia.

No, Barrett thought.

The shrieking stopped at the front of his door. He heard enormous, labored breaths. Then something else. It sounded almost like a human crying, but wetter somehow, more alien. Barrett smelled it now. It smelled like yellow dog shit on the bottom of your shoes. Barrett retched, despite himself, and the crying stopped immediately. There was a pause, three or four seconds that felt like an eternity. Then suddenly, whatever was in front of Barrett's door took off, sprinting south, screaming. Barrett listened intently. The tongue and mouth were clearly malformed, ill-suited for language, but Barrett heard what it was saying distinctly.

"DON'T HURT ME! DON'T! NO! NO! NO! NO! NO—"

Barrett stayed still as he listened to it trail off, heading to the river. After about five minutes of silence, Barrett tried to stand up again. His ankle was killing him. He could see it swelling through his socks already. He sat on the couch for a moment to rest, and accidentally drifted off to sleep.

He awoke with a start and immediately chided himself for passing out, grumbling. Barrett saw his muddy jeans on the floor and slid them on best he could. He buttoned them as he took a tentative step out of his front door to try to figure out what had happened.

No footprints. He frowned. He started walking toward the river and saw that three of his trees that stood over the small cliff on his property had been smashed completely in half, about six feet up. Large splinters were thrown everywhere. They were hit by something blunt. He put his hands in his pocket and sighed, bracing himself against a tree as to not put weight on his ankle.

The early morning sun was rising. There were cars going up and down State Highway 333 normally, like nothing ever happened. It was spring, and the world was fragrant. He stared down toward the river, and his mouth fell open.

There was a path of smashed trees leading all the way down to the Missouri River. The brown river glistened in the distance.

꩜꩜꩜

BEFORE ROSE SENT HARPER to live with Amelia, Amelia had to clean. There were dozens of boxes to move, and she started carrying box after box into the unfinished basement below, stacking them to the ceiling. When she ran out of space there, she moved things into her own room, which she had managed to keep some of the clutter out of. She even stacked some boxes into the shower of her master bathroom, since she typically only took baths. Her closet was too full of old clothes to manage much more.

Eventually, she was able to clear out the living room except for one corner, and cleared the guest room full of Edi's old things for Amelia. She took the two books, *The Riverside Ascetic* and *The Trees of Iron County*, and placed them on her bedside table. She put a padlock on the door leading down to the basement.

On the day Harper was set to arrive, Amelia brewed a pot of coffee and sat at her kitchen island tapping her foot. She had expected Rose to come inside with Harper, have a discussion with her about boundaries and rules, help Harper settle in, and leave.

Instead, Harper arrived at the front door with a large pink suitcase and a backpack, frowning hard and avoiding eye contact.

"Hey, dear," Amelia said.

"Hi," Harper replied.

"Get in," Amelia said. "Harper, do you drink coffee?"

"No. I haven't tried it."

"Try it. I made a whole pot, and I'll drink it all if someone doesn't help," Amelia said.

"Mom never let us. School said we couldn't bring it, too," Harper said.

"You see her here? Any school stuff here? Dump your stuff here, we'll take it up later. I was hoping I could tell you something first," Amelia said.

"Oh," Harper said.

Amelia poured a cup of coffee for Harper, adding some sugar and cream.

"So—" Amelia started, sitting down, clasping her hands in her lap, "some bad shit happened, and, well, that's that, and if you ever want to talk to me, I'm here. But also, well, this is a lot to, uh, address within two minutes of walking through the door, and I know it, but, well, I had a daughter, a little older than you, not much, and that was the last girl your age, well, that I've had in my house, or even talked to, so if I ever, you know, act odd, or get emotional, that's part of the reason why. And I just want you to understand that, because the room you'll be staying in was her room."

"Oh, ok," Harper said.

"Yes, well—try your coffee."

Harper took a sip.

"It's okay. It's different."

"You'll get used to it," Amelia said. "You hungry?"

"No, sorry," Harper said.

"Maybe later," Amelia said.

The two sat there at the kitchen island, silently alternating sips of their coffee for a few moments. After a minute, Harper put her arms down and buried her head in them. Amelia patted her shoulder while she cried.

"I'm not saying things are okay, honey. I'm not saying that. But I will say what I felt like. At the worst, I felt like it was going to last forever. And just, well, it doesn't, even if you want it to. Do you want me to show you where your room is?"

Harper nodded without revealing her face. A week later, her parents decided to pull Harper from school.

Harper was in gym class. It had just gotten warm enough that the kids were able to run track outside instead of playing dodgeball in the gym. After each student completed their four laps, kids were essentially allowed to do what they wanted to fill out the rest of the hour. Some of the kids played basketball, some threw around a football, but most just sat on the bleachers and talked with each other. After coming back to school after everyone knew what happened, Harper didn't say a word. She sat as close to the teachers as possible and never ate lunch. Gym was really the only class where she was left to her own devices. Her first instinct was to hide in the bathroom, but she knew if some girls saw her go in there, they would follow. Harper decided the safest course of action was to walk in circles around the track all class.

The danger in this plan was that whenever she walked in front of the bleachers on the track she saw everyone look at her. The next go around they whispered. She started walking really quickly past the bleachers, and really slowly the rest of the way.

The taunts of children are rarely creative. The ones that whispered, emboldened by the laughter of others, resigned themselves to yell something quickly and muffled to Harper as she passed.

"Mouth!" a chubby kid in a camo shirt yelled.

Harper turned.

"How's that mouth!" he yelled quickly.

Harper looked at her feet and kept walking. It elicited a hushed half-laughter that flared up quickly and was shushed by groans. A few of the kids walked away in exasperated protest.

Harper rounded the track, empty faced. She began to jog when she approached the bleachers again.

The chubby boy pretended to cough and said, "Poison pussy!"

A girl in a teal polo punched his arm, avoided looking at Harper, but still laughed. Harper hurried her pace. As she crested the corner, she heard a small scuffle behind her, and turned to see an older guy, one of Derek's friends (whom she had never been introduced to, she just recognized him from various social media photographs) grabbing the camo kid by the back of the neck and sneering in his face.

"It's not fucking funny, bitch. He'd be fucking alive if it wasn't for her. My uncle is the fucking sheriff, man. He told me the texts she sent. She fucking threatened him to make him go over there, basically. You think that's funny? Turning this into a fucking joke?"

"I got you, I'm sorry," the camo kid said.

Derek's friend released him. The coach was approaching now, saying, "All right, all right, let's go, c'mon."

Harper ran back inside. No one stopped her or said anything. She got dressed quickly in one of the bathroom stalls so that she would be safe in case any girls followed her. She cried silently. She composed herself briefly when dressed, wiped her eyes, and walked calmly out of the bathroom stall. The locker room was still empty. She turned out of the locker room back into the school building proper and headed for the nurse's office.

"I'm sick," she announced.

There was a kid lying down on a small vinyl couch as the nurse pressed a cloth to his forehead. Fluorescent lights flickered as the nurse turned to address her. Harper stood straight up, looking directly at her, one hand on her bookbag strap.

"Is that so," she said.

"Yes. My stomach," Harper said.

"Let me take your temperature in a minute," the nurse said.

She stood up and took her hand off the wet cloth. She removed her plastic gloves and walked over to a sink and began washing her hands.

"Just have a seat, hon," the nurse said.

"May I use the bathroom first?" Harper said.

"Of course," the nurse said.

Harper walked into the bathroom and locked the door. She looked for a light switch and found none. After a few seconds of flailing around, the lights just flicked on. Motion detector, or something. Harper got on her knees in front of the toilet. She put the lid up. She placed her middle finger as far down in her throat as possible. There was a first gurgle, a burp, and the bitter and acidic taste of stomach acid flared through her mouth and nose. She focused on the taste, the acrid, pervasive thing that clung to her nose hairs so tightly, and tried to do something she had read online. Just stick your finger back and "press the button."

She puked. Not much more than a mouthful. There wasn't much food in her right now. It was mostly a thin, orange liquid flecked with the bready remnants of her cereal breakfast. She watched it, determined, spitting into the toilet every few seconds. The thin orange strand of spittle landed on top of the water and drizzled outward, becoming translucent, mixing with the water in the bowl, the tiny flecks of cereal drifted aimlessly, as the orangish acid formed a spiral pattern in the water before dissipating.

She listened for sounds outside the door and heard none. She pressed her middle finger down her throat again, for either emphasis or catharsis, and puked only a handful of acid into the mess below her. Harper breathed hard for a few seconds, not moving. The lights turned off in the bathroom. She raised her hand up and waved them around. The lights flicked back on. She spit a few times, stood up, put the toilet seat down, washed her hands, rinsed out her mouth, spit again, dried her hands off, flushed the toilet, stepped outside, and sat down.

"You okay, dear?" the nurse asked.

"I puked," Harper said.

"I heard you. I'm going to take your temperature, okay?"

"I just want to go home," Harper said.

"Let me take your temperature first, just to make sure."

The nurse approached.

"Hold out your tongue, hon," the nurse said.

Harper looked at the nurse with her mouth closed. Her face started trembling. She didn't break eye contact. First the lips opened, the eyes welled, and then it all sort of spilled out when the face leaned over, and immediately, inconsolable, fat, blubbering tears. Total and complete wailing, just the sounds of pure anguish that only teenage girls and Italian mothers are capable of making. The boy lying down all of a sudden felt better and went back to class.

The nurse got low and looked at Harper's face and said "honey," repeatedly, like it was a mantra. She placed her hand on her shoulder and just watched her up close, touching her, saying, "honey," and nodding.

Honey, honey, honey, honey, honey, honey, honey. Honey. Honey.

Harper cried so hard she couldn't think normally. She thought only in single words and images, cycling through them in her brain. From her parents, to Derek, to Amelia. To the word "SLUT" emblazoned on her garage door. These thoughts, these people and faces and images, all swirled together like flotsam she puked into the toilet, and they cumulated into rehearing the phrase "he'd still fucking be here, dude," that Derek's friend yelled on the bleachers, because she recognized that she had the same pain that he did, but was ostracized from participating in the same mourning ritual as everyone else, because of her role, fair or not. She let out one final howl, one final blubber, and as a large bubble of snot emitted from her nose, the nurse wiped it away, and said, "Honey, lie down."

Thirty minutes later her mother, Rose, arrived. She wordlessly guided her into the parking lot. The few students that saw her leave said nothing. Rose drove her to Amelia's house.

"Do you want to keep going to school?"

"No," Harper said.

"I think that's okay," she said, "for a while."

I am never going back to that school ever again, Harper thought.

She sat stationary in the car and watched the woods scroll by. When Rose dropped her off, she walked inside and saw Amelia hurriedly try to hide a book from view.

"You're home early," Amelia said.

"I'm sick," she said.

"You look like shit, honey," Amelia said.

"Thanks," Harper said.

"Want some coffee?"

"God, you with your coffee," she said.

"I don't wanna drink it all myself."

"Then why make so much?"

"Because what if someone comes by and wants some?" Amelia said.

"You're crazy," Harper said, half-laughing through her snot.

Amelia shrugged and took a sip. It was early afternoon now, and the sun came rushing into the hybrid kitchen/living area through the skylight, bathing everything in natural light, and making the room warmer. Harper stared up at the sun just peeking over the edge frame on the roof. It was so different than the white, almost medical looking lightbulb panels that filled up her school. She breathed and slumped in her chair.

"Your posture is awful, good lord," Amelia said. "You know what my mom used to do if I sat like that? She would come behind me when I was a kid and jab her thumb in between the vertebra in my spine real quick to get me to jolt up. Old school."

"What were you reading when I came in?"

"Eh, nothing," Amelia said.

"God, you're so cagey. Every other older lady I know is like, desperate to talk about the book they are reading at any given time," Harper said.

"Older?"

Harper laughed, "You know what I mean. And you're just trying to change the subject."

"Okay, okay, I'll tell you. But you gotta tell me why you came home early. I hate beating around the bush and being sensitive with my teenage-handler gloves on."

"Deal," Harper said.

"It's my daughter's book, Edi. The one who—the one whose room you are staying in. My ex-husband came over about a month ago and demanded to read one. I guess, well, neither of us ever have read any of them. Too hard, mentally. Well, I gave him one, and, even if he doesn't know, I feel like he shouldn't go through it alone. So I've been reading one too. *The Riverside Ascetic*."

"She wrote two?"

"Three," Amelia said, "and don't think I forgot our deal. Why'd you leave school?"

Harper bit her gums and looked down.

"I'm never going back to that school ever again."

Harper's tears started welling up in her eyes. She placed her head face down on the counter and started crying.

"Oh, no, oh, here it comes, it's okay, it's okay, sweety, it's okay, I got you, I got you," Amelia said, squeezing the girl. "Oh, God, honey, you got no idea how long never is, no idea, it's okay, it's okay, I got you."

〰〰〰

An Excerpt from *The Riverside Ascetic*
By Edi Markham

I HAVE BEEN ON a forced march for three days. After twelve hours of walking, Torbil sets up camp and loosens my binds so that I can write down what has happened in my journal.

He does not seem to be, from observation, the greatest fighter I have witnessed. However, his name comes up more than anyone. He seems to just play everything right. When he can win, he always fights. When he can't, he doesn't. He survives.

Ignatius Torbil first came to the Recorder's attention when he was a slaver for a trade company from the Kingdom of Cam.

It was the assassination of the Lake Boss of Cam that branded him an outlaw, and started the descent. Countries other than Cam were willing to work with him still, until he upset the nation of Sedna as well as the Church of New Gods by hitting a diamond transport in their capital. His actions seem not to be motivated purely by money. Torbil was known to attack caravans, banks, and temples. He seemed perfectly willing to kill women and children. The Recorders showed a special interest in him after he hung a living girl from a tree on top of a hill so that her struggling would be a distraction to his escape. This itself wasn't too jarring, but it was the fact that he left so much gold at the scene untouched. No one knew why. He went from bandit to demon in the minds of the people. Horror stories about him were spread at every tavern throughout Armin.

At camp, he throws me my journal and loosens my binds. He skins a rabbit and chops its head off. He throws it in a small black pot over a fire and stares at me. I stare back, not out of defiance, but because I have to watch.

"May I ask you a question?" I asked.

He nodded, staring.

"Why did you kill the Lake Boss?"

"Why do you ask?"

"The knowledge isn't there," I said, "in our records."

"No, I mean, why that question? You led with that question. Why?" he said.

Torbil wasn't even looking at me anymore. He was staring to the west. We were almost at the coast of the nation of Veti. Calm, cool forests rolled toward a sandy, foggy coast.

"I believe it is a crucial piece of information. Though maligned, you were considered legitimate before. You could have retired without incident. You were by all means considered to be a wealthy man. Now if you are found, you will die. To me, following this train of logic, something happened that I do not know about. You suddenly became sadistic."

"Are you curious?" He asked, grinning.

"Personal curiosity is of no pertinence to a Recorder," I said.

"Shut the fuck up," Torbil said.

He seemed legitimately upset. He stood and hunched over me.

"I refuse to fucking buy it, you stupid fucking kid. They can't just grind out the humanity in you to a dust and let the wind take it away. You're scared, you're curious, you feel pain, hurt, just like anybody fucking else. Only reason you don't fucking do shit is because you know your order would kick your ass out if you did, and you're so fucked and brainwashed that you think you couldn't possibly exist without that as a core part of your identity. And you know what? For all your serenity, your logic, you still don't know shit. You don't wanna know where you're going? Or why for the last five years I've run back and forth across Armin with my dick in my hand pissing all over everyone's stupid fucking faces? Really? The Lake Boss? Fuck."

Torbil withdrew from his menacing position and poked at the cooking rabbit in the small pot. He exhaled loudly and dramatically.

"The Lake Boss was in possession of something he shouldn't have had. Something not from our world. I've been–I've been broken long before that, though. The Lake Boss, he really didn't matter," Torbil said.

"What did he possess?"

I wrote quickly.

"This," Torbil said, reaching into his pocket.

Onto my lap, Torbil threw a thin, square case. A hyperrealistic painting of a desert vista with four faces of four old men at the top. They looked foreign, unlike anyone around here. Perhaps they were Treebrayers, or the red-necked northerners of Cam. There was something written above the faces in a language I couldn't understand. I focused on the material. It felt like glass, but much weaker, with grooved sides. I could tell something was inside.

"Open it," Torbil said.

I ran my fingers on the grooves trying to find a latch, pulling at the sides. I began to pull harder.

"Do not break it," Torbil said.

I traced the weak, malleable glass-like substance to the corner, lifted, and it snapped open, the cover revealing an object unlike anything I had ever seen before. It was a circular object, rigid but flimsy looking, impossibly thin, at the center of the case. It was silver and beautiful. The same foreign language on the cover was written on this bizarre, alien disc. I went to remove the disc from the case, and Torbil snatched it from my hand.

"I've never seen anything like that before. Why'd you take it?"

"Lake Boss used to show it off when he was drunk. Said he took it from a bandit who crept out of the swamps and tried to stow away on one of his ships when he was younger. When he showed it to me, I started trying real hard to get everyone as drunk as I possibly could. All either company men or rich mercs who used to work for Cam, fucking around on vacation at Osage Lake, the big oasis to the east. If you've never been, it's a shit show. Complete revelry. Everybody goes home with bumps on their lips. So, everybody turns in but me and the Lake Boss. We got the... disc, whatever it is, on the table between us. And the more I keep drinking...I start to read it. I could read it. And I ask him question after question about it, he knows jack shit, he doesn't even care or want to figure it out. And I start reading out loud.

"'Waylon Jennings Willie Nelson Johnny Cash Kris Kristofferson. Highwayman.'

"He leans in. I read it again.

"'Waylon Jennings Willie Nelson Johnny Cash Kris Kristofferson. Highwayman. At the bottom here. Compact disc. Columbia Records.'"

"'How can you read it? What language that in?' he asked me," Torbil said.

I sat there with my legs crossed and my hands in binds. Torbil talked not to me, but himself, eyes on the thin grass on the ground. Looking but not seeing anything except whatever was going on in his own head.

"When I found those slaves on Pahusk...I learned something. The island teaches you things. The longer that you are on it, you just see nothing but prophecy. No outcome is too mundane. Carved into the bark of trees, things like 'the wind from the north brings cold rain in three moons'. 'Muddy boots will stain the furs of the eldest woman's house when the third rain falls.' It's so ripe with prophecy that the tribals on the island are fucking bored by it. But on the third night on the island, the night after I scouted out the village, we camped alongside a large cliff to hide our smoke from them. On the cliff was something written in large, red letters in a language I didn't know. Anyway, long story short, I got really drunk that night, and before I went to sleep, I thought I read what the cliffside said, bathed in the orange light of the campfire."

"What?" I asked.

"It said, 'The Gods have Cancer.'"

"Cancer?"

"Cancer. I don't know what it is either. But I thought nothing of it, I was so drunk, I fell back asleep. I remembered it as I read the case that said Highwayman in front of the Lake Boss."

"So you still didn't answer, why kill him?"

"Because," Torbil said.

Torbil faced me. His face conveyed no emotion. I started to smell the rabbit cooking behind him. He squatted real low. He got an inch from my face. I smelled his sweat.

"I can read the language of the Gods, and he can't. I can take it, so I did. I made a choice. It's why you are here right now. I am not the same as the rest of you. And if I can read the language of the Gods, that means I have some purpose. If I have a purpose, that means, I think I have a choice. And I've found more signs."

Torbil reached into a sack, and I heard light, melodic clunking as he dumped a series of bottles out onto the ground.

"Read it," he sneered at me.

I grabbed a bottle. Seemed foreign. Wrapped in a red and white scroll, color faded from time. Something alien written on it."

"I can't," I said.

"Budweiser," he said.

"What?"

"I don't know either," Torbil said.

Torbil spit, gathered the bottles back into the leather sack, and poked at the rabbit. He fumbled to roll a cigarette and dropped the contents of his tobacco onto the ground.

"Fuck," he said. "Do you ever think the world is a big, nasty, fucking accident? The Gods have Cancer. Waylon Jennings Johnny Cash Willie Nelson Kris Kristofferson. I think that's a guy. Maybe he knows. I learned about prophecy. And prophecy only ever predicts events. It doesn't predict outcomes. That means I have a choice. I don't know what the choice is, or what the events will be, but I am different from everyone else, and it has to do with the Gods, with this world, everything. And I'm the one who gets to make the choice. I'm sure of it. Me. Tell me, you mutilated, passive little pointless thing, how does that make you feel? It's me! Out of everyone! Tell me, and don't lie!"

ᚎ ᚎ ᚎ

DANIELLE CIRCE SAW A man walking up her gravel driveway from her kitchen window as she washed dishes. He was wearing a clean black suit with a starched white collared shirt underneath it. He wore a plain black tie. His hair was short and parted at the side.

Danielle Circe did not know that this was The Company Man. He was carrying a briefcase.

The name chili comes from the chili powder that is required to make the chili. Heard you got an interesting goat? Is this Circe farm? Heard you have an interesting goat.

Danielle rinsed her hands off and put on a light coat. She walked out her front door to greet the man walking up her driveway.

"Car break down?" Danielle asked as she stepped outside.

The Company Man smiled the smile he had practiced. He was hoping that she would smile back, but she did not.

I'm going to have to ask the company to give me a brand new smile.

"Yes, my car has broke down. Is this Circe farms?"

"Yes, yes, it is. Heard of us?"

The Company Man stopped walking and looked around the fields for a few seconds. He did not see any goats. This was disappointing. He then turned to regard the woman in front of him.

"Yes. I have heard of you. I was looking for you, but then my car broke down," said The Company Man.

"Well, at least you found us. Reception is really bad out here, so you aren't the first to wander up to my doorstep," Danielle said.

"Yes. My reception is bad, I'm sorry. I'm sure you are busy. But I am happy that I found you, at least," The Company Man said.

"I'm Danielle. And your name is?"

"I'm Mr. Mann," The Company Man said, "and I have been led to believe that you have a unique and/or interesting goat here at your farm? I was hoping I could meet with him," The Company Man said.

"Are you from a news station or some TV studio or something?" Danielle asked.

"Yes," The Company Man said.

The overcast sky broke for a second and the sun touched down onto the ground. Danielle shielded her eyes with her hand and beckoned The Company Man onto her porch. For a split second, it seemed like his suit glittered a bit as the sun hit it. Green and black.

"Well," Danielle said, sitting on a folding chair, "last time he was on the news it didn't go so well. I think it might be best to leave him be."

"What can I do, for you, that would allow me to see the goat?"

"Ha!" Danielle blurted, "Pay my mortgage."

"How much is that?" The Company Man asked.

"Oh, stop."

"I think that is something that can be arranged. I don't know what a mortgage is exactly or how much they cost. And I understand that they are paid for in American currency."

"Eleven hundred dollars, try me," Danielle said.

The Company Man reached into an empty briefcase and pulled out eleven hundred dollars. He handed it to Danielle with a blank look on his face.

"Is this satisfactory?"

Danielle hadn't touched the money yet. She hardened her eyes and cocked her head to the side as she stared at his face.

"Who did you say you worked for?"

"Like you said," The Company Man said, "a news station or TV studio or something. May I see the goat, please?"

Danielle took the money and counted it. It was all there. She pointed to the barn past the south field and started leading The Company Man there.

"What do you want with the goat? His name's Elmer, by the way," Danielle said.

"I just want to see the goat. After seeing it I will figure out what to do next."

"Awful tight-lipped about this. And throwing a lot of money around, not that I'm complaining. It's just very odd to me," Danielle said.

"People have stuff to do all the time. This is just another one of those things," The Company Man said. "You know us news station or TV studio types."

"It's right over here. Let me slide this open."

Danielle walked through an open door into a short, square barn. A few bales of hay were stacked in the corner, and the floor was covered in hay. A chicken-wire fence about six feet high separated two pens of goats, one for males, one for females. There were eight goats in total, and each pen had its own free area fenced in outside.

"He's, uh, Elmer is the white one with the brownish red legs. Um, uh—"

"Thank you," The Company Man said.

The Company Man leaned forward slightly and examined the goat. His head seemed to crane back and forth in unnecessary ways as he squinted. His feet stayed still. Danielle looked at The Company Man warily. She hadn't even put the money in her pocket yet.

"So, now wha—"

"This is the goat," The Company Man blurted. "Would it be too much to ask to ask you to go back inside of your home to leave me alone?"

"What? Why?"

"I will give you another eleven hundred dollars if you go back into your home and leave me alone with the goat for fifteen minutes," The Company Man said.

"What? Um, well, I guess…okay."

The Company Man reached into his empty briefcase and handed Danielle another eleven hundred dollars. He stared at her until she warily turned around and began to walk back to the house. He watched her walk down the path flanking the field and didn't turn to look at the goat until he ascertained that she was back inside her house.

The Company Man opened the chicken-wire fence and walked toward the goat in question. Elmer. The Company Man stood right in front of the goat and looked around. There were three more goats on this side of the pen, all sort of clustered around Elmer.

"Excuse me," The Company Man said, addressing the other goats, "I will give you all eleven hundred dollars if you will step outside and allow me to talk to Elmer alone."

The goats didn't stir. Elmer bleated, and the three begrudgingly bleated and walked outside. The Company Man watched them leave, and he went into his empty briefcase and took out thirty-three hundred dollars for them and threw it at their feet outside.

Elmer got to his feet. He never once made eye contact with The Company Man. He walked to the other side of the small pen where there was a little bit of hay out to eat.

"FUUUUUUUUUUCK," Elmer bleated.

"YOUUUUUUUUU," Elmer bleated.

"You go by Elmer now," The Company Man said.

"Bahhh," Elmer bleated, "hhhhhHNNN."

"Seemed a little brazen of you to go on the news, seemed sloppy. Not like you, I suppose. I'm here to check in. What you got for me?"

"Beh. Beh beh. Yeh. Yeeeeeh. YEEEEEH."

"It worked then. You got my full, undivided attention. Inform me of your prepared statement," The Company Man said.

"Meh meh. Hnnnnnn meh. Bleh bleh, HNNYEEEUNG."

"Him being overweight is not pertinent information. Please stick to relevant information."

"Hyehyehyehyehhhhhaaaaa," Elmer said.

"How long ago was the storm?"

"Hyeh. HAAAAAAA. Byah. Byeheyeh," Elmer bleated.

"You have proof it is an anomaly?"

"DOGS. DOOOOOOGS."

"And where are these dogs, Elmer?"

"WEEEEEEEEEEEST. WEEEST. FUUUUUUUUUUCK," Elmer replied.

"This will be taken care of," The Company Man said. "Thank you."

"Hyeh. Nnnnyaaah. HAAAAHHHH."

"Me? *I'M* not going to be doing anything," The Company Man said. "You know how this works."

"SHIIIIIIIIT," Elmer said.

"There are things that are and shouldn't be and there isn't anything you or I can do about it but help it play out its course. It's in motion already, somehow," The Company Man said.

"Hyeh. Nyah, behhh. AHHHH," Elmer bleated.

"Really? Bigfoot?"

"Nehhh," Elmer said.

"This will be bleak," The Company Man said.

The Company Man picks up his briefcase and begins walking north, back toward the house. Upon reaching the gravel driveway, he makes a perfect ninety-degree turn and starts heading back to State Highway 333. Danielle watches his back creep down the shallow hill and waits until he is out of sight before heading to the goat barn to check on Elmer.

I really hope that guy didn't just pay me two grand to fuck my talking goat, she thinks, *oh my God, I'd never forgive myself.*

As Danielle heads down the path flanking the southern field to the goat barn, she sees Elmer standing on a large rock, and breathes a small sigh of relief. Danielle walks into the enclosure and circles Elmer, checking for any type of wounds or marks. Nothing. She begins to walk away, grimaces and frowns, and turns back toward Elmer. She climbs up on the rock below him, pets his back, and lifts up his tail to look at his asshole. Danielle lets go of the tail, gives a sigh of relief, and hops down onto the ground below.

Danielle looks to the left and sees one of her goats chewing at the edge of a pile of money. She pushes him aside and starts stuffing the money that hadn't been eaten into her pockets.

When her husband gets home from work later, he will ask her if anything interesting happened today, and she will look at the television and say, "No, not really."

◆◆◆

Barrett was in a large, black medical walking boot for his right ankle. He had set up his ancient desktop computer on his kitchen table and was reading a cryptozoology website while drinking a bottle of Budweiser beer.

Pig Iron sat on his bedside table with a bookmark from a national pizza chain's child-reading program in it about twenty pages from the end.

The doctor had told him it was just a sprain, and, as such, a cast wasn't necessary. He had offered Barrett some pills, but Barrett declined, because he said you can't drink while you take them.

"At your age," the doctor said, holding his ankle.

"I'm under no illusions, doctor," Barrett said.

"Well, let's do what we can and get you home. Let's see if we got a boot around here. Six weeks, at the very least," the doctor said.

Barrett was reading a website detailing the suspected behavioral habits of the creature known as Bigfoot. He had a notebook next to his beer with a red pen on it, but he hadn't taken any actual notes yet. He sighed and took a drink of beer.

I'm losing my mind.

I know what I saw.

Makes no difference.

Barrett read.

Says Bigfoot was first seen by the Native Americans, primarily in the north. Salish people by the northwest and Canadian Native Americans. Canadian Native Americans. That ain't right. Canadian Indians. Native Canadians. There really ain't any Native Americans that I know of out here. Every blonde lady that owns a bead shop says she's one, I guess.

Missouri is not a location that is associated with Bigfoot sightings. Many cryptozoologists do not consider any part of Missouri to be a territory of the potential Bigfoot species. Over the course of many conferences and online discussions, the potential habitable territory of Bigfoot has been determined to be a region called the Bigfoot North Region. This territory stretches from the

American Pacific Northwest to the northern, non-arctic regions of Canada, then goes eastward over the Great Lakes, under the Hudson Bay, stopping in Western Quebec.

Barrett tapped his plastic, black medical boot against his linoleum floor as he read from a website called *The Bigfoot Consensus Project*.

ABOUT BIGFOOT

The creature commonly referred to as "Bigfoot" isn't a recent phenomenon that simply oozed into American folklore in the last fifty years. Even before Europeans landed in North America, the First Nations Tribes of Canada, the Salish, and a multitude of other Native tribes had depictions of similar creatures in their art as well as tales of their existence in their stories. Now, these descriptions can be wildly different, with some depicting the modern day creatures' known as Bigfoot as veritable boogeymen, kidnapping children who had the audacity to speak their names, some depicting them as little different from humans, just hairier and wilder, more autonomous, true beings of nature, and some refer to them as humans "Elder Brothers," shy, natural creatures with their own traditions and cultures, burying their dead and roaming the wilds. I would say to the person reading this, imagine the variety of depictions a human person can have. The same individual could be described as feral, wild, violent, or as peaceful, wise, and generous.

We here at the Bigfoot Consensus Project believe that all these depictions are about the same singular race roaming the temperate forests of Northern North America. For example, all of the stories depict the Bigfoot creatures as taller than average, stronger than average, with limited speech function, and covered in head-to-toe hair. They are described to have simian features.

We are able to state our hypothesis, that the creature commonly known as Bigfoot, while not depicted as foolishly and incorrectly as he is in the media, indisputably exists based off of a multitude of evidence, from tribal stories, to footprints, to pictures and videos, to the similarities in encounters, to environmental cues and population and territory estimations.

The estimated region where the Bigfoot race is estimated to live contains nearly fifteen million people. However, of that region, eighty percent of it contains absolutely no human residents. Is it not unreasonable to think that maybe, just maybe, there is something going on that we could not possibly know about? Are we, as humans and so-called Scientists, so sure of ourselves that we could possibly dismiss the idea completely?

Barrett killed the last of his beer and placed it on the table down away from him. He reached toward his ankle and pulled up another bottle of beer from the pack by his feet on the floor. Barrett typed in "MISSOURI BIGFOOT" into the search engine. The first thing that popped up were stories of a local creature he had never heard about, named Momo the Monster. It was supposed to be slightly smaller than a Bigfoot with a big clumsy head and a distinctive skunk-like stench. The thing Barrett definitely did stink, but it wasn't like a skunk. The thing Barrett saw smelled like freshly laid shit. Plus, his daughter never wrote about Momo, his daughter wrote about Bigfoot. Barrett shook his head.

The next listing was an article written by a small county newspaper in the Ozarks. It was about a supposed ufologist in the region who was designated by some UFO agency to collect all the reports in the area. The guy was a local chiropractor who was appointed by some nonprofit started by some French guy to be the lead investigator in Central Missouri. He started sharing Bigfoot stories.

"I had pulled over to check my tire, and I felt a large, leathery padded finger gently stroke my face and run off. I saw the back. All hair, huge, grunting."

"My husband hasn't been the same since he went on a walk behind our house a few days ago. He came back covered in scratches and abrasions and said that he had been thrown down a hill through the brambles by a big ape. He says Bigfeet isn't real, but really, is that more insane than him saying that there is a large ape throwing men down hills in Missouri?"

"One feller called to tell me that he saw bright lights in the sky outside his farm. I went to check and saw burn marks in the crops in his field. All soy, all scorched black. No other signs. Just a black circle and the crops all laying down flat. The next night, he sees the lights again, and rushes out. Nothing at the circle, but in the trees he said he saw a large, bipedal hominid lowering to the ground in a beam of light. He said it was clutching at its genitals and screaming."

"There were mysterious logs being thrown onto the highway. Too big for a human to toss. Not good."

Barrett read all night, until the sun came up. It was a familiar feeling to him. He often allowed the nights to drone on, buzzing silently around him, until the orange light broke. It wasn't something most people paid attention to, he thought. Drunks stay up all night, of course, or people on drugs, but it isn't the same. There's an activity, a bustle for them. Social and chemical. Even when he was younger he could drink until the sun came up, but it wasn't the same as being mostly sober and alone and feeling that pang of shame in your throat when the sun broke. Barrett read somewhere that staying up all night was a sign of intelligence, but Barrett thought that that was just probably written by a guy who stayed up all night a lot.

He powered down the computer when confronted by the morning sun. Going to sleep wasn't really something he wanted. It felted like a forced resignation. Barrett sighed.

"One trip outside," he mumbled to himself, and began to put on his left shoe. They said he could take the boot off only when he slept, but he never really did.

The air outside was crisp and cool. Taking the few small steps onto the unvarnished oak stairs was a bit more challenging with one foot covered in plastic armor. The humidity was intense. The air was wet but there wasn't any liquid. Barrett lurched his way toward the trees in front of the cliff. The spot where he saw Bigfoot and fell.

"I know what I saw," Barrett said.

Barrett used his big boot to kick a path into the loose, wiry brush at the base of the trees. A myriad of small plants and dead weeds growing into and over each other's corpses year after year, just starting to bud green. He stepped over what he could to get closer to the cliff just a few feet away.

He had never got this close before. He didn't like it. To most, it was a spectacular view. Objectively, it was. It oversaw the whole city of Armin, the bridge leading there, the Missouri river. At night, it would have been breathtaking. Barrett liked having the buffer of trees. His house was obfuscated from the view of any of those on Main Street in Armin below.

Barrett got to the edge and stared straight down. Mud, dead trees, and a few pools of stagnant water, waiting for a rainfall so they could be swept into the river. Nothing but floodplains between him and the river. Occasionally, a church with a short memory would try to turn them into a soccer field. He stared back at his feet and to the left, scanning for the creature he saw.

He had read hints on what to look for online.

1. Bigfoot follows elk/deer herds. They are his main source of food.

2. While squirrels, mice, voles, raccoons aren't something the Bigfoot hunts, their presence means that the local ecosystem is healthy.

3. If an area can support wolves or coyotes or bears, it could be a territory that Bigfoot roams. A typical Bigfoot territory will span nearly a hundred miles. They mark this territory by snapping trees in half and leaving them pointing in certain directions.

4. Bigfoots require a large source of nearby fresh water. Lakes and ponds are ideal.

5. Wild plants and berries are a necessary part of the Bigfoot's diet. Without fresh fiber, the Bigfoot is known to have diarrhea.

6. Look for areas that don't have a lot of active hunters. Private property or difficult terrain is a plus. For this reason, in recent years, many temperate Bigfoot have found themselves heading for swampy or marshy areas.

7. Bigfoot likes to rest on high ground that has lots of cover. They like to scan their territories while idle. The Bigfoot is a creature that considers himself a complete outsider to all humans. They interpret the world as being constantly at war with them. They will seek out locations that are unpleasant for humans, fetid or dangerous or both, and camp there until human activity ceases.

8. Bigfoot are known to occasionally make elaborate tree or rock structures in the wild. Stacking stones that are impossible for a human to lift in elaborate, cairn-like structures, or snapping thick trees in half and leaning them onto each other like the bones of a teepee. The exact reason for this is not known. It could perhaps be the intelligent Bigfoot's moment of artistic inspiration or a more elaborate familial communication with other Bigfoots.

9. Listen for exaggerated animal calls. The Bigfoot will often mimic other animals calls to gather information from the forest. Keep in mind that when dealing with Bigfoot, you are in THEIR home, in THEIR arena.

10. Look for big piles of shit. Because the Bigfoot is the biggest thing in the woods, their shit will be biggest too.

11. There are reports that Bigfoots can see infrared light and are very bothered by it. This explains why the Bigfoot has seemed to evade being spotted on thermal or infrared imaging.

12. You should be physically fit and in good health if pursuing a Bigfoot. The advantages that human physiology has over the Bigfoot is our lateral quickness, endurance, and agility. In open territory, a Bigfoot's long strides would overtake a human easily if they are agitated enough. Bigfoot are known to defend themselves by throwing rocks and logs at their pursuer, and anyone who wishes to track a Bigfoot must have the general health to withstand a hit and the maneuverability to avoid and evade any would-be Bigfoot out there attempting to put down their pursuer for good.

The soil at the top of the ridge was slick and clay-like. Barrett stepped tentatively, feeling his large boot getting caked in soil pretty quickly. Barrett was staring up, at about the eight-foot mark, evaluating all the skinny oaks that bordered the hill. He only had to take a few steps before noticing one was snapped very high up, at about the nine- or ten-foot mark, and the upper trunk of the tree was leaning from the snap all the way down to the disturbed clay soil below, pointing westward toward Barrett. Barrett shambled over hurriedly, his black medical boot caked in muddy clay now, and he stared at the trunk, both powerfully snapped and delicately laid down on the ground.

"Well," Barrett said to no one.

He looked at the break. It seemed so clean, so effortless, like if Barrett had snapped a twig on the ground. His vision slowly clambered downward as he heard a low, infrequent buzzing, and on the ground he saw a few flies circling what was easily the biggest shit he had ever seen in his life. Right next to the huge pile of shit, Barrett saw a clump of hair, what appeared to be a large toenail, and an enormous footprint.

"Good lord," Barrett said, "this seems like a freebie."

Barrett suddenly scanned around nervously.

"Who's there?" he yelled. "What kind of prank shit is this? I'm not falling for it."

He saw nothing and was answered only by the sound of cars rolling down the highway in the distance. From the snap and the shit pile, Barrett had a crystal-clear view of the town of Armin over the river. People seemed to be parking their cars, talking in front of shops. He saw old, overweight men carrying in cases of produce into small, riverside restaurants. He saw a woman walking down the sidewalk with a coffee. It could have been Amelia, he couldn't tell. She was blonde and in sunglasses, but it was far, and Barrett hadn't slept in a while. There was a family that had just unloaded out of a minivan at a park by the dock and the kids were throwing rocks in the river. The day was blooming in front of him. It was a real town full of real people. Just people living their lives.

Barrett picked up a smaller stick and started poking through the Bigfoot shit. Whoever this Bigfoot guy was, he ate a lot of corn.

EMERY WOKE UP TO a buzzing sound that he couldn't immediately place. He shifted in his recliner to check under his own ass, feeling out the chair with his palm. He placed his hand in the crease in the cushion by his right hip and heard something hit the floor. The buzzing resumed on the floor. Emery slapped the recliner shut and rocked back and forth three times, building up the momentum to get out of the chair. Once on his feet, he slowly turned back toward the chair, placed his hands on the armrests, and got down on his knees. He ran his hands underneath the recliner and plucked out his old flip-open cell phone. Then he crawled back to the front of the recliner, placed his hands on both armrests, and propped himself up. Once standing, he grabbed his tennis-ball walker (all the balls had managed to stay on since he lost the dogs) and headed slowly for the kitchen. Emery sat down on one of the hard kitchen chairs and opened up the phone to see who had called. It was his daughter, Carrie. He dialed her number.

CARRIE: Hello?

EMERY: Hey, pumpkin.

CARRIE: What were you doing? This is like the third time I called. You still didn't respond to the text I sent yesterday.

EMERY: Oh, I always forget to check those. I was, uh, in the chair, and had a hard time getting up.

CARRIE: Is anyone there with you?

EMERY: I'm fine.

CARRIE: That's not what I asked.

EMERY: It's what you meant. How's the Big Apple?

CARRIE: Same as ever.

EMERY: Come back and visit. I'll pay.

CARRIE: I can't afford to take off of work, Dad. We don't get vacation time with this job.

EMERY: Well, they should give you vacation. You should tell them.

CARRIE: They don't care, Dad. I'm one of, like, a hundred people.

EMERY: Could they take you off the schedule for a week? It's just a grocery store. Whatever your pay is, I'll pay it.

CARRIE: No, Dad, it's like a six hundred dollar ticket, then you got to pick me up from St. Louis, then it's like eight hundred bucks to miss a week of work, and they'll take me off of overtime priority… it's just a bad idea, Dad, no. You could always come here, though.

EMERY: Eh, my doctor says I shouldn't travel.

CARRIE: He says you should do physical therapy, too. He says you shouldn't be drinking so much. He says a lot of stuff, Dad.

EMERY: Yeah, well. I'm old.

CARRIE: You're not that old.

EMERY: Well, I feel old.

CARRIE: Yeah, you lean into it.

EMERY: How's that guy of yours? The boyfriend? You both should come visit. I'd make room.

CARRIE: He's okay.

EMERY: ----

CARRIE: ----

EMERY: ----

CARRIE: What's the point of staying there, Dad?

EMERY: Well, I live here. Where would I go? New York?

CARRIE: I asked you before, Dad. You said you couldn't leave because of the dogs. It's been a couple months. They haven't come back.

EMERY: It's just, it is a lot to ask.

CARRIE: Is it though?

EMERY: (Sighs) Listen, I've been through a lot. Just, in my life. And life is constant and I'm tired and I've spent all of my life in Missouri. I got my brothers and sisters right where I want them, about an hour away. This is where I'm staying, this is where I'm dying, and it's just going to have to stay that way. And this isn't because I think what you are saying is ridiculous. If I had the gumption in my heart to do it, I don't think I would. I'm just tired, honey. I'm tired as hell. And even if you get me up there where you and your boyfriend can come see me once a month outside of the city, away from your mother and her boyfriend and everything, I'd still live and die the same way. I've lived my life a very specific way, without fuss. And you been fussing about this for awhile, and I need you to know, you already know, you need to know I'm staying here. It just is what it is. But I love you, and I thank you for caring. But I'm just tired, honey.

CARRIE: You're just so ignorant, Dad. That whole damn state has crept into your bones and died.

EMERY: Well, there it all is then.

Emery heard a click, and a dial tone. He slowly clambered to stand and walked over to the kitchen sink, shuffling his feet the whole time. He reached up and grabbed a small coffee mug that said Me Want Coffee on it. He poured some instant coffee into it, filled it with water from the faucet, and placed it in the microwave. He listened to the microwave hum for a full minute without moving or having a single thought in his head. When it dinged, he took a small spoon and stirred it. He held it delicately with one hand and shuffled back to his walker by the kitchen table. He shuffled with the walker back to the recliner, rigidly wobbled in front of the chair, and threw himself backward into it. He rolled back and forth to get his ass in the right position before extending the legs. Emery ran his hands through the crevices of the recliner until he found the remote control. The TV was showing some poker event that came on after he had fallen asleep. Emery changed it to put on the movie *Con Air*.

Emery looked out the window. He looked at the phone in his hand. He opened it up and turned it off. He sighed and clambered up from the recliner and headed to his front door and opened it.

There was so much property. An acre of flat grassland leading south to some forested hills that marked the end of the Missouri River Valley. Supplemental Route QQ was the only visible sign of civilization, and even then he only saw a vehicle roll by every fifteen minutes or so. The air was cool but the sun was baking so the air was humid with the smell of grass.

No one saw this place like Emery did. No one. It was like his own private universe. There's a kind of dignity in solitude that was hard to quantify. It's really easy to convince yourself of the nobility intrinsic to isolation, especially after having a long, gray life that was mainly determined by other people.

Emery had walked off of his porch to the short, sparse grass that ran alongside his gravel driveway. He kicked off his house shoes. His gray toes were wrinkled with sweat, and it felt good to plant them on the thin yellow grass. He stared at his feet. There was a dime-sized patch of gray hair on the nubs of his big toes. He was a bit north of the proper time to trim his toenails.

The ground beneath Emery's feet darkened as his wiggled his toes. A big fat cloud fell over the sun like a rug. He looked up at the road. The world was suddenly dim and dull around him as it was swamped by the overcast sky. He sighed and looked back at his feet.

Emery was sliding his loafers back on when he witnessed another shift in color below his feet. The ground grew even dimmer. The cloud seemed to harden in the sky and saw no traces of movement at its edges. It seemed frozen in the sky, and it was getting darker. Around him, the air took on the image of a weird twilight. Light peering around corners in an orange corona. A purple tinge to air around him. Emery backed up, heading toward his door as the air grew darker and darker. He turned around and started walking to his door, unsure of himself, and his right shoe fell off. He turned around to look at it and it was vibrating, slowly. Emery started coughing and fell to one knee, still clutching the walker, staring at the vibrating shoe, which began to levitate a few inches off of the ground.

Emery heard a bark. The shoe hung in mid-air. Emery turned to look but coughed into his hand. The air felt dense around him. He coughed with his eyes closed and clenched his eyes. He observed green and purple fractals form in his mind's eye as he hacked over and over into his hand. The density of the air remained, and he occasionally heard a weird popping sound.

Then another bark. And another. He opened his eyes, and the fractals remained, overlapping his own vision for a few moments as the blurriness cleared and he looked into his hand, which was drenched in blood that was thick and pasty. He wiped it on the yellow grass and looked up. The sun was out again. His shoe was firmly on the ground. The bark again. He looked.

Lulu came trouncing out of the forest, whining.

"Lulu?"

Lulu licked his face and cried. She jumped all over him and buried her tongue into his face.

"Easy, easy girl."

Lulu started licking the blood on his hand.

"No, no, you don't want that. Lulu. Lulu."

Lulu jumped up and down on Emery as he slowly stood back up with his walker. He made his way over to his once floating loafer and put it back on.

"Did you do that?"

Lulu kept headbutting his knee.

"Where'd you come from, girl?"

Lulu stopped. She pulled back a bit, and took a step toward the southern woods, and barked.

"In there?" he said.

3

THE ROOM ONLY OTHERS SEE

An Excerpt from *The Riverside Ascetic*
By Edi Markham

"Have you ever seen someone die?" Torbil asked me.

"Yes," I answered.

"How?"

"The Kingdoms of Veti, Cam, and Sedna will invite us out to observe their battles during times of war. They will also request Recorders to accompany their generals on campaigns where they are fighting against bandits, Orcish or Human tribals, Myconids or monsters."

"So, tell me when you saw someone die," Torbil asked.

"I came of age at the tail end of the Diamond Wars, around eight years ago. I was called to Record the battle of Chubby Neck," I said.

"And?"

"There were casualties in the battle," I said.

"What were their names?"

"I did not know. I was up on the bluff in the Winter Hills overlooking the descent into Vetian territory."

"I fought in the Diamond Wars," Torbil said.

"I know," I said.

"I met a few Recorders. Miserable little mutilated freaky fucks. Pointless. Generals invited them only so they could be written about. Pure fucking vanity. When your order ever showed up uninvited, they just put you in cages. Miserable."

"Their vanity is not our concern. We aimed to Record the war."

"You never get up close," Torbil said.

"Is that a problem?"

"You never get up close. You never see it leave. You never see people die slow. Dying is a number to you. It measures the war to you. That's all. Have you ever seen anyone die up close?" Torbil said.

"No," I said.

"Okay," Torbil said, "that's all I wanted to know."

He stood up, and pulled at the chain around my waist.

"We're marching west. I realize all we've been doing is moving farther and farther west. That won't last forever," Torbil said.

"Where are we heading?" I said.

"You know, I've been waiting for you to ask me that. I really have. It's been, what, how many days now that I've been dragging you around? Cooking rabbit for you? Yelling at you and calling you a little nasty weirdo with mutilated genitalia?"

"It has been two weeks," I said, shaking.

"Why are you shaking?" He said.

"It should not be my concern where we are heading. I am supposed to merely observe and document. It is irrelevant. I made a lapse in judgment," I said.

"You didn't answer my question," he said.

"It is irrelevant."

"You wanted to know, so you asked. It's simple. For the first time in two weeks, you asked. It's fucking great. I'm honestly so happy you asked. You do want to know, right?"

"If you tell me, I will document it."

"No, no, no, fuck no. Do you want to know?"

I remained silent. This seemed to upset him, and he dropped the chain. He approached me menacingly. I stood still.

"I don't give a fuck what you say or how you act, Recorder. But regardless of whatever front you put on or what you are like, you are human whether you like it or not. Do you understand me? You are a fucking human being whether you like it or not. It makes me fucking sick to watch you try to remain neutral, surrounded by all this fucking wretched shit. Why fake it? Why? The world reeks of piss with all these people and gods and magic and you just fucking watch while pursing your lips. Fuck."

Torbil turned and began walking away. He did not pick up the chains he had bound me in. I followed, dragging my chains behind me.

"We're going to the Emerson Bridge," Torbil said.

I remained silent.

"I got to go up north. The Vetian Army found some mural the barbarians and those tree men, the Cedrus, worship. I'm going to go read it."

I remained silent.

"I also would very much like to see how you react if I kill a guy in front of you. If I told you all you had to do was say "stop," and I wouldn't kill him, would you say it? It's very interesting to me to know."

I remained silent.

"It would be so interesting to find out."

※※※

AMELIA PUT THE BOOK down. Reading Edi's books made her feel so grim. It's why she had such trouble reading Edi's stuff when she was in college. All death and tragedy and seven-foot-tall talking mushrooms. To Amelia, it all felt like such a disconnected tapestry. How do you learn about death, think about death, by evaluating it in the context of books where there are Gods, magic, and resurrections? What was she trying to express?

Amelia thought herself into a headache. She sat at the kitchen island and propped up her forehead with her hand. She heard Harper shuffling down the stairs from the bedroom. It was about two o'clock in the afternoon and this was the first Amelia had seen of her today.

It had been about two weeks since Harper dropped out of school. Things had not gone well. She had spent the majority of her time on her laptop watching TV series or internet videos. She stayed up all night and slept all throughout the day. Amelia frowned. Rose used to stop by to check in every single day, but after Harper dropped out the visits became rarer and rarer. Not that Harper seemed to notice. She just sulked.

It was a dreary house before she got here, Amelia told herself as Harper came shlubbing down the stairs in sweatpants and an inside-out hoodie.

"Hey, kiddo," Amelia said.

"Hi," Harper responded.

"Coffee?"

"It's two o'clock."

"It's morning for your ass," Amelia said.

Amelia took the tone of a person who feels like they should say something about someone but does it in a fake jokey way in order to not upset them.

"I couldn't sleep last night," Harper said.

"Why?"

"Did you tell anyone I'm staying here?"

"No. Only one that knows is your mom. I haven't told anybody. Have you?"

"No. I deleted everything. All the social media. My mom deactivated my phone and gave me that burner, everything. It's fucking awful. I feel so empty. I know that's like, simple and lame to say, but every impulse in my brain is like, 'check my phone, check my accounts, talk to people.' But now, oh, I can't, everyone hates me and wishes I was dead and blames me for him dying."

"I'm sorry, honey, I know it sucks," Amelia said.

"I snuck onto it. I took your iPad and I logged into Facebook. Someone spread a rumor that I'm pregnant from him and his cousin posted that if that's true he was going to give me an abortion with a shotgun and it got thirty-three likes."

"Jesus fucking Christ. Oh, my God. I need to call the police," Amelia said.

"Don't. Amelia, don't. His cousin's dad is a sheriff anyway. It'd just stir stuff up. There's no, like, lawyer stuff or police stuff that can fix this. It can't be fixed. It just is," Harper said.

Amelia frowned and closed the book. She bit her lip and stood up. Harper was leaning on the kitchen island with both her elbows, looking out the window.

"Can I give you a hug?" Amelia asked.

"I don't need a hug," Harper said.

"It's not for you, it's for me," Amelia said.

Harper nodded. Amelia put her head on Harper's shoulder and breathed deeply.

"You're not a very touchy person, are you?" Amelia said.

"No," Harper said. "My dad always said I was like a cat. I want to be in the room, but with my distance. Exactly three feet away from people at any given time."

"I can't believe someone would say that," Amelia said.

"The cat stuff? It's fine, I don't care," Harper said.

"No," Amelia said. "The stuff about the shotgun."

Harper stood upright. She walked to the fridge and opened it. She took two diet sodas out and placed them in the large center pocket of her hoodie. When she turned around, her facial expression was mostly neutral and slightly grim. Her eyes seemed completely flat in her skull and her jaw seemed locked in place, but her lips were completely straight. She faced Amelia for a few seconds before walking with the sodas in her pocket to the base of the stairs.

"I just have to realize that, because of this, and this isn't melodrama, this isn't like, wrong, that part of my life is completely over. That there's no going back. And I don't know if it can even work normally or if I can ever be normal again."

"Harper, hold on, don't go upstairs," Amelia said, walking toward her.

"I don't want to talk right now. I can't even cry about anything anymore. I just feel dead. I feel like I'm already dead."

Harper started walking up the stairs.

"You shouldn't say that," Amelia said. "You really shouldn't. High school, honey, it's a small bubble. And it's popped. It's gone. All these people you knew...most of them you would have forgot, anyway. It's such a tiny, shitty part of life, and when it's good, it's worse, because it's a fucking trap and you end up wasting parts of your life being wistful for it. Listen, we... Maybe we should just go somewhere. Even for a little bit. We'll just get in the car and drive."

Harper paused at the top of the stairs.

"I think someone knows I live here. Last night...I couldn't sleep last night. I kept thinking rocks or something were hitting my window. Pebbles. I was too afraid to look. I don't care for me, you know, if they know I'm here. But I just don't want them messing up your house. But it kept going all night. And just like, dogs howling? Everywhere. I thought I was dreaming or something. Maybe because I'm not sleeping...I don't know. I just don't. I'm...Amelia, I'm going to go lie down."

"Harper," Amelia said. "Tomorrow I'm going to drive us to somewhere nice. Somewhere we can just try to feel normal for a little bit. Someplace with no past. St. Louis or something."

"I don't know," Harper said. "I don't know if I have the energy."

"I don't care," Amelia said.

Harper went into the guest room and shut the door. Amelia paused at the base of the stairs, standing there flippantly with her hands on her hips. There was a powerful, motherly storm of meddling brewing within her. The base of the stairs/top of the stairs discussion had been a staple between her and Edi. Like this, it was usually about leaving the house, but for different reasons.

Feel dead already dead social media bullying feel dead already dead...

Amelia's face hardened into a frown. She pursed her lips together and headed to the kitchen. She took a large plastic container out from under the sink and placed all of the sharp knives in the kitchen inside of it.

Manically over and over, suicide suicide suicide she's going to suicide suicide risk social media bullying dead feel dead see it all the time on the news all the time in documentaries people always talk about how bad it is but when it comes to their town no one gives a shit no one is SMART enough to grieve correctly so they just RUIN other people it's very simple and NOW she is going to suicide or she might and I have to be prepared she's up all night she can get anything—

She looked through the cabinets and took out all the medicine and threw it in the box. She stared at a bottle of vitamin C for two minutes straight and placed it in the box. She opened the fridge and looked at a bottle of wine for a minute before putting it back in. She looked at the chemicals under the sink and put the bleach inside of the box. She went to the garage and opened the garage door. She hid the garage door opener in her purse with her car keys. She decided that she would sleep with these in her room with her bedroom door locked. She rummaged around in the bathroom that her and Harper shared and got rid of all the razors.

At this point, the plastic box was full of all kinds of dangerous things. She wondered if it was worse to centralize it all like this. She thought deeply for a second, what else, what else…and her eyes went pale for a second as she carried the box down to the basement.

She placed the plastic box at her feet and snapped the lid on. She wrote "HALLOWEEN DECORATIONS" on the lid so that Harper wouldn't open it. Amelia sighed and took out her cell phone and called Barrett. Of course, he didn't answer. So she left a voicemail.

"Barrett, hi, it's Amelia. I have a thing going on here, I can't really talk about it, but I was hoping if you could come over and pick up a box for me. And, well, all your old guns are here, too. I just need you to come over and pick them all up. I can't have them here right now. Call me back whenever you get this."

Three canvas gun cases for two .22s and a hunting shotgun stood propped up in the corner of the basement. On the floor, there was a small, black case holding a 9mm handgun.

Amelia stared at them and scowled and tapped her foot on the ground. She exhaled loudly and walked up the stairs.

◈◈◈

HARPER FELL FACE DOWN on the mattress after she closed the door to her room. Her mind was short-circuiting. So much bad shit had happened. The first boy she ever slept with died immediately, everyone found out, vandalized her house, fantasized about killing her, and now she was sleeping in the guest room of an old woman whose life had been completely pulverized.

She listened to Amelia running around the house, rummaging around and banging stuff together. She focused in on her own feelings and tried to decide if she was sad right now or not. She couldn't tell.

Before everything, she had reacted to sadness differently. Despondency or grief would illicit large displays. Slamming doors, crying loudly, acting out, blaming others, vague and sad sounding social media posts ending in song quotes. There was an air of melodrama, an air of performance. The lows were low, always questioning life itself and tragedy and feeling so sad that she thought her heart would fall out of the bottom of her body, but usually it just took a night's sleep to get back to a place of relative normalcy.

It was like that at first, after Derek died. Her emotions took over and decided everything for her. Whole days in bed, the hysterical crying, the long, drawn-out periods of melancholy without tears where she could stare blankly at her laptop for four hours, and then it would all hit again, and she would be in the whirlwind cycle of emotions. It took a few days until she had moments where she felt like things might be okay again, but, she would then immediately feel guilty about those moments. Guilty that he was dead, and she wasn't, and that others and Harper herself expected her to mourn darker, more bleakly, and more sincerely. At this point, Harper would feel better after willingly losing control, drowning herself in the depths of her melancholy, blaming herself, and hating herself for him dying. This made her feel less guilty, to lay herself onto the bed of spikes. Maybe, if she mourned hard enough, hated herself hard enough, everyone would forgive her.

After a while, that didn't work either. She would crucify herself against her mattress and only leave bed to piss. Her face held a grayness to it, and she either slept or stared blankly at the world.

It was a nice, dark room, with everything in it consumed in a dark gray outline. The guilt and the sadness about it all was still there, it was just the mourning that started to feel fake. It didn't feel right. In fact, worst of all, nothing at all felt right. Enjoyment felt perverted, sadness felt performative, and disassociation felt unnatural. The only thing was to just be blank and stare at her laptop, letting time pass continuously, hoping that maybe, just maybe, time was the cure. People always said about things like this that life goes on. But for Harper, the life that she had had literally couldn't. The town, the people, the baggage, it was too heavy. And if life can't go on, a new one had to be built, or she had to die, and she wasn't ready to pick between those two options yet.

Harper lifted her face from the mattress and grabbed her laptop. She sat in front of it for the next hour, watching a documentary series about various cults. A woman was telling another woman that when she was younger, around twelve years old, she had been sexually abused by a powerful elder in the Jehovah's Witnesses, and the laptop died right when Harper thought to herself, *I'd kill to be a victim instead of what I am now,* almost as if it was punishing her interior monologue. The charger for the laptop was downstairs, and Harper reacted to it turning off by staring at it for fifteen seconds and then leaning back to lie down.

She drank the warm soda that was in her hoodie pocket and looked at the wall.

I wish it was night so I was tired and could go to sleep, she thought.

Harper lay down for five minutes without moving. She thought about sneaking downstairs to grab the charger. She realized she would have to, eventually. She got up and sat at the edge of the bed and looked at the bedroom door. A clean, white door, in a white room. It looked too intimidating to open. Harper stood up and turned the lights on. She decided to occupy herself in the room by being nosy and going into the closet where Amelia kept a bunch of boxes.

All of the boxes were identical white cardboard boxes with matching white lids. She took the tallest one off the top, and it was heavier than she expected, and she managed it to the ground with a thud. Harper sat down next to it and popped the top off. It was full of clothes. At the top, a series of sweaters, all cable knit, and mostly earth tones. Wide-necked, women's sweaters, in forest green, tan, gray, and purple. A little too big for her, Harper thought, but that would be fashionable. She could wear it with a shoulder out. She looked at the tags and saw they were relatively new brands, and Harper realized really quickly that she was holding Amelia's dead daughter's clothes.

Harper felt a guilty panic as she thought about trying them on. She stood up and peeked in the rest of the boxes. Jeans. Graphic T-shirts with either cartoons or superheroes on them. Leggings. Shorts. It was all here. Harper listened carefully. She couldn't hear Amelia moving around.

She scooted one box to the door to block it if Amelia opened it and began to try on the sweaters. She looked in the mirror and adjusted her body to different angles. She didn't even feel guilty about it. As she put them on, she thought about Amelia's daughter, Edi. Her mom, Rose, had told her a little about Edi when she told Harper of her plan to get her out of town for a while.

Her name is Amelia. I've known her for years, and I really think this will be good for both of you. See, she lost her daughter about, I don't know, close to five or ten years ago. Leukemia. They didn't catch it fast enough, and there were complications. They didn't know until she had all these weird bruises on her arms, and they took her up north to the University to get looked at, and they diagnosed the cancer. So they immediately started the treatment, and for a few days everything seemed okay, but then she got an infection and died within one night. Just overnight, and Amelia and her husband were devastated. I know after there were issues between them, and they got a divorce. Amelia's kind of been on her own since. She's got this big house about twenty minutes from here, away from the school, away from town, on a hill in the woods. You can stay there, honey, until everything dies down, and people realize it's not your fault and stop harassing you. I'll visit you every day, okay?

Edi's purple sweater was Harper's favorite of the bunch. She put it on and looked in the mirror. She wondered what Edi would think about her wearing her clothes. All Harper knew about her was that she went to college for English, she wrote a lot of, like, nerdy Dungeons and Dragons style books, and was kind of introverted. Amelia kept a picture of her on the wall. It was her senior picture from school, most likely. She had thick, black, and curly hair. She looked a lot like Amelia. She had a bit bolder features than the wispiness Amelia seemed to have, but the same serious facial expression. She had very well-defined, thick eyebrows, and wore cat-eared eyeglasses.

It's less of a picture of someone and more of snapshot. She imagined Edi in the same sweater she was wearing now. Probably a little taller, a little bigger. Harper imagined her as a bit bookish, a bit shy, and a bit standoffish to people. Harper imagined her as reacting coldly to male attention, and then later complaining to friends that boys simply didn't like her. This was all projection, of course. Harper was painting a portrait of Edi in her mind, and the more vivid the image got, the worse she felt for Amelia.

She's been so nice to me, Harper thought, *and I've been such a bitch. She's tried so hard. I should try harder.*

Harper sat down on the floor in the purple sweater. She smelled it. It still smelled of laundry detergent. Some kind of floral scent. That meant Amelia had cleaned them all before packing them away. After Edi had died.

I should ask Amelia about her daughter. I think it might make me feel better. Especially if she wants to take me somewhere away from here. Especially if someone knows I'm here and is throwing rocks at my window.

Harper took off the purple sweater and slid it underneath the bed. She put the boxes back where she found them, removed the box barricading the door shut, and put her hoodie back on. She stared at the door for a few seconds, and climbed back into bed.

Unsure of what to do, Harper folded her hands into her lap and stared. She felt a weird energy within her body that she didn't know what to do with. It wasn't a feeling of normalcy or anything she had felt before. It was completely new. She took a couple deep breaths and looked around her. She looked to the bedside table and, for the first time, actually read the title of the book that Amelia had left sitting there. A book of computer paper bound together by a plastic spine.

The Trees of Iron County, by Edi Markham. The first thing she had ever wrote.

Harper picked it up and started reading. She made it three words before she heard a knock on her door. Harper took the flimsy book bound with plastic and placed it under her blanket.

"Come in," she said.

"Hey," Amelia said.

"Hey," Harper said.

"You okay?" Amelia said.

"Yeah, I think so," Harper said.

Amelia stepped inside the room and leaned back against the door frame. She crossed her hands and stared at Harper. Harper shifted uneasily.

"I got a hotel room for us. In St. Charles. Just for a few days. I figure we can find someplace out there to go and pretend to be normal people at. Does that sound okay?"

Harper leaned back and looked at the ceiling. She took a deep breath.

"Okay, yes. But why? I mean, really?"

Harper sighed and made a disgusted face. She held up her arms in question and glared at Amelia. Amelia did not move. She remained on the wall with her arms crossed, and shifted her focus from her to the wall.

"You don't know me that well. Has my mom even talked to you about how much longer I'm supposed to be here? What if someone knows I'm here? I think last night, someone was throwing rocks at my window. What if they come in here, and, I don't know, trash your place? Or maybe one of his family shoots me like they said they would. In your house. Then I'd feel guilty about that too. Maybe I don't want to be your problem? Did you or my mom ever think of that?"

Amelia let the words hang in the air. She licked her lips and looked back at Harper.

"I didn't think of that, no," Amelia said, "I just—"

"I just don't want to be anybody's burden or disappointment or be hated by anyone," Harper said, looking at her own hands in bed. "I just want to just be left alone. Just forever, maybe. It's the only time I feel okay."

"Like the world is a slow, draining place, and everyone in it just helps it to wear you down," Amelia said, looking at Harper.

"Yeah," Harper said.

"I haven't really left Armin since I came back to it. When Rose asked...I didn't care why she asked, Harper. I'm just lonely. I thought I would be okay if I was just by myself, and I was for a long time but now I'm lonely and I just want to take a vacation from it. So we are going, okay?" Amelia said, her eyes beginning to well up.

"I'm sorry," Harper said.

"Just, Harper, just pack a damn bag for tomorrow, okay. If it makes you feel better, yes, we're going for selfish reasons," Amelia said, wiping her eyes.

"It actually does make me feel better," Harper said. "Don't cry. I'm sorry."

"It's fine, we're fine. I'm fine. I'm fine," Amelia said.

Amelia wiped her eyes and straightened her clothes before walking out of the room even though there wasn't anyone else in the house.

◉◉◉

THE DOGS WERE WHINING and rotating back and forth through the brush.

"I know," he said.

◉◉◉

THE GAS STATION ATTENDANT was counting the money in his register as his coworker grabbed her stuff to leave. He stuck all of the money in excess of two hundred dollars in an envelope and forged his coworker's signature on it. He wrote the date on it and slid it into a small safe they kept in the back office.

"You good?" she asked.

"Yeah," The Gas Station Attendant said.

"You look like shit, man," she said.

"I'm sorry," The Gas Station Attendant said.

"Don't apologize to me," she said, "it's not my problem. Take care."

"Bye."

"Why would you apologize to me? I was being rude," she said.

"Yeah. I—uh, I almost said sorry again."

"Okay," she said.

"Okay," said the Gas Station Attendant.

Two old guys were sitting at a table near the warming tray for the breakfast sandwiches. They were sipping coffee and reading the newspaper and mumbling. It wasn't very busy for the morning. The Gas Station Attendant rubbed his eyes and went into the back office. He filled up a bucket with a purple cleaning solution and hot water. He was placing the mop in the bucket when he heard the bell on the front door ring.

The Gas Station Attendant approached the register. Emery had walked in. His freshly shaved face looked slightly unnatural in the daylight. His pooched gut sat on the middle bar of his walker. He was wearing an oversized tan T-shirt with a front pocket on it. The Gas Station Attendant watched him closely to make sure he was getting around on his own okay. Falls are bad business.

"The whole track of it. Messed up. That whole mile stretch by the creek. There were like five trucks out there this morning. A couple sheriff cars too."

"At the grass farms?"

"Yeah."

"For what?"

"I just said. The grass was messed up. All tore up. Mud everywhere."

"What did it?"

"Probably some asshole on a truck. Either a kid showing off, or a drunk driver, or maybe both at the same time."

"Eh. Kurtis is a rich guy. He'll be fine. He just wants some pity. Poor baby."

The old men started laughing.

The Gas Station Attendant grabbed a cleaning spray and sprayed the plate glass front counter. It contained a display with all of the different types of lottery tickets for sale. The Gas Station Attendant yawned, and Emery approached with a single medium-sized bag of dog food.

"That'll be all?" The Gas Station Attendant asked.

"That'll do," Emery said.

"Seven twelve."

"Here," Emery said.

"You need help with that?"

"No, no, I'll manage."

"Two eighty-eight's your change."

"All right," Emery said.

"All right," said the Gas Station Attendant.

The door chimed. A dad came in with two kids. Two old guys chatting near the soda fountain stopped talking until they passed. The Gas Station Attendant sighed. His manager approached him.

"Hey," the manager said. "You ready for this double today?"

"I guess," The Gas Station Attendant said.

"You sure you can go for sixteen hours? You don't look like you got much sleep."

"I didn't. I haven't been sleeping well lately," The Gas Station Attendant said.

"Well, I can call and get someone else to do it," the manager said.

"No, I got it," The Gas Station Attendant said. "It's good to just get away from my house for a while. I just, I can't rest there, I don't know."

"Well," the manager said, sticking his hands into his pockets, "let me know, I guess. I'm going to run the safe over to the bank."

"Okay," The Gas Station Attendant said.

The Gas Station Attendant continued mopping.

A large, square-faced man pushed the door open. He immediately walked for the back where the beer was kept. The

Gas Station Attendant had seen him here a lot. It was Barrett. His phone rang as he went to grab the door handle to the beer. He flipped his phone open.

"Hi, Amelia. Yeah, I saw it. I was on my way over. You told me to come over, so I'm coming. I know it's early, but it's daytime, and I didn't see your message yesterday. Well, yeah. I mean, I did. I thought I did text you back. Hold on. Wait, I can't check it while I'm on the phone. Well, I'm coming over. It doesn't matter now. I did. I texted you back. Yes. I'm at the gas station now. What do you mean? I'm getting gas. Why else would I be at the gas station? Look, it doesn't matter. Okay. Okay. Two percent or low fat? No. About what? No, I haven't finished it. No. I'm coming over. We can talk then. Let's just talk then. Okay. Okay. I'll see you soon. Bye. Bye. Bye, Amelia. Okay, bye."

Barrett looked at the cold beer they kept in the fridges and then the warm beer they let sit out in giant square piles and he grabbed a thirty-pack of room temperature Busch Light and walked to the front. He grabbed two great big packs of trail mix as well. He walked to the back to grab a gallon of two percent milk. He walked awkwardly up to the counter, the trail mix slipping from his hands as he struggled with the milk and the beer. The Gas Station Attendant stopped mopping and put down that classic yellow sign. He walked to the back of the counter.

"Anything else?"

Barrett didn't even say anything, he just pressed his bottom lip up and shook his head side to side.

"Fifteen thirty-five," The Gas Station Attendant said.

Barrett wordlessly put his card into the little digital stand in front of him.

"All right, receipt?"

"No, thanks," Barrett said.

"Have a good one," The Gas Station Attendant said.

"I'll try," Barrett said.

❖❖❖

Barrett walked up to his ex-wife's front door like a dog before the hand falls. He knocked. The humidity of summer had appeared before the heat. She lived on the edge of town, with her empty grass lawn ending immediately at the thickness of the woods, and Barrett listened to the sizzle of bugs from within it while he waited patiently.

He had been to this front door plenty, but never inside. It had small windows to the left and right of the door, but they were blocked by white lace drapes.

The door opened before he even heard footsteps, startling a lost-in-thought Barrett.

"Ope," Barrett said.

"Hey, you. You okay?"

"Yeah. Just—you're so quiet. I didn't even hear you walk up," Barrett said.

"Yeah, well," Amelia said, smiling slightly.

"Well, here," Barrett said, handing her the gallon of milk.

"Thanks," she said. "Come inside, c'mon."

"Oh, I get to come inside now?" Barrett said.

"Yeah, I guess you do."

"I thought I was an outside dog."

"Sometimes people let the outside dog inside."

"Well, I won't question it anymore, else you change your mind," Barrett said, smiling.

"Coffee?" Amelia asked.

"Yeah. What number cup you on?"

"Five or six. Who counts? Cream, sugar?"

"Just some sugar," Barrett said, "cream's been making me feel sick."

"You're getting old," Amelia said.

"Someone has to," Barrett said.

It was just as humid in Amelia's kitchen as it was outside. Barrett seated himself at the smooth, cool marble island in the center of her kitchen. He kept soaking everything in, looking back and forth throughout the room.

"What is it?" Amelia said.

"Man, it has been a long time since I lived with a woman," he said.

"Yeah, it has," Amelia said.

"Everything's so clean. I mean, there's so much stuff, and it's still clean."

"Yeah, I'm sorry for all the stuff," Amelia said. "I'm in the middle of a process."

"Don't bother me none. Don't tell me you're moving, are you?" Barrett said, nodding his head toward all the boxes.

"Nope, couldn't leave now. Too old. What would I even do? If I sold, you know people in town would kill me," she said.

"Suppose that's right," Barrett said, taking a sip.

Amelia took a sip of her coffee. She looked out the window above the sink at the grass creeping up to the forest. Barrett stared at his knuckles as he gripped his coffee and marinated in the silence. Amelia took a deep breath and looked at Barrett. He glanced up and smiled.

"Do you remember the end of Edi's freshman year of high school? When she locked herself in the car?" Amelia said, turning to look out the window again.

"Yeah," Barrett grunted. "That was a bad year. For her, for all of us."

"Whenever I think about you, Barrett, I always think of that moment in the car."

"Why?"

"I couldn't have got her out of that car in a million years. I remember I got out of the car, I was a little mad she didn't want to talk to me, and I see her in the front seat not moving, and I just kept walking inside. And then, ten minutes later, she's still out there. And when I walk up she locks the door. And, lord help me, I lost it. I started pulling on the handle, and she starts crying, telling me to go away, cussing at me, she had never, ever done that before."

"She was a kid, Amelia. It happens to kids."

"I just remember you picking me up and taking me inside, and then I huffed and puffed, and I went to the window to see what was going on."

"Oh, Lord, yeah, now I remember."

"You were putting your belly against the window. I remember it vividly, I swear."

Barrett started laughing.

"Why remember that?" he said.

"You were skinny as a twig but for the beer weight, so you had this little pooch, and Edi was still crying, but obviously, like, turning away from it. Screaming at you, oh my God, oh my God. Looking back, it was a spectacle for anyone driving by, I'm sure."

"Hell, it didn't work. She was in that thing for another hour."

"But that's the thing, too. You just sat on the front step waiting on her after that. Just lounging on the concrete. I went to go get dinner ready, you just sat out there for an hour. And then next thing I know, you and her come inside and you tell us we're going to go on a vacation to Alaska."

Barrett chuckled.

"Well," Barrett said, "she brought it up, and I didn't know how expensive it would be."

"God, you're a fool," Amelia said, smiling.

"It's still America, so I thought it wouldn't be that bad," Barrett said.

"What did she say, by the way, when she came out? You guys never told me, you just kept telling me, 'I got this, I got this.'"

"She said she didn't have any friends," Barrett said.

"Oh, God," Amelia said, "that's so awful. What'd you say?"

"I said, me neither."

Amelia just frowned. She placed her cup down on the marble island and sat on the stool next to him. She leaned her head on his shoulder.

"That makes me so sad, Barrett, honestly. That breaks my heart."

"Well, it made her feel better. It made me feel a lot better, too, just to say it out loud I guess. It was a bond between me and her, I suppose. I guess I gave her the sad sack gene. For that, I am sorry."

"You were a good dad," she said.

"I was a shitty husband," he said.

"I guess when it comes down to it, I would prefer to have a man be a good dad and a bad husband than the other way around."

"I'm sorry for everything, Amelia," he said.

"Me too," Amelia said.

They took sips of their respective coffees as they stared each other in the eyes.

"I have a question for you," Amelia said.

"Oh, nuts," Barrett said.

"After she died, Barrett," Amelia began.

"I don't know, Amelia, I don't know, I don't know if I want to get into all of that," Barrett interrupted.

"You don't think about it? About us?"

"You ended it," Barrett said. "Ain't nothing to think about. I understood."

"You just never said a word about it, even when, you know, you knew I was thinking about it," Amelia said.

"Ain't nothing to say. After Edi, after that, ain't nothing to say. Haven't said anything important since, either," Barrett said, picking at something on his knuckle.

He exhaled directly into his coffee and watched it ripple. He felt the weight of Amelia's eyes on his forehead. He felt something swell up in his throat, either a feeling or stomach acid, and he coughed. Every breath he took floated toward Amelia. The gravity in the room was hers.

"I just thought that maybe, after all this time, one day, we'd be able to talk about it. The divorce. Talk like we used to. Think it could help both of us, at least," Amelia said.

"I'm not...I'm not stupid, Amelia. It might. And I don't want you to think, that, well, I blame you. I know why you wanted to leave and I know, probably, I should have fought harder for us. But after Edi, I just, I couldn't fight anymore. I couldn't fight for you or myself or anyone. I just had none left I guess. I think you made the right choice. I know it was hard. Hard to look at each other after. But, things are what they are. I love Edi and miss her every day. I can tell you that. But about you, about us? I still got my pride, I guess. And you left and I get why, but you left, and now you want me to, what? Talk about the divorce? I still got my pride. You left me, you don't get to then, demand a conversation. You ended the conversation right then. Right when I had to move to that little house I'm in now. The conversation ended. I can't talk about it now," Barrett said.

"Wow. Okay. You're the dumbest man that I have ever met in my life," Amelia said.

"Yeah," Barrett said.

"Every man out here thinks he is John Wayne. I swear to God," Amelia said, "I just thought maybe you'd feel better. Invite you over here, give you some stuff, but you had to go climb up on the cross. Hope you like the view."

"I just don't want to talk about our divorce," Barrett said.

"Fine. Here," Amelia said, thumping down a large, plastic tub on the kitchen island. There was a piece of paper taped to the top that said 'Halloween Decorations.'

"What?"

"It's why I called you over here," Amelia said, sighing.

"The guns are in there?" Barrett said.

"What? Oh, no. Those are still in the basement. This is something else I want you to take," Amelia said, "pills, knives, sharp things of the sort. Chemicals."

"Why?"

"I told you," she said.

"What? Your voicemail said you couldn't talk about it."

"Oh," Amelia said, squinting. "Well, have you heard?"

"Heard what, Amelia? If it hasn't been on during a baseball game, then I haven't."

"I figure the town is gossiping about it now, it's been so long since she left her parents' house," Amelia said.

"Who?"

"The girl," Amelia said.

"What girl?"

"You know exactly the girl I'm talking about, even if you don't know her," Amelia said, sipping her coffee. "You remember that boy who died?"

"Yeah…I remember that. Sad thing. Sad shit all around. I mean, what do you even do about shit like that? Can't even blame anybody. Can't even get mad. It's just some stare-out-the-window type shit. That's all you can do."

"Well, don't be so loud."

"What?"

"The girl is upstairs," Amelia said, whispering.

"What girl?"

"Jesus Christ, Barrett," Amelia said.

"Can you stop dancing and just tell me?" Barrett asked.

"The boy that died, Derek, he was driving home from her house early in the morning. Didn't take them too long to find out. So, once it got out after people started talking, they all started going for her," Amelia said mournfully.

"Well there's your someone to blame," Barrett said.

"Barrett."

"I'm not saying I do. It's not…I'm just saying, like, it's hard to process things that happen without a focus for it, you know. Just a random death with no moral. I bet people were almost relieved when they figured a girl was behind it. They didn't have to just stare out their windows no more," Barrett said.

"They've done awful things, said awful things, to such a young girl that's just scared and hurt as much or more than the rest of them," Amelia said.

"I know, I know, I'm on your side, trust me," Barrett said, putting his arms up defensively.

"Well, she's here," Amelia said.

"She's here," Barrett said in a monotone. "Like upstairs?"

"Yeah."

"Doing what?"

"Sleeping, I think."

"You think she's going to kill herself?"

Amelia frowned.

"You know something," Barrett said, "you said the same thing about me."

"I know," Amelia said, "and I'm sorry."

"I kept telling you, too."

"So what?" Amelia said. "If you were going to kill yourself, you wouldn't have told me anyway."

"Why'd you think I was going to kill myself, anyway? I mean, there was Edi, and our divorce was bad and all, but I don't know why you put up that big of a fuss with the lawyer to get the guns. You wouldn't tell me neither."

"I read an article," Amelia said, looking at her feet.

"You read an article?" Barrett said, quizzically.

"Yeah?"

"Well, what'd the article say about me?"

"Stop," Amelia said, smiling.

"C'mon," Barrett chided.

"It said that divorced men above the age of forty had a significantly higher risk of suicide than women of the equivalent age," Amelia said.

"That's it? You swear? It was only that?" Barrett said, laughing.

Amelia's face weakened a little bit. A frown split her smile, and she covered her hand with her mouth. Her eyes clambered upward, and she looked out the window.

"You know," she said.

"Okay," Barrett said, raising his hand, "you don't have to say, hon."

"That's not it," Amelia said, sighing.

"Well then?"

"There isn't anything to say," Amelia said.

"What do you mean?"

"I mean that is the whole reason, Barrett. I read that article, and I couldn't get it out of my head. For months. I mean, I did what I needed to do, what was best, but you know, I'm the one who left, not you. And I read that article and I was positive. I was positive. I just knew you were going to kill yourself. It made so much sense at the time."

"I wasn't going to," he said. "You got to trust me on that."

"Oh, Barrett," Amelia said.

"I wasn't going to," Barrett said, a little flustered.

Amelia put down her cup on the island and rounded the corner. She sat down on the stool next to Barrett and placed her head on his shoulder.

"You know what?" Amelia asked.

"What?" Barrett said, nervously.

"I still think I saved your life by making such a fuss," Amelia said, "I really do."

"You didn't," Barrett said.

"I did."

"Okay," Barrett said. "If it makes you feel better."

"It does."

The bugs churned in the forest outside. Barrett stared away from Amelia and saw a hummingbird on a feeder through the window. Amelia kept her head on Barrett's shoulder. The air condensed in the room. It was a balmy seventy-two degrees outside, but humid enough to sweat. The white room caught the light from the west through the front door lace doilies and the dimness of the room cast shadows everywhere. Amelia sighed and lifted her head from Barrett's shoulder. Barrett glanced upward when he heard footsteps upstairs.

"Suppose that's her," Barrett stated.

"Yep," Amelia said. "It's morning for her."

"Suppose I should grab the guns and go before she sees me," he said.

"Suppose so," she said.

Barrett turned to look at the hummingbird at the feeder. Amelia followed his gaze.

"Well, ain't that nice," she said.

"Yeah, that's nice, ain't it."

"I'm sorry I divorced you," Amelia said.

"Yeah," Barrett said. "I'm sorry you had to."

"Here, I'll show you where the guns are in the basement."

"Yep," Barrett said, groaning as he stood up.

ф ф ф

BARRETT HAD STOPPED AT a fast-food restaurant on the way back from Amelia's home. He clambered up the two short steps into his home clutching onto a brown paper bag, three gun cases, and a small black gun box as he stumbled up the two steps into his trailer. He never locked his front door. He angled his body sideways as it clicked open, and he ambled toward the plaid couch in the center of his living room. He threw the black gun box and the brown paper bag onto the middle seat of the couch and went and propped up the three guns in the corner. Barrett sat on the edge of the couch next to his gun and food and took his boots off.

"Holy smokes," he said, leaning back.

Barrett ate three value menu hamburgers while a rerun of yesterday's Cardinals game played on a regional sports channel. As he plopped the last bit of the last burger in his mouth, he placed the gun box on his lap. He undid the clasp and opened it. Within it was a spare clip of ammo and a loaded 9mm handgun. He sighed.

He grabbed the pistol and unloaded the clip. He checked the gun like he was taught to do as a boy. He reloaded the gun and leaned forward. He read the side of the box. Glock 17 Gen4 Semi-Automatic Pistol.

2001

"DO YOU KNOW WHAT kind of tree that is?" Barrett said.

"I don't know," Edi said.

"It's a pine tree. And what did I say about pine trees?" Barrett asked.

"The mushrooms don't grow there," Edi said.

"No, they can grow there, but that if they do, they tend to taste bad, real bad, like pine needles," Barrett said.

"What do they taste like?"

"Well, here," Barrett said, shifting his direction.

Barrett approached the pine tree and pulled off some needles. He walked to Edi and got down on one knee.

"Smell them," he said.

"It smells good," she said.

Edi turned to Barrett and smiled. Her canine teeth had just fallen out on both sides so her two oversized front teeth stood unflanked in the center of her mouth. Barrett smiled and Edi put her hand over her mouth and frowned.

"Don't laugh," Edi scolded.

"I'm sorry," Barrett said. "You're just so cute."

"No," Edi said, "I'm not."

"Ah, hell girl, yes you are, whether you like it or not," he laughed.

"There," she said, stomping off over the dead needles on the forest floor.

There was a small creek separating her from her destination. She jumped onto a rock sticking above the water in the middle of the shallow creek. She slipped on the algae but kept her footing, but it messed up the trajectory of her second follow-up jump, and she ended up getting her other foot soaked in the river. She continued running off, forcing Barrett to follow.

Barrett jumped over the creek and said, "Ope."

"Are your socks wet?" He called out, following her.

"No," she lied.

"You gotta be careful," he said.

"Okay," Edi said.

"Did you spot some morels?"

"Yeah, on the side of the hill."

Barrett removed a crumpled-up plastic grocery bag from the back pocket of his jeans. He found the handles and shook it open. They were currently in the hills of Iron County, somewhere in Mark Twain National Park. This was Barrett's favorite spot to look for morels. He took Edi as often as she wanted to go. Amelia despised hiking, so it was Barrett's intention to get his daughter to like it while she was still young so he had someone to do it with. She wasn't too keen on it, but he got her to come simply because he promised her that she could go to the stone swimming holes in Johnson Shut-Ins after a few hours of foraging. The area they were in was a small basin between two large, slow hills, where the tiny creek would flood if it rained. There was an abundance of pine and cedar trees, which is why most mushroom hunters avoided it. However, Barrett had a spot here, a clearing where the trees broke and there was a lot of disturbed soil getting good sunlight and staying moist. Perfect for mushrooms. He'd been able to clear over seven grocery bags there once, when he was younger. Back then, he'd freeze them and eat them all year. Amelia didn't like the smell or how much room they took up, so nowadays he kept a little for himself and sold the rest for forty dollars a pound on the internet.

"What we got?" Barrett asked, approaching Edi, who was crouching with her knees drawn up to her chest, looking down.

"I think they are morels. They look like morels. Can you cut them open to be sure?" she asked.

Barrett smiled and took out his pocketknife. It was a good-sized haul. Over a dozen mushrooms, pretty healthy looking too. He plucked up the closest one and cut it open.

"It's hollow in the middle, see?" Barrett said. "What does that mean?"

"It's a real one!" she said.

"So, Edi, how do we pick these?"

"Pinch them at the base so that the underground part of the mushroom stays underground so it can grow more mushrooms around it later."

"Exactly," Barrett said, beaming. "You know, you're kind of a genius at this."

"I just wish they tasted better," Edi said.

"I think stuff tastes better when you find it yourself," Barrett said.

"No, it doesn't," Edi said, "stuff tastes how it tastes."

"I don't know," Barrett said. "I just think it's cool I guess. It's cool to find stuff in the woods and eat it without having to go to the grocery store or something. Makes me feel like how it must of felt thousands of years ago, you know, in the wild, fighting to survive."

"Dad," Edi said, "you're a dork."

Barrett laughed.

"Holy smokes, you sound like your mom."

"I'm just kidding," Edi said. "Can we go to the Shut-Ins now to swim?"

"All right, girl, but let me get one last spot. Last year, this clearing gave me three bags. You know how serious mushroom hunters are about spots around here?" he said.

"What do you mean?" Edi asked.

"A lot of guys walk the trails around here, in the forests, right? So, they know their favorite spots from the trails. Mushroom guys will actually not walk to their best spots if they know other people are around because they think other people will follow them. I've seen guys actually try to hide behind stuff on the trails if someone walks past while they are picking some. It's ridiculous. It's so embarrassing. All for mushrooms," Barrett said.

Edi laughed. "Have you done that before?"

"Are you kidding?" Barrett said. "Of course. About this spot up here."

"You are a dork."

"Yeah, I suppose so. But who cares, I'm old. Anyway, follow me, girl."

Barrett led Edi over a hill full of cedar trees. The slope was low and gentle, but it still was a pain on the calves trekking up such a thing. At the top of the hill, he looked down and saw a lot of brush in the next valley. He sighed and tucked his jeans into his socks.

"Watch out for ticks. Ride on my shoulders, okay?"

Barrett hoisted Edi up. She was staring up through the trees at the sun poking through the canopy above, and she was thinking about swimming.

"Will it be too cold to swim, you think?"

"No, no, not in the shallow ends," Barrett said, walking through the brush below.

"Are we eating dinner with mom, or in the car?"

"Maybe both, if you can keep a secret."

Edi laughed. Barrett hopped down into a small creek bank. You could see the roots of the trees nearby poking out the side of the soil, coiling into the creek bed below. He turned right and followed the creek down its length. Tiny red and gray rocks flanked the creek, resting in a silty, rust-colored mud. Barrett walked with Edi on his shoulders in silence. He was humming some ditty to himself as he approached a small hillside where the sunlight above pierced the canopy and rested on some soil where the brush disappeared above the creek bed.

"Bingo," Barrett said.

He crawled out of the creek bed and put Edi down on the rocky, steady soil. Even from a distance, the rich brown color of the mushrooms was undeniable. The hillside was full of them.

"All right, girl, time to make the money," he said.

Barrett began pinching mushrooms from the ground and throwing them into plastic grocery bags. When the bags got halfway full, he would tie the handles loosely together and then tie them again to his belt buckle. He did this for three bags before he looked up and noticed Edi at the top of the hill.

"Edi! You find any?"

"Dad," she said, looking away from him.

"Yeah?"

"What's that?"

Barrett's internal monologue immediately went *fuck fuck fuck fuck* as he hurried up the hill toward her.

"Honey, come to me," he ordered, as he rushed to her.

Edi didn't move. She was fixated in a single direction. Barrett smelled it before he saw it. Noxious. Acrid. Ammonia. He had heard things. He knew the country and the land and he knew the people.

"Does someone live in there?" Edi asked, when Barrett reached her and pushed her behind him.

An eight by eight by four wooden building with a handmade door. All slats and frame. Simple. A small concrete ring surrounding a small pit. The door was open but no sound stirred inside. Empty.

"Jesus," Barrett said.

The M-Word hung quite a shadow in Missouri. It was often whispered and rarely said. People were afraid to even say they knew anything about it in fear that they would be accused of having taken part in some of it. And that wouldn't even be devastating to the one's own reputation, but that of the extended family in general. A good man knew nothing of meth. A good woman knew nothing of meth. Even if all they knew was the tragedy of their friends and family having been tainted by it, that taint spread to them through gossip and backhanded rumors. Eyes were closed to it.

It was the destruction of the illusion of Norman Rockwell. The last semblance of a real America in the face of encroaching big city life. The country was supposed to be a better place, someplace kinder and more real, and meth didn't fit into the narrative. The rich country folk designated that those who partook were of bad stock. The poor that didn't partake said that it was a blight on the weak-minded. Either way, it was all a collective defense mechanism. And because of this, everyone decided on the narrative of what a meth addict was. This way, it made it easier to isolate them from the rural experience and cast them as an anomaly. They were decrepit, sallow things with sunken cheeks who scratched holes into their necks. They were temporary and doomed things. And everyone, at this conclusion, tried to move on with their lives.

But it persisted. Barrett knew the real guys well. There were a couple guys at the dealership, and they had a myriad of family members and friends that did the same shit. Guys that did meth just on weekends. Guys that did meth only at night, and only a little. Women that only did meth when they got in fights with their boyfriends. People that said that they didn't have a problem as long as they only snorted it. It seems insane to say that there are casual meth users. It didn't fit the narrative. It doesn't mean that it isn't a serious problem. It's just that, like it or not, meth existed out here, and it existed for a reason.

"We should go," Barrett said.

"Okay," Edi said sheepishly.

Barrett grabbed her by the hand and turned to walk her away. That's when he heard the crunch of leaves behind the shed, a large yawn, and the sound of a walking man coming around the bend.

"Shit," Barrett whispered.

"What?" Edi loudly asked.

Fuck fuck fuck fuck.

Barrett saw the figure of the man as soon as the man saw him. He was about fifty yards away, zipping up his fly, trying to stand upright but wobbly.

His eyes fixated on the revolver that the man had tucked into his jeans. Barrett held up his hand to the man. The man did not appear to react. He simply started walking jerkily toward Barrett.

"Go to the creek, Edi," Barrett said.

"Why?"

"Go to the creek."

"Do you know him?"

"Yeah. I know him real well," Barrett said. "Go to the creek and wait. Now. Or you ain't gonna go swimming later."

"Jesus, fine," Edi said.

Edi stomped down the hill away. The man approached.

"The fuck you doing out here?" the man asked.

"This was my secret mushroom spot," Barrett said.

"Fuck," the man said, laughing, "saw that the other day."

"You?" Barrett said.

"C'mon man," the man said, bashfully, "you know ex...you know exactly what I'm doing. You don't got to play coy," the man said.

"Well," Barrett said, "I won't say nothing. I should be going."

"Hell, man, I'm sorry your girl had to see it, or know about it, I don't know what she knows, sorry, but I know it's a bad scene but I didn't think, I mean, I'm out here, so don't worry about it, okay, or call anyone, okay, because, you know, it's not exactly like I'm winning in life out here, man, so, state park or not, I'd appreciate it if—"

"I get it," Barrett said.

"I want to, I want to, I want to," and the man started fidgeting with his hands, and reached downward, and Barrett glared at the revolver and immediately punched the man in the nose without thinking.

The man tumbled once feet over ass and Barrett rushed and followed him as he hit his back and struck him again in the neck with his fists. He placed his knee on his right arm and grabbed the gun from the man's jeans. He cocked back ready for another punch.

"Fuck, f-fuck, man, I just wanted to s-shake your hand, as a man, I just wanted to shake your hand," the man said.

Barrett punched the man as hard as he could in the stomach. The man wretched and spit. Barrett stood up as he rolled to his side and began to disassemble the pistol. He began walking toward the creek. He jogged lightly down the hill and jumped into the creek bed. He saw Edi about two dozen yards away, throwing rocks into the shallows. Barrett threw the gun and its bullets into the water and jogged toward Edi.

"We're leaving," Barrett said.

"Okay," Edi said.

Barrett scooped her up and held her like bunch of firewood as he jumped out of the creek bed and headed through the woods to his car in the south. He ran, and Edi noticed, but kept quiet. Upon reaching the break in the forest and spying the parking lot where the trail started, Barrett put Edi down.

"Let's go, honey," Barrett said.

Edi said nothing. She walked to the truck and got in the passenger side and put on her seatbelt.

"Who was that guy, Dad?"

"Old friend."

"What happened?"

"Do you want to go swimming?" Barrett asked.

"Don't ignore me, okay," Edi said.

"Ah, shit, fuck, fuck," Barrett said.

"Dad!" Edi exclaimed.

"I'll tell you on one condition, okay?" Barrett said.

"What?"

"Don't tell your mom," Barrett said.

"Okay, okay," Edi said.

"Do you know what meth is? Okay, well, I can tell from the vacant stare that you don't. But here it goes. Meth is a drug that people take to feel good, but the thing is, it makes them weird, scratchy, paranoid people who hate, I don't know, dirty countertops. It feebles your brain and makes your skin cracked. It's not good. And it's not their fault, they just got trapped. Meth is like a big trap. And that guy was a meth guy who was making meth. You know how it smelled? That's a meth smell. And the thing is he scared me and we got into a fight and now we're driving away but don't worry, because we are away, and we don't live near here, and we're fine, and now we are going to go to the Shut-Ins to go swimming, and after, we are going to eat burgers and get milkshakes. Do you understand?"

"I think I understand," Edi said, frowning.

"Yeah? Are you okay then, honey?"

"Yeah. But, Dad?"

"Yeah?"

"Did you win the fight?" Edi asked.

"What?"

"Did you win?"

"Yeah, honey, Daddy won the fight."

Edi smiled as Barrett started the car.

The next day, Barrett drove to Washington County to buy a 9mm handgun for three-hundred and twenty dollars. He had planned to take it with them next time they went mushroom hunting. But she never wanted to go again.

1919

January 16, 1919. The Armin Reporter
MISSOURI RATIFIES—ARMIN WILL SURVIVE
Missouri ratified the federal prohibition amendment today. The house concurred 104 to thirty-six after the Senate had passed the amendment by a vote of twenty-two to ten. Speeches were made by many members of the Senate and House for the amendment and they were met with wild applause. Even dissenting Senators acknowledged the fervor and vowed to honor the wishes of the majority.

One year from today, every winery, saloon, distillery, and brewery must close their doors as the sale of liquor in any form will be outlawed.

While many business owners and citizens in Armin are fearful of the events to follow, many Churches and Citizens rejoice. The Anti-Saloon league holds weekly meetings and anti-liquor societies, sororities, and fraternities have organized in Armin and surrounding areas. The realization that victory has come to these organizations has been met with a bittersweet feelings to the members, who have expressed some fear about the repercussions to the local economies, as the local wineries have been a powerful industry for such a small town.

Kathy Garland, a local homemaker and organizer for Women Against Liquor, states that she is not worried about the impact on the local economy.

"God does not reward temperance and willpower with punishment. I am sure that Armin will be blessed. Even if there is a bit of troubling times, I would prefer that than to live in a country that embraces lewdness and degeneracy."

The Schneider Winery is an award-winning winery and one of the top ten largest wineries in all of the USA. It employs around one hundred and thirty men. It had been primarily shifted to making alcohol for medicinal purposes for the US Army prior to the end of the war and had been preparing to resume full-time winery purposes, but now it appears the Winery intends to shut its doors for good. Paul Schneider, the owner of the Winery and son of the founder, declined to comment.

Silas Weber, a long-time employee of the winery, had this to say.

"I will head to the city to try to find work as I do not think I can find work here. I just don't see it happening. I just see most of us, the guys I work with, their families, trying to go up north or to St. Louis to try to find some industry."

Many of the remaining wineries have planned to fight the amendment in court on the grounds that it was not adopted by two-thirds of the congress and that the seven-years limitation on it invalidates the measure. They further claim that a ban on liquor violates the simple promises given by the Constitution.

Even if this process lasts some time legally, it appears that the law enforcement is on the side of the drys. As soon as the amendment was ratified, the local wineries and saloons were notified of their termination dates. Many local businesses plan to sell before that date takes place.

"I just don't see it," says Allan Markham, proprietor of the Goat's Rest Tavern in Armin on Main Street. "Everyone in this situation will most likely sell their business and property. I do not intend to leave town. I will do what I have to and provide for my family. I am dismayed that I have to close the doors of my business, but if this is what people want, I understand. I understand, and I bear no ill will toward anyone."

2018

THE KURTIS GRASS FARMS daytime office was a small, rectangular steel building. It had four rooms. One main lobby area, with pamphlets and pricing in it, where Bev sat and handled phone calls and some orders (Ernie in the warehouse handled all the corporate orders). There was a small conference room where the employees could meet up once a month. There was a small, closet office that contained a disconnected phone, a lone computer monitor, and some files from 2013. Mr. Kurtis's office was at the back end of the building. It was decorated with bright green carpet, a leather couch, and plenty of dark wooden furniture. He had a *Sports Illustrated* magazine that featured the Mizzou Tigers football team framed on the wall.

He clattered away at his desk on a laptop computer. He was sending an angry email to an administrator at Armin High School asking if any of the students' cars were covered in mud and grass this morning.

"Mr. Kurtis?"

Beverly had walked in. She was a middle-aged woman with a short haircut and a lot of eye makeup. She had big aquamarine earrings on that draped down to her shoulders.

"Yes, Bev?"

"There's a guy here to see you," Bev said, "suit and tie guy. Mr. Mann."

"What for?"

"I'm not sure," she said.

"Well, did you ask?"

"Yeah," Bev said, "but I got distracted. He's kind of a...fluid talker. And I didn't want to ask again to be rude."

Mr. Kurtis sighed. Bev was a good woman. He didn't even really move enough sod to justify a secretary. She was his brother's widow, though, and family looks after family. It made sense. Plus, people liked her. And Mr. Kurtis understood that people generally didn't like him.

"I don't see any cars in the parking lot," Mr. Kurtis said.

"He just walked right up," Bev said.

"Hmm. That's weird."

"Yeah. It is. But he's dressed nice, so I figured someone must have given him a ride," Bev said.

"I guess," Kurtis said. "Send him in."

"Mr. Mann?" Bev said through the door, "Mr. Kurtis will see you now."

The Company Man walked through the door. The windows were open in this room, and The Company Man could feel himself breathing.

I cannot smell the river here but I know it is still there, he thought.

Mr. Kurtis stood up and approached The Company Man with an outstretched hand with his fingers pointing at him and his palm adjacent. The Company Man returned this gesture by clasping the outstretched hand and shaking it once, at which time the body contact stopped, and Mr. Kurtis gestured toward a seat. The Company Man sat into the seat that was gestured at.

This is going perfectly, he thought.

"So, Bev didn't fill me in, Mr. Mann. What have you come in for today?" Mr. Kurtis asked.

Chili is named after the chili powder they use to make it, The Company Man thought.

"You had an incident during the night," The Company Man said.

Mr. Kurtis looked out the window to the south. His field of Kentucky Bluegrass had been trampled and torn up. The current theory was that a kid on a dirt bike or in a car had dragged a large tree behind their vehicle and tore up the grass. Ernie thought it was a bear, but that seemed idiotic. But every explanation seemed idiotic.

"Yes, I did," Mr. Kurtis said, "and this concerns you?"

"I am very concerned, yes," The Company Man said.

"Do you work for Agri LifeCo?" Mr. Kurtis asked.

"Yes," The Company Man sputtered out, "I work for Agri LifeCo."

"So, I take it you guys got my call? It's funny, when you guys messed up processing my first month's payment it took you over a week to even return a phone call. Now, one single thing happens and it's your money, you send a guy the next day. I find that funny," Mr. Kurtis said.

"Yes, I find it funny as well, and I am the guy that they have sent," The Company Man said.

"You know that whole field was insured," Mr. Kurtis said.

"Yes?"

"Yes, sir," Mr. Kurtis said. "I have it all right here. Do you want to see them?"

"No. It means nothing to me. I would like to see the field that was affected."

"You can see it to the south, there, right out that window," Mr. Kurtis said.

"I am going to go outside and take a look at it," The Company Man said.

"If you want to, be my guest," Mr. Kurtis said.

I am your guest. A mortgage is the name of the amount of money that is eleven hundred dollars. The meal known as chili is made from a powder named chili and that is what they have named it.

The Company Man stood up from his chair and headed toward the back door. He walked past Beverly without making eye contact and walked out the front door. He spent a few minutes walking south on the (now dry) Kentucky Bluegrass field. He came to the vandalized part. He relaxed his shoulders and exhaled and stared straight into the air. Beverly and Mr. Kurtis watched him from the window.

"Bev, what's he doing? Can you tell?" Mr. Kurtis asked.

"I don't know. He's just looking up," Bev said.

A few moments passed. Mr. Kurtis turned to sit down at his desk.

"I got work to do," Mr. Kurtis said. "Let me know if he does anything else."

Bev stared at The Company Man. His shoulders were slack, and he was staring straight into the air. The light from the sun grew dimmer as a large mass of clouds rolled over it. His neck started to slowly loll over to the left, farther and farther down, until the once taut and straight back was a slumped and loping thing. His right arm reached down into the mud tracks in the grass with no artistry and The Company Man pulled up a handful of sloppy dirt from the ground.

"Oh, my," Bev said.

"What?" Mr. Kurtis said.

The Company Man took a step forward, dirt in hand. He sunk his black shoes into the soft dirt below, staining his white socks. He took the handful of soggy dirt and wiped it on his forehead, face, and mouth.

"OH, dear. Oh, my," Bev said.

"What? Bev. Bev, what is it?" Mr. Kurtis said.

"I don't think he works for the insurance company," Bev said.

"What?"

Mr. Kurtis pushed himself away from his desk, stood up with a groan, and headed to the window. He spotted The Company Man, caked in dirt, pointing his finger to the southwest. He watched in a mixture of confusion and fear for a few moments before The Company Man started walking to the southwest. Mr. Kurtis clambered into his pick-up truck and started driving down Supplemental Highway QQ in order to cut off The Company Man.

The Company Man had no urgency in his gait. He walked straight as the crow flies. His stare was fixated on the woods to the southwest. Mr. Kurtis rolled down his window as he approached him.

"Buddy, who the fuck are you?" Mr. Kurtis asked.

"I'm your guest," The Company Man said. "That's what you said."

"What?"

"Be your guest. That's what you said."

"Real funny."

"Yes. Funny. I agree," The Company Man said.

"You ain't from the insurance company," Mr. Kurtis said.

"Oh?"

"Yeah. The insurance company was supposed to pay me out for the lost sod. You just rubbed yourself in dirt and left. What the fuck did you do that for?" Mr. Kurtis said.

"Ah, yes. Payment. How many mortgages do you want?"

"What?"

"Will this do?" The Company Man asked, spilling out fifty-five hundred dollars onto the gravel road below from out of his mud-stained briefcase.

"What the fuck?"

"I really do have to be going," The Company Man said.

"Wait, buddy—"

"I really have very important business going on all of the time," The Company Man said.

Mr. Kurtis scooped up the money and threw it into the bed of his pick-up truck as The Company Man meandered calmly across the highway and immersed himself in the woods to the southwest.

And the Company Man had a thought.

Because you just had to, didn't you? You just had to? You couldn't be like me and the goat. You couldn't just be a Their Guest.

I am Their Guest, and I know their secrets, I speak their language of mortgages and cryptic chili secrets, and I have Found YOU, and I have FOUND you.

◈◈◈

IN AN IDYLLIC LOOKING wooded glen, a felled tree rests on clean dirt. It is flanked by great, yawning oaks reaching upward, congealing together in a sea of green in the canopy. Light glides in through the canopy, diffused just perfectly enough that it bathes the idyllic looking glen in light so soft and warm that the new summer particles in the air look like bubbles in the breeze.

Two figures are holding still in the orange afternoon light.

One is a tall bipedal ape covered in thick, oily hair.

One is a four-legged goat with wet, wicked eyes darting all over the place.

"Listen," the goat said.

"I'm sorry, this isn't—"

"HNNNNGGG FUUUUUCK. COME ON. BLLLEEEEEEEEE-HHHH HYNNNHHHHHGGGGG."

"It's not that bad," the tall bipedal ape said.

"Hyehh," the goat bleated.

"Do not scold me," the ape said.

"Hyeh. Hyehh."

"I do not understand why we had to meet in secret. I could have come to the ranch, it's not a—"

"FUCK. You. FUCK YOU, HEEEEEEE," the goat yelled.

"Hmm," the bipedal ape said.

"Listen," the goat said, "I think you need to tone it down about thirty percent. Because this is going to be trouble for all of us. Just play ball with me. That's all I'm asking. How many people have seen you?"

"I am sorry. I just don't think that—"

"HYEEHHHHHH. FUCK YOU. SHIT. FUUUUUUCK," the goat said.

The goat turned away from the tall, bipedal ape. Sounds of barking rapidly approached from behind the ape. A myriad of dogs appeared and attempted to surround the goat. The goat remained steadfast and bored.

"You, you don't get it," the tall, bipedal ape said.

"Nyehhh," the goat said.

The barking dogs got closer. They bared their teeth and inched in. They were emboldened by the lack of movement from the goat. They angled their mouths appropriately, snapping their jaws, and got ready to kill it.

"Please, please stop," the tall, bipedal ape said.

It wasn't clear who the tall, bipedal ape was talking to.

The goat turned around. All the dogs jumped instinctively back. It took a few slow steps east, heading toward the highway and away from the tall, bipedal ape. The dogs watched for a few seconds, still barking, posturing, circling. The tall, bipedal ape didn't move.

"I need you to stop right now," the tall, bipedal ape said.

The goat kept walking and the dogs kept circling, snapping. A few darted in close and darted back out without making any physical contact. The dogs got closer. The goat kept walking, undeterred.

It was midafternoon. The only sounds emitted from the whole forest were the chorus of bugs and the occasional chattering of unseen birds. The lighting was overall pretty pleasant and unspecific. The sun had craned down just under the leaves and swept horizontally through the woods. It was cast on all things. Ten dogs were barking and acting like they were going to kill a lone, uncaring goat, while a tall, bipedal ape watched worriedly.

As the dogs circled and snapped closer and closer, one, emboldened, enraged, decided to make contact. A beautiful golden retriever, immaculate in teeth and coat minus the soft red tinge of blood on his chest. The dog sprinted toward the goat, did a quick hop, planted all four feet on the ground about a foot away from the goat, and lunged its sharp teeth toward the goat's throat, aiming to tear in and drag it to the ground, suffocating and killing it.

In the moment that the dog made contact with the goat's throat, a shockwave of energy burst out, raising the dirt from the ground and blasting it outward, painting it against the bark of the nearby trees. The tall, bipedal ape cried instantly. As the dust cleared, the goat remained unscathed. The goat was surrounded by eleven dead dogs, their eyeballs all dislodged from their heads, with blood oozing out of their ears.

"There's easier ways of going about life. You're just wallowing in it. I don't quite know what your problem is. You're obsessed with your own misery. It don't mean anything," the goat said.

The tall, bipedal ape cried.

"I wash my hands of you, then," the goat said.

The tall, bipedal ape groaned.

"FUCK. YOU."

༆ ༆ ༆

LULU WHINED.

"You ain't going outside again, Lulu, you're an inside dog now," Emery said, chuckling to himself.

Lulu whined.

"If you go outside, honey, you get the leash," Emery said.

Lulu kept scratching at the door with one paw and looking backward at Emery, who was smiling to himself in his recliner watching cable television, one hand on the remote, the other balancing a soda can on his stomach. Next to the recliner was Emery's walker. All the tennis balls at the bottom had been chewed in half.

It had been two days since Lulu came to him out of the woods. He had brought her inside immediately and locked the door. She was uneasy the whole time, nervous, pacing around and barking at the slightest sound. He fed her deli meat all day in an attempt to calm her down, but all it did was give her diarrhea that, in his condition, Emery was only able to handle by sitting down on the floor to clean. When he was finished, he took a shower and shaved his long, gray beard. He hadn't seen himself like this in ages. His face had been aging in secret behind the hair, and he shrugged at the revelation.

"Well, then," Emery said, scooping the hair up out of his bathroom sink with a paper towel.

When he came outside, Lulu didn't recognize him, and barked at him for nearly a minute before she felt comfortable enough with him just standing there to come and sniff at his outstretched hand. When she settled down, Emery headed for his truck and made his way to the gas station to buy some dog food. After two days, Lulu still hadn't settled down, and fixated her agitation by scratching at the front door.

Now, when Emery did let her outside, he started putting her on a leash. She didn't like it, especially since it wasn't that long, and she typically liked to go to the bathroom out back farther in the fields. So Emery had to shuffle along with her for two odd minutes each time while she dragged him out away from the house to take a dump. After doing her business, she then became fixated on the woods to the south, trying to drag Emery toward them.

"Easy, girl, easy," Emery said.

It took all his strength to drag her back into the house each time. He would be wheezing for minutes after sitting down in his recliner. His back would feel on fire.

"I guess you need your exercise, girl," Emery said to Lulu.

Lulu looked back for a second before looking forward again to scratch at the door.

"Just give me a week, okay," Emery said to Lulu.

Emery shuffled up, grasped his walker, hobbled over to his desktop computer, opened up a web browser and searched for "physical therpy."

4

THE ROOM NO ONE CAN SEE INTO

THE TREES OF IRON COUNTY
By Edi Markham

Page 56

I DIDN'T KNOW HOW to feel about it. A person carries things with them in life, guilty feelings for others and themselves, burdens and fears, all these little gray shadows cast over their hearts. The hardest ones to explain are the ones that don't seem to have a source. Implicit guilt, or implicit self-hatred. I've tried explaining this to what few friends I've had and either people don't get it or are Catholic.

I always thought that it was a universal feeling, that everyone, on some level, felt unlovable. Because how arrogant would a person have to be to believe that they are lovable? That the love people have for them isn't conditional, but inherent? It hurts to even think about. It makes me feel like a scab on the skin of the earth.

I think that's why I keep following it. I lose sight of it most of the time. I take its directions by following the moans and roars. When I do lay eyes on it, even, I don't know what to think. Black hair bordering on purple and those milky, yellow-green eyes. I'll catch eye contact with it for the briefest of moments before it whips its head around.

I don't know how to feel about it. The longer I walk behind it, the more I think about, just, well, desperate things. Like love and self-value and fear and sadness. It's like it casts a wake behind it that's not just the smell, not physical in any means. It's emotional. It's like how my dad describes hangovers.

One last time. It's been forever. He had been trying to get me to go look for morels with him for years since I was a kid. Well, a little kid. I'm still a kid now, I guess, legally. I used to like it until I didn't. I never felt less graceful than I did in the woods. Spider webs, sticks, bugs, creeks, the little jumps and sliding down hills, well, it made me feel like shit. I wasn't good at maneuvering through it so I just felt like a clown, always falling, tripping, feeling like something flew into my mouth. It wasn't for me, and I knew it. And if he ever paid attention to me for a second he would have seen it too. But he liked it too much for me to bother to tell him.

I did feel bad for him, though. He said we never do anything together anymore. He was right. I was getting older. I'm changing. So I said yes.

Now, look at me. In a parallel dimension following around a nine-foot-tall ape walking on two feet. I call it Bigfoot just because it hasn't given me it's real name yet.

I still think I'm in Iron County. The sun just never rises. There's this purple-gray bloom of color that shoots in between the black outlines where trees should be, the ground is this melded brown-green color. All the plants look obfuscated and effervescent like watercolors. And I just follow the whining. Time is losing its meaning to me. It's hard to stomach. And I can't stop thinking about this sinking feeling that I carry within myself. Not as sharp as sadness, but bleaker. Not as poignant as pain, but lamer. Just quiet, droning suffering that makes you feel like a loser. And I can't escape it while I'm following this thing. But the thing is, that is why I follow it, too. I feel bad for it. And I don't know why, but I will keep following it.

My father had led me to a hill full of mushrooms. He gathered the mushrooms while I climbed the hill. At the top of the hill, I saw a man. But he wasn't human. He frothed at the mouth and gurgled a pale purple foam. He lumbered at me like a sleepwalker. My father told me to run, and I did. And then he screamed. And I never looked back.

You know how I said I felt awkward in the woods? I tripped into the creek bank. Shallow water, no deeper than two feet. I'm not even sure I was completely submerged. But I woke up in this world, to the moaning. To the ape sitting on the hilltop.

I don't know where my father is. I don't know.

It's harder to describe the feeling of being displaced in something…else. Especially when the world never really felt like your home.

◖◗◖

HARPER DOG-EARED THE PAGE and closed the spiral-bound book. Amelia and Harper had gone about thirty miles north to the interstate without speaking.

"Was that your ex-husband?" Harper said.

"You were awake for that, huh?" Amelia said.

"Well, I saw an old guy getting into a truck, and you guys talking downstairs woke me up, so," Harper said.

"Well," Amelia said, "did you hear anything?"

"Just mumbles. Then he left carrying some stuff. And all the razors are out of the bathroom so I couldn't shave my legs this morning. So I'm guessing it's stuff like that," Harper said.

"Yeah. Listen, I'm sorry, but—" Amelia started.

"I understand," Harper said, "but you don't have to worry."

"I always have to worry," Amelia said, sighing.

"No, you want to worry," Harper said, "gives you something to do."

"Excuse me?"

"It's a choice is all," Harper said. "I'm not even your kid."

"A person asks for help, you help them," Amelia said.

"I didn't ask for help," Harper said.

"Your mother," Amelia said.

"She asked for help, which is easier than actually wanting it," Harper said, looking out the window. "Where is she now, even? Drinking her teeth red on wine watching *Family Feud*, I bet."

"You never, ever truly know what's going on in someone's head. It's a good idea to not pretend to know," Amelia said.

Amelia eased onto the ramp and accelerated down the freeway. The woods and hills of the south started to pass by. To the north, all they saw were fields and farms. The plateau of northern Missouri blended into the south here. All the way to Iowa, in the north, there were golden fields and gas stations and little else. Amelia drove with one hand on the bottom of the steering wheel, like she was holding a beer in her lap. Harper tucked her knees into her chest and stared out the window.

"Why'd you divorce him?" Harper asked.

"What?"

"I mean, my mom said it was because your daughter died. I'm reading her book, by the way. It's really depressing. But anyway, like, just because of what happened to your daughter, most couples still wouldn't divorce, I think," Harper said.

"You're young," Amelia said.

"Thanks," Harper said, "but why?"

"It's hard to explain to someone who hasn't been there before, meaning, a woman my age," Amelia said.

"Talk to me like I am one. Try me," Harper said.

"What do you think love is like?" Amelia said.

"Don't change the subject."

"I'm not. What do you think love is like? Like, if you had to verbalize it."

"Okay," Harper said, "I don't know. I think it's like, this swelling in your heart, right? And it just kind of pours from the inside of you, the deepest part inside, and you just care for someone so much that your heart feels like it's going to burst at all times and want to be with that person for as long as you possibly can."

"Not a bad answer," Amelia said, "for the first part of love, anyway."

"I'm pretty sure love is just love," Harper said.

"Yeah, kind of. It's hard to explain. Marriage is a whole different thing from just love, you know? Love can come in all different types of forms, really. Pining, wanting, caring, protecting, absorbing. And the wanting of love, I guess, is the most powerful, but it also isn't sustainable. I think that's why young people who get married get divorced a lot. It's hard to *want* someone when you *have* them, you know? So, love has to mature the same way people do. And, you know, it's different out here in the country. My mother got married when she was eighteen. I was twenty-six when I got married, and people thought I was an old maid. Most of the girls I went to school with had already had multiple kids. I mean, how old do you want to be when you get married?"

"I don't know if I ever want to get married," Harper said, "I don't even like thinking about it."

"Right. There's no pressure for you. I was pressured by everybody. Find a man and be in love and get married."

"Were you in love when you got married?" Harper asked.

"I think so," Amelia said. "It was always hard to tell with Barrett. He was even older than me, but acted younger, and he made a damn fool of himself pretty often, but alone he was sweet and kind. He'd just bring me cups of water, all of the time, even if I didn't ask for them. He just looked out for me. He didn't smell bad and he worked, and that meant a lot back then, believe it or not."

"That still means a lot now," Harper said.

"The bar is low, I guess," Amelia said, laughing.

"Anyway."

"Anyway," Amelia continued, "I didn't think about feelings much until he proposed, then I panicked. I mean, I only ever thought, he's suitable, he makes sense, he's nice, and he's normal. But when he proposed, I really started paying attention to him and how I felt. And I realized I never met anyone like him before. He was protective, strong, and honest. He cared for me and I knew I could trust him with all of me. I noticed then, well, he never felt comfortable with anything because he just seemed always a little sad. Never nothing crazy, he didn't cry or nothing, but just a quiet, noble sadness. And I liked it. It was endearing."

"Did you say yes when he proposed?" Harper asked.

"Oh, wow, no. I made him wait for two months before I had my answer," Amelia said.

"Oh, my God," Harper said, laughing. "You're evil."

"Well, I didn't want to say anything I'd ever have to regret. I had to be sure," Amelia said, chuckling. "I guess I really didn't think of how he'd take it. He did lose a good amount of weight though. In retrospect, I should have waited another month or two, and he would have had abs."

The women laughed in the car as it sped down the interstate highway. They drove for about three minutes in silence. Harper stared out the window with the spiral-bound book in her lap, and Amelia fidgeted with the radio trying to find something she figured they both could enjoy.

"Don't worry too much about love, anyway," Amelia said.

"I don't," Harper said.

"It really messed up a whole generation of women, I think," Amelia said. "Not love itself, but the hunt for it. When you're really desperate for something, you never, ever find it. And if you can't find something you need, it drives you crazy. And if you do find love, after all that mess, and it isn't exactly how you pictured it in your mind, that'll make you resent love in general. And that sours people's insides, I've seen it."

"Do you love your ex?" Harper said.

"Yeah, I'll always love him, whether I like it or not."

"You never answered me, though," Harper said. "Why'd you get divorced?"

"Look, love is great and all, but there's more to a marriage. Partnership, cohabitability, respect, self-respect, it's all a lot of stuff. Hard to express," Amelia said.

"I guess I get it," Harper said, looking out the window.

Amelia drove on. The highway weaved east, gliding through farmlands of soy and low, sloping hills, flanking woods swelling with green in the early summer. The weather was hot and humid. It wasn't a long drive, but it was the farthest both Harper and Amelia had been from their hometown in about a year. They alternated between the pop radio station and the country station. Amelia controlled the dial.

"Look, you made me think about it and now I can't stop thinking so I'm just going to say this to get it off my chest," Amelia said.

"Okay," Harper said.

"I gave my whole heart to that man. It took me awhile, but I gave my whole heart to that man, and I loved him hard, in my own way. We relied on each other for everything. We were a family. And then we had a kid, and things became more intense than I could ever imagine feeling, and I thought, wow, at long last, after everything, I'm happy. And the worst thing happened, and I lost my daughter, and he, well, he as a man always had the urge to go find some dark cliff edge and teeter on it, right, and I pulled him back once, when he was younger, and I just didn't have the strength to do it again. And I absolutely refused to follow him into that bleakness, that black hole. I refused."

Harper paused a few beats to see if Amelia was done talking.

"I'm sorry," Harper said. "About everything."

"Me too," Amelia said. "But you know—what are we supposed to do? What can anyone do?"

"Well," Harper said, "life keeps going whether we like it or not."

"You're pretty smart," Amelia said. "You know that?"

Harper smiled and turned away.

"You want my advice? Towns like Armin were made to be left. I wouldn't sweat a drop over what comes out of anyone's mouth from there," Amelia said.

"You're still there," Harper said.

"Yeah, well," Amelia said.

Amelia fiddled with the radio. The song was being lost to the static.

⊮⊮⊮

"Your surgery was a year ago," the receptionist said, "and this is your first appointment?"

"Yep," Emery said.

"Well, we can see what we can do. You got insurance?"

"I should," Emery said, passing them the insurance card he got with his pension.

"You can have a seat," the receptionist said, gesturing toward a row of chairs.

Emery groaned as he eased himself down from the walker into the chair. The room was sterile and light blue. Magazines were neatly folded and a TV hung in the corner of the room playing a daytime talk show. A man in scrubs appeared to be scolding a box of cereal. Emery felt anxious. All this fuss for an old man. He wondered if Lulu had chewed up the laundry room where he penned her yet. Outside dogs don't like being caged up.

"You're a little late," a man in a gray T-shirt tucked into athletic pants said.

"Suppose so," Emery said.

"Well, I'm Dr. Farthing," he said.

"Okay," Emery said, "I'm Emery."

"So," Dr. Farthing said, "thankfully, we still had your file here. They sent it over after your surgery. So, most recent thing you had done was that spinal fusion surgery, right? How's it felt since then?"

"Stiff," Emery said.

"Okay, come back here with me," Dr. Farthing said.

He led him down a brown and blue hallway. Emery used the walker as little as he could to walk, making it a few steps each time before he had to put any serious weight on it. The doctor kept glancing backward at him as he showed him the way. The hallway opened up into a sterile-looking gym with stretching tables, resistance bands, exercise bikes, padded boxes, and exercise balls everywhere. There was a counter and cabinets built into the wall next to the stretching tables, with a fridge and freezer built into it. Emery sighed as he passed it all. The doctor gestured at the exercise table and Emery approached.

"Have a seat," Dr. Farthing said.

Emery gingerly placed his ass on the padded table and grunted. Dr. Farthing pushed the walker to the side and grabbed him by the legs and slowly swung him over to the length of the table. He got Emery to be completely on his back, and Emery panted lightly.

"So," Dr. Farthing said, "why a year?"

"Just didn't see the point," Emery said.

"Why?"

"Just a whole lot of trouble. Ain't too bad to use a walker. I'm old, anyway," Emery said.

"You are not that old," Dr. Farthing said.

"I feel old," Emery said.

"Well, you're as old as you feel," Dr. Farthing said.

"I guess so," Emery said.

"So, let's get you feeling less old," Dr. Farthing said.

"Sounds good," Emery said.

"So, if you didn't see the point then, I'm guessing you do now. Where do you wanna be?" Dr. Farthing said.

"Just a little better, I guess," Emery said.

"What changed?"

"Excuse me," Emery said.

"What changed? You didn't see the point, now you do, you got a goal in mind? Ditching the walker or something?"

"Well," Emery said, "I want to take care of my dog better. And she wants to go for a walk in the woods."

"Perfect," Dr. Farthing said. "I can work with that."

"I know it's silly," Emery said.

"Who cares? Every reason to get better is a good reason. I got your back. Now, let's loosen you up, huh?"

1937

From The Desk of Fuhrerprinzip Fritz Julius Kuhn, Addressed to St. Louis Office Leader Barry Siegfried, Regarding Placement of

Midwest German American Heritage Sites and Discrete Locations
for Boy Camps Amidst Troubling Activity in Congress

Siegfried,

I am deeply troubled by your report out of Armin. I am deeply
disappointed in your understanding of the scenario. What we
have there is a bucolic, German-hearted settlement in a wide open
wilderness that seems ideally suited to what we have requested for our
New York and New Jersey departments. I have read the newspaper
clippings! A hundred years ago they promised that all the children
there would be raised speaking German! For Goodness sakes, it is
named after a legendary Roman-killing General! A stalwart!

There's a darn statue of the guy! Of a thousand-year-old
German! What doesn't work about this? If I am understanding
correctly, you are telling me that this town was hit hard by
PROHIBITION? Is this a joke? A settlement of nearly pure German
blood decimated by congressional afterthought! It's on a river,
for goodness sake! A prime trade route! It heads straight to the
Mississippi, then to the Gulf! And prohibition is over, for goodness
sakes! I'm very confused, Siegfried! Very!

That is the top cultural location for our flagship Midwest
camp. There isn't anything else that works. You also told me—
had the audacity to tell me—that the denizens of the small town
aren't particularly empathetic to Adolf Hitler and prioritize their
American identity over that of the German, which I absolutely
refuse to believe. Absolutely. Why, they aren't surrounded by
anything over there. No blacks, no Jews, no nothing. This should
bolster their pride and easy living. Why—what they set out to do
one hundred years ago is exactly what we have been doing with
planned communities in New York.

So their economy is struggling. Fine! That means they haven't
tore down any of the original buildings. Perfect! You tell me that

you can't stoke that kind of fervor out there—that is, and will be, a failure on your part.

What kind of power play are you making here, Siegfried? Have you run off with the Gund's money already? Do you intend to make me look like a fool?

"The future of our country's anti-communist and nationalist leaders will not come from the countryside—they will come from the centers of industry and from the centers of culture. You can't stoke the fire necessary out here, so removed from everything. It's a bad idea. Armin is a lonely, isolated place that has been ground into dust more and more with every decade of its existence."

Do you know how stupid you sound?

Don't write back until you have cost estimates! Time isn't exactly on our side!

◆◆◆

THE GAS STATION ATTENDANT watched the evening news. He had stripped himself of his gas station uniform and was sitting on his couch in his underwear and socks. He was drinking a cup of black tea and sipping loudly in the comfort of his own home. The news kept talking about things from either Columbia or St. Louis. Every few minutes he would stand up to peer out of the front window of his home at the encroaching riverbank in front of him. The brown water was coming forward. It had lopped over the dredged banks of the Missouri river and had started oozing through the sparse grass toward his home.

"Gonna get a snorkel," he said to no one.

"Shit!" he said to no one.

When the news switched to coverage of the flood, he put his mug of tea down mid sip. He placed his elbows on his knees and leaned forward on his couch.

"Record rainfall to the northwest and melting from the Rockies have combined to cause flooding all along the Missouri River this week. Multiple towns in Buchanan County have been ordered to evacuate as the water levels keep rising. Residents downriver are told to be ready for continued flooding coming their way. The national guard has been mobilized and sandbagging efforts have already begun in Howard, Cooper, Boone, Cole, Calloway, Osage, Warren, Franklin, Howe, and Duden counties. Residents near the river have been advised to temporarily evacuate, as waters are expected to keep rising as much as a few inches to a few feet," said the man on television. "Now, protests have continued in—"

The Gas Station Attendant knew his history. He knew how often this river flooded. He had grown up as much in it as on it. Even the first accounts of the river, even in pioneer days, painted it as a temperamental little bitch. *It cuts corners, runs around at night, fills itself with snags and traveling sandbars, lunches on levees, and swallows islands and small villages for dessert.* That's what George Fitch said about it a hundred and twenty years ago. The constant dredging and manicuring of the Missouri River nowadays was a hint to its traveling past. The river used to just decide a new course every year. It was less of a river in the classic sense as a loose collection of rain and meltwater coalescing every spring and summer and deciding in unison that the river should take a new channel this year, often running through towns, houses, farmlands. Hundreds of years ago, every year, the government would try to persuade the Missouri River to stick to a single course, a single riverbed, and nearly always it was in vain. Simply put, as it was, the Missouri River was useless to all manner of business, agricultural, commercial, and manufacturing. If the river couldn't be predicted, how could it be effectively monetized?

The Gas Station Attendant didn't know which river he preferred. Nowadays, of course, civilization won. The river was dredged and channeled and kept its same course from source to mouth. The Gas Station attendant thought that there was something romantic about this muddy, shitty, mostly useless river being a bucking bronco of sorts, fighting against anyone that tried to claim it. On the other hand, that bucking bronco was now going to flood and fuck up his house. Because it never quite really got tamed.

See, when the river was properly channeled and aimed, it still had the problem of being too damn low most the time. Barges couldn't go through it. It was a silty, brown water, prone to sandbars and whatnot. They built a dam up north to periodically flood, and this solved the problem for a bit. But, The Gas Station Attendant thought, nature usually wins anyway. Because that's when the floods started.

Floods. They always call it a natural disaster. People think of it as inevitable, I guess. Been floods since the Bible days and no one really could point a finger at no one about anything. Just the same shitty, fighting river, fighting back. Ain't nothing natural about the flooding. You took this… thing, this big behemoth of a waterway stretching from the Rockies to the Mississippi and you put a leash on it, you took all the plants and the animals along it and you replaced it with flat fields of corn and soy, but you didn't change what the river is naturally, it's a wild river, prone to inconsistency and travel, and just when you think you got it by the neck it's going to wash you all away. And no matter how many levees or flood storage you design up north this thing is never, ever going to be what you want it to be. And it's no one in particular's fault. Just all of man versus nature. Pretty simple story.

"Sometimes we win," The Gas Station Attendant said to no one, "and sometimes we lose."

The Gas Station Attendant walked to his front window. Trickles of brown water rested on the unvarnished wood that was his front steps. All he could hope for was that he had built the foundation high enough. All he could hope for was that his carpet wouldn't get wet. He opened his front door and sat on the front steps in his underwear. The sun was still high, slowly creeping west, and the first tinges of yellow-orange light started bouncing off the brown water and flittering through the leaves of the trees nearby.

"Flood storage, dams, basins. All this stuff, huh. And you beat it, is that right?" The Gas Station Attendant asked the water.

"All this water, just gonna dissipate into the air, run off into the ground to run off back into the river, to get dumped in the Mississippi, to get dumped into the gulf, to go back into the air, or whatever," The Gas Station Attendant said.

"You know if I ever had any money," The Gas Station Attendant said, "any money my whole life. If I was the type of guy to ever know what to do with a little money my whole life, I'd look at all of this water, all of you, I'd look and I'd think, why, if I could get you in a dam to churn out some electricity, or clean you up and get you on some crops, or take you out to Nevada or something and sell you to drink, why, I could have a lot of money from this water right here. But nope, you just gonna creep on into the mud, down river, wreck a few homes, kill a few crops, and keep it moving. If I had a little money, I'd look at you, water, and tell you what a fucking waste you are right now."

The Gas Station Attendant spit into the low, encroaching water approaching his stairs. He took a deep breath and looked out on the swollen river in front of him.

"Fortunately," The Gas Station Attendant said, "I ain't never had shit my whole life, so I wouldn't say that to you."

⍾ ⍾ ⍾

THERE WERE THREE GUN cases in front of Barrett on the coffee table and one 9mm handgun in a small, black, plastic case on his lap. He had no idea where to put them, so they had just been out and around the last couple days. The weather had warmed up. It had rained a few times, so the air was thick and suffocating. Everything was hot and wet and the river had flooded past its banks and soaked the lowlands through. From his house on the hill, Barrett had full view of the Missouri river, bleeding out into the town of Armin to the south. They had even had to sandbag Main Street. News said it was only going to get worse.

May and June. That was when the river swelled. Before they had dammed it a couple hundred times up north, the river used to bloat twice a year about. The spring thaw and the summer thaw, when the snow sitting on the Rocky Mountains melted. It would flood everything. Edi was just a baby in 1993 when the big flood hit Armin. It made its way up to the steps of the courthouse and everything. The whole lowlands was covered all summer. It wasn't as extreme now as it was then. Most of the little riverside roads were shut down, about two feet under the water. The people that had bought the cheap property of the floodplains in the area kept their houses dry by building them up on raised foundations, though the flooding was bad enough that if they left their house they were bound to get their socks wet at the very least. A few days of dry weather up north and they'd be fine, as the muddy water would creep east to the Mississippi.

Barrett was restless. The heat made him shift back and forth on his couch. The TV was showing some movie about some guys trying to steal a bunch of diamonds for a girl. Barrett glanced uneasily at the copy of his daughter's book sitting on the coffee table. It was clumsily earmarked on the last dozen pages or so. Barrett sighed audibly to no one. He felt heat emanate from his throat.

He thought about getting a beer from the fridge and immediately remembered there was no beer in the fridge so he started putting his shoes on so he could go buy beer to put in the fridge. Hopefully the gas station wasn't underwater yet.

Barrett pushed the screen door open. The thickness of the air had seeped into the house already but the heat was fresh. It felt like perfect mosquito weather. Barrett spat and hiked himself up into his pick-up truck.

"Had to get out of the house," Barrett said to no one.

Barrett took a right out of his driveway onto the 333 and took a left onto the Q. He was daydreaming about the ending of his daughter's book and missed the turn into the gas station and decided to keep driving past it. The Tin Nickel was about a mile ahead. He could drink a few beers there in some proper air conditioning and clear his head. He drove slow and looked to the river to the south. The behemoth had spilt over the banks. The trunks of the trees of the lowlands rested in about a foot and a half of water. The corn field by the gas station had started to sop up rain. It had nowhere to drain, and you could see whole patches where the corn started to slump. Barrett shrugged. All the crops were insured, anyway.

Barrett pulled into the gravel parking lot of The Tin Nickel. There was only one other car there. A little green Sonata. That meant Carol was bartending.

Something took Barrett's attention as he slid out of his truck. There was a series of trees to the side of the bar, slightly up the hill a bit, that had appeared to be split in half. Not huge trees, mind you, but still, about a foot thick from end to end. Four trees, split at about six feet above the ground, with the severed parts of the tree placed almost gingerly on top of each other. Barrett breathed and felt the heat of his throat.

"Holy smokes," Barrett said.

WATER, WASTED

Barrett thought about his daughter writing about Bigfoot. He remembered the passages. He remembered the smell of shit from his backyard. Eight feet tall.

"Mother fucker," Barrett said. "It's all fucking real."

Barrett immediately began walking up the hill. He still had a small hitch in his step because of the fall, but he managed all right. Upon getting to the trees, he reached up to touch the fibers. It wasn't sawed, he could see. Didn't look like lightning either. The wounds of the tree smelt like brute force. No rot, no wetness.

"Mother fucker," he said. "Edi, what the fuck?"

He spun around in a fit of self-awareness. Barrett tried to see if anyone was looking at him. Just a few passing cars from the highway, nobody probably paying attention. Carol hadn't come out. It felt like it was just him and the woods. Satisfied, Barrett turned back around to look farther up the hill. It sloped up slowly, and it appeared that the whole of the woods here seemed to be one big, slow hill. Barrett looked to the ground for footprints and found nothing. The undergrowth of the forest had dried out all of the mud and dead leaves from spring and winter.

Just going to take a look, Barrett thought.

Barrett moved slowly up the hill, watching his footing carefully. He was concerned with twisting his ankle on a rock or hitting a bit of loose soil and falling on his face. Even if he fell, the hill wasn't dramatic enough where it was a death sentence or nothing. Barrett just still wanted to get a beer and couldn't bear to show up with his shirt muddy.

It was near the top of the hill that Barrett started to feel weird. He felt like he was breathing directly from his heart, and not his lungs, and his breath became short and labored. He coughed for a minute and found a rock to sit on. He noticed a lot of footprints in the mud and dirt near the top, but nothing the size of the thing he had seen. It looked like dogs or children. There was a suburb nearby so Barrett didn't think much of it. He just tried to catch his breath. He caught his breath and turned cold when he looked back down the hill at his car.

Standing next to his car, way in the distance, was the figure of a man. He couldn't make out many details and started to strain his eyes as he peered down. A figure wearing a black suit with a white shirt. He could make out a hat, too. Even though he was about a half-mile away, Barrett was taken aback, because this man seemed to be able to see Barrett with perfect clarity. He was standing in a way that seemed devoid of humanity, his arms perfectly vertical at his side, his posture immaculately straight, staring directly at Barrett. And he slowly raised his right hand, raising his palm to Barrett almost like he was about to wave, but he just stopped there, like how Indians did to say hi in movies in the fifties. Barrett struggled to stand, placing his hand over his mouth.

It all felt foreboding. It felt unfriendly. He looked around him to see what he should do. The way he came up was intimidating to go back down on. With his knee, he felt way more comfortable going up than down.

What the heck? Do I know this guy? Does he know me? Should I go back down there? Is he just being friendly? How'd he see me? I'm so far up here, surrounded by all these trees, there's no way…there's no way…

Barrett spied a gentle incline that looped around the top of the hill. It went a bit northwest, but he figured he could double back down after walking to the highway. If Carol asked anything, he'd just tell her that he thought he saw a Hen of the Woods mushroom. And then he would ask her if she saw the Jehovah's Witness looking fella standing by his car. Solid plan.

Barrett walked through the woods and felt it mighty hard to think. There was a density in the air that wasn't just from the humidity. Almost like a drumbeat. Almost like static. He hurried along, following a declining patch of limestone through to the north. It ended in a small creek bed holding stagnant water, and he slapped a mosquito trying to nibble on his neck as he stepped over the creek. His head was starting to ache bad. He pinched the bridge of his nose and clenched his brow as he kept walking. He saw the woods end into a big field of grass and hobbled forward through it.

As he stepped onto the fresh-cut grass, he felt his headache evaporate. He placed his hands on his knees and focused on breathing.

What the hell was that?

"Excuse me, sir? You okay?" a man asked.

Barrett turned to face the man and shook his face a little. He saw a somewhat portly man (not that Barrett was no prize himself) holding a walker in one hand and a dog leash in the other. Barrett turned to look at the dog. It was a brown lab. It wasn't barking or excited or scared or anything. The brown lab just stared at Barrett as he stared back.

"Sorry," Barrett stammered, "this your property?"

"Yes, sir," Emery said. "You okay? You lost?"

"No, no, I just, I'm sorry. My name's Barrett. I just thought I saw something in the woods, I mean, I did, but I started feeling so sick, pain in my head, I just, I tried to get out as fast as I could, I'm sorry," he said.

"Well, I'm Emery," Emery said. "You need a glass of water or something? You look a little spacey."

"No, no," Barrett said, "I don't want to be a bother. I should get going."

"This is Lulu," Emery said. "She went missing for a few months and then came creeping out of those woods a few weeks ago. She went missing with a bunch of my other dogs, but she's the only one that came back. She always barks at the woods, tries to run into them, tries to get me to go in with her, but, um, it's hard, on account of my condition."

"Sorry to hear that," Barrett said.

"There's something weird about those woods, that's for sure," Emery said. "You know what? Water won't do. Let me get you a beer, how about that?"

Barrett's ears perked up. Lulu turned from Barrett and looked into the woods. On the top of the hill, cascading down toward them, there was the distinct sound of a crunch. Barrett and Emery turned to look in silence. Lulu started barking and thrashing against the leash.

"Let's grab that beer real quick. Emery, was it?"

"Yessir."

"Yessir."

Emery dragged Lulu back toward the house as Barrett followed. He wiped his nose as he thought of the Jehovah's Witness looking fella standing by his truck. He looked at his fingers and saw blood. He wiped it on his jeans and followed Emery.

❁ ❁ ❁

AMELIA AND HARPER CHECKED into the hotel room. It was a modest room with two beds and they threw their bags onto their beds and laid down.

"All right," Amelia said, "just a minute. Then we go eat something and look around."

"Okay," Harper said, scrolling through her phone.

"You okay?" Amelia said.

"Yeah. The drive was nice. I'm glad to be out of that house. I'm just tired," Harper said.

"Yeah," Amelia agreed.

"Why St. Charles, anyway? This is just, like, a suburb right?"

"Edi liked it here," Amelia said, "she just—well, sorry, I think I talk about her too much."

"No, it's okay," Harper said.

"I don't want to impose. I mean, what happened happened, and I understand it's a little bleak," Amelia said.

"No," Harper said, "I like it when we don't talk about me."

"All right," Amelia said. "We'd come here alone because Barrett couldn't stand the crowds. There was a used bookstore she liked around here. And then we'd go to the mall and there was some awful store—oh, God, what was it called—where she would go and buy like, fingerless striped gloves that went all the way to her elbow."

"Oh, my God," Harper said, "was she like, Emo?"

"I don't know what that means," Amelia said.

"It's like a type of music, or something, for emotional kids, wore black and stuff."

"She did wear a lot of black as a teenager, before college. I didn't like it," Amelia said.

Harper sat up and started going through her suitcase.

"Do you need to shower before we head out?" Amelia asked.

"No, I'm okay," Harper said.

"I'd love to get something to eat. Some nice little place with tables on the sidewalk," Amelia said.

"I need to get new clothes," Harper said. "My mom gave me some money."

"For what?" Amelia said.

"For my comeback," Harper said half sarcastically.

"Are you serious?"

Amelia looked at Harper with a mixed face of shock and hurt. Harper responded with a puzzled look. Amelia just looked, mouth agape, brows down, waiting for Harper to speak.

"I'm going back to school in the fall," Harper said, staring at the wall to avoid Amelia's gaze, "Whether people like it or not, I'm going back to my fucking school in the fall. I don't care what anyone says."

"Are you sure?" Amelia said.

"Yeah," Harper said.

"Are you ready? But what if—"

"I'm ready," Harper said. "It doesn't matter. My mom didn't take the news that good either. But I'm sick of everything. I'm sick of the bubble. I'd almost welcome some crowd of kids ripping my hair out at this point. I'm going back."

"What about, like, going to school up north in Howe County? Or down in Washington? It's not far, and it'd be safer," Amelia said.

Harper looked at Amelia and deliberately said nothing. She just looked. Amelia averted her gaze and started going through her suitcase pretending to look for something.

"I just think, I worry, that you're wasted on that small town," Amelia said.

"I don't want to be rude," Harper said.

"What?"

"I don't want to be rude, okay," Harper said.

"What? What am I missing?"

"I think you hate that town more than anyone," Harper said, "so why don't you leave? You keep acting like I can, and maybe one day I will, but I'm still a kid, and that's my only home, and I'm alone, and no one wants to just leave. I don't want to leave. I want things to go back to how they were. I was happy, I really was happy. You're the one who isn't, or you weren't, or you never liked it growing up, or whatever. I just want to go back, and I'm going back, no matter what."

Amelia's back was turned to Harper as she rifled through her suitcase. She kept rifling all throughout the speech and suddenly stopped. She just stopped moving altogether, without turning around, and buried her hands in her face. And then she started crying.

"No, no, no, no, I'm sorry," Harper said, springing up and walking toward her.

Amelia said nothing and held her left hand out at Harper to impede her. Harper stopped in her place and fidgeted. She made little movements with her hands in futility. She kept waiting for Amelia to speak but she just kept crying. She just kept crying. And Harper stared at the back window of the hotel. The curtains were slit just a bit so that the light crept in and reminded her of the world outside the room. There was an office building across the street next to a cobblestone road. Harper couldn't decide if she felt guilty or not, but she knew nothing would change her mind at this point.

After a few moments, Amelia exhaled one big, long breath and wiped her face. She appeared to have composed herself instantaneously, and began putting some wedges on and straightening her clothes.

"Come on, get ready," Amelia said, "we're wasting time in here all crying and carrying on. Don't want to stay out too late and get robbed. It's a fairly large city, you know."

"It's a cobblestone street. No one's been robbed on a cobblestone street in, like, a hundred years," Harper said.

"We got to go get lunch and then we got to go get you some new clothes for school," Amelia said.

Harper put her shoes on and followed Amelia out the door. Amelia swung open the car door and put her sunglasses on as fast as possible.

"I just want a tuna melt," Amelia said, starting the car. "I want a tuna melt so damn bad. Is that okay? Sound good?"

"Sounds good," Harper said as Amelia pulled out of the parking lot and onto the cobblestone road.

⦿⦿⦿

EMERY POPPED OPEN THE beer and handed it to Barrett. Barrett's nose was visibly bleeding and he appeared disheveled and in a daze. He kept flinching at nothing and stretching out his jaw.

"Are you sure you're okay, bud?" Emery asked.

"Yeah, yeah, I'll be fine," Barrett responded.

Barrett pressed the beer against his forehead and took slow, deep breaths.

"You're bleeding," Emery said, standing up, holding his walker.

"Must of caught a spell of something up there," Barrett said, eyes closed.

"What did you see in the woods? Whatever you saw, I'm guessing Lulu saw it, too. She's going crazy," Emery said, gesturing at Lulu, who was still scratching at the corner of the door, whining.

"You said you found her in there?" Barrett said, opening one eye to look at him.

"Yessir," Emery said.

"Hmm," Barrett said.

"You never said what you saw in there," Emery said.

"Aw, it's nothing. Thought I saw a Hen of the Woods growing at the base of one of them trees. Then the slope became too much, and I started getting this splitting headache. Got all dirty running out. Ugh, I'm a mess."

"I think I'm going to call someone for you," Emery said.

"What?"

"Should I call 911? Your nose is bleeding real bad and you seem all sorts of confused, coming out of the woods like that. I just wanna look out for you."

"No, no, you can't, man, Emery, was it? Don't call nothing. I just need a minute, okay? It'll stop," Barrett said.

"Okay, okay," Emery said, "Your call."

"You, you uh," Barrett stammered. "You moved out here about a decade ago, right? I think I heard about you."

"Yeah. I worked for a plant out in Jefferson County for a while. Retired. Came down here to get a lot of land. I always wanted a lot of land," Emery said. "You?"

"Born here," Barrett said, "stubborn. This area used to all be, uh, Ralph Eaton's land, right?"

"Yeah, I bought it from him," Emery said.

Lulu started scratching at the door, turning around to look at Emery. The slow whine started turning into small barks she aimed at the wall.

"Hush, Lulu."

"You wanna hear a story about Eaton? Why he sold, I think," Barrett said.

"Sure."

"All right, so up north a bit, there's that ridge, right? Before the woods? That's where Eaton started a ranch. I think the old barn's still up that way, all falling down."

"Yes, yes, it is," Emery said.

"Anyways, he had cancer, right. And he had it for a real long time, honestly. He never seemed to beat it and he never seemed to die, he just seemed to—I don't know, have cancer. He just had cancer for a real long time. And when a guy has cancer the only real news you don't expect is no news, you know? Anyway, he had cancer for a real long time, but that's not the point. So he, before this, he had a head a cattle. Back then you used to get tax breaks for having cattle on your property, implying you were breeding or selling or whatnot. Ralph Eaton had a twenty head of cattle, but this guy in town, Don Hamill, he convinced him to partner up and get another twenty head, and while Ralph was sick, he would take care of them all, and when they bred some and sold some they'd split it fifty-fifty."

Lulu started growling at the door and barking. She was trying to jump up and hit the door handle. Emery grabbed the leash and pulled her away, and she started this low, whining cry.

"Stop, girl," Emery said. "Anyways, go ahead."

"So, it had been a while for Eaton, and he wasn't getting worse, right? So he decided to drive on out to the old barn one day. He had been staying in a rental closer to the college where he had been getting his chemotherapy. Wanted to surprise Don, I guess, I'm not sure. So he shows up to the barn, and guess what? Out of all the forty head of cattle, the whole ridge is abandoned. There isn't any feed, any hay, any cattle. It's empty. Ralph Eaton kept his cool, apparently. He had a guy he knew who lived north of the grass farm that was the closest thing he had to a neighbor. He goes over to the guy, his name was, uh, they called him Buster, I don't know what his real name was, and he goes, 'Buster. What happened to all my cows?'"

Lulu pulled on the leash and snapped. She was flailing and barking and pulling as hard as she could, trying to get at that door. She didn't make eye contact with Emery or Barrett in the slightest. The dog was single-minded.

"Jesus, girl!" Emery exclaimed.

"What's wrong?" Barrett said.

"I ain't ever seen her like this," Emery said. "The hell is going on?"

Barrett stood up. He took a gulp of beer and looked through the window that rested over Emery's kitchen sink. He saw nothing but the woods ahead of him but felt a familiar pang in his head, blunt and cold.

"I don't see nothing," Barrett said.

"Buddy," Emery said, "your nose is bleeding again."

"Shit," Barrett said, wiping it onto his jeans.

"Come here," Emery said. "I got paper towels in the bathroom."

"The bathroom?"

"I ran out of toilet paper and I just—"

Barrett stepped away from the kitchen sink and took a few steps toward where Emery was leading. Lulu all of a sudden doubled backward and followed, sprinting between Barrett's legs, almost knocking him over.

Then the roof split open over the sink and the glass window blasted into the kitchen like rock salt. Emery and Barrett both hit the ground like sacks of shit and the ringing in their ears only subsided to reveal the panicked barks of Lulu as they whipped their heads around to see that a tree trunk as thick as a telephone pole had pierced Emery's quaint home, split it like an axe and revealed the big blue sky. The contents of the kitchen had spilled everywhere, and they both heard the giving of what was left of the roof in pitiful creaks as they scrambled to their feet. Lulu rushed to scratch at the door again, barking and whining, and Barrett helped Emery to his feet. The magnitude hadn't reach them yet as they scrambled outside and collapsed onto the long, hot grass.

"What the hell?" Emery yelled.

"A tree feel onto your goddamn house," Barrett said.

"There ain't no trees a hundred yards from my house!" Emery protested.

Barrett slowly ambled to his feet and rounded the corner to get a full view of the damage. The ringing in his ear intensified as he traded glances between the house and the tree line.

It was the top half of a twenty-foot-tall tree, splintered at the bottom like it had been ripped in half, and it had caved in half of the house, smashing the lumber and the vinyl siding to splinters.

"You ain't going to fucking believe this shit," Barrett said.

Emery stood up and approached. He had left the walker inside, but still had Lulu's leash in his hand. He walked in a very measured manner, favoring his back, as he turned the corner to see the tree that had crashed into his home.

"Oh, my," Emery said. "Where'd it come from?"

"Something threw it," Barrett said.

"No way," Emery said. "There's no way."

Lulu sniffed at the air suspiciously. She was quiet now, but the panic was apparent. Barrett looked into the forest.

"I was right," Barrett said. "I was right. I was right this whole time. I didn't even think I was right."

"About what?"

Lulu stared directly at Emery and resumed barking. She was pulling on the leash away from the forest, spinning around, panicking, and wrapping the leash all around herself. Emery leaned over and started untangling her.

"We should go," Barrett said.

"Why?" Emery asked.

A thunderous moan echoed from the center of the woods.

The sound of insects stopped. It was quiet as church. Emery and Barrett looked around. Lulu tried to drag them away from the woods. A bird fell to the ground in front of Emery, and he heard something in it softly crunch. Then another. Then another. They turned around to see birds falling slowly but surely all around them, cracking into the ground, the trees, each other.

A thunderous moan echoed from the center of the woods.

"I—I got a truck! Over here!" Emery screamed.

The two old men and the dog hobbled toward the pick-up. Barrett positioned himself in the driver's seat as Emery lagged behind with Lulu. The keys were in the ignition already, and Barrett started it as Emery and Lulu hopped in.

The thunderous moan echoed out from the woods again.

"LULU," the voice boomed, "LUUU LUUUU. HOME!"

And as the low moan turned sharp as it screamed "HOME," Barrett immediately accelerated off of Emery's short dirt road and spun out onto Supplemental Highway QQ. Barrett drove home without thinking, and the men spent the whole time catching their breath.

"You hurt?" Barrett asked.

"Caught some glass on my forearm here," Emery said, "but I'm fine. You?"

"Bruised. Fell pretty hard when it hit. Knee wasn't doing too well before."

"It said Lulu," Emery said.

"You sure?" Barrett said.

"Think so," Emery said.

"Shit," Barrett said.

"Dang," Emery said.

"Shit," Barrett said.

Barrett turned onto Q. He saw his car parked in the parking lot of the Tin Nickel and looked for the man who had waved to him beside it. Nobody was there. Just Carol's car sitting next to his.

"So what happened to the cattle?" Emery asked.

"What?"

"The story you were telling, with Ralph Eaton. He went there and there was no cattle. What happened?"

"Oh," Barrett said, pinching his nose and wiping down. "So the neighbor says that there hasn't been cattle there since the Fourth of July, which was four months ago. And it turns out that was exactly when Ralph had started this round of chemo. So the guy, Don, convinced him to buy all them cows and then he just robbed him of them blind because he knew he was sick. Don had just left town, and this was right when meth was getting big, so people said it was because of that, who knows, but the whole thing burned Ralph's guts up so much he sold the property immediately and just moved to the college town to be closer to the hospital."

"Good lord," Emery said.

"Yeah," Barrett said.

"That's bleak," Emery said.

"Yeah," Barrett said.

"Why, that's no good at all," Emery said, as Barrett came careening up the gravel road leading to his house.

"Whole point I left the house," Barrett said, resting as the car slid into park, "was to buy beer. And now look at all this. Guess you oughta make what phone calls you have to make. But buddy, do me a favor. Wait an hour before calling the cops. Just give me an hour. I'm beggin' ya."

"Yeah, yeah. An hour, sure. What the hell the police going to do about a log in my house anyway. I just need a moment to rest. Just...a moment," Emery said.

Emery eased himself out of the truck. Barrett beelined into his home and grabbed his copy of *Pig Iron* from the coffee table, and turned to the earmarked page near the end.

◈◈◈

Chapter 38 of *Pig Iron*
by Edi Markham

AISIR WOKE UP TO a low, throttling burning feeling all over his body. He immediately spat up bile and rolled to his side, retching. He clenched his eyes closed and went to wipe his mouth. He felt as if his arm was dead and replaced with nothing but painful humidity. He opened his eyes to see what was wrong, and saw that he no longer had an arm. At his elbow, there was an entanglement of moss where his forearm should have been.

Aisir growled and rolled onto his back. A smattering of images and memories and wants and desires flooded his brain all at once. He tried to breathe. He thought of his mother. He thought of being a child alone with her in the high, dry hills above the Kingdom of Cam. Lawless territory. Unclaimed. He remembered chasing a rabbit with his bow and stepping on a loose rock, falling down, twisting his ankle. He remembered crying. He remembered his mother pulling him up hard by his ear, glaring at him, hating his weakness.

"You are a red elf. We are hated by even the Gods. We won't give them the satisfaction of crying. If you cry, I will cast you out now, and have a new child not cursed by your weakness. Do you understand?"

Aisir thought about his breathing. That's what she had said to do. Think only about your breath. The images go away. Just the pendulum of breathing. Aisir felt all of the pain in his body center on his stomach as he tried to stand. He thought he might shit himself.

"Sorry," came a low, grumbled voice behind him.

It sounded like its teeth were so big that the words couldn't fit through them. Aisir froze. He heard brush clear and the sound of two steps. Then it stopped.

"Sorry. Sorry. Sorry. Sorry."

Aisir looked around him without moving. He saw his sword laying next him. He had been placed down on a mat of peat moss on a dry patch of land elevated above the moisture of the swamp. He picked up the sword slowly with his one good hand.

"Sorry. Sorry. SORRY. SORRY."

The low, guttural voice pleaded. It became harder and harder to understand with each word. It just ended up sounding like a mashing of S's and R's. Aisir turned to face Bigfoot. He was standing in the cattails just out of the water. His face in his large, leathery hands. Aisir touched his neck lightly.

"Where's my arm?" Aisir said.

"SORRY," Bigfoot screamed.

"Where is it?"

"GONE," Bigfoot screamed.

"...well, yeah, I figured. Shit. Shit. This hurts really fucking bad, you know that?" Aisir said.

"SORRY," Bigfoot screamed.

"Is that it? That's it? Go fuck off, already, please. Get the fuck out of here. Fuck. Everything is so fucked," Aisir yelled.

Bigfoot just stood there, lolling back and forth, staring at him.

"Which way is west?" Aisir asked.

Bigfoot pointed west. Aisir found his pack on the ground by his sword, slung it over his shoulder with his sword hand, and walked in the direction Bigfoot pointed.

"Big fucking help you were," Aisir said as he passed Bigfoot.

Bigfoot just stared. When he passed, Bigfoot stared at his feet.

"Just got to keep going fucking west, I guess," Aisir said to himself, "because if I don't find her, no one will. Fuck, I hope Henbit's okay."

At that moment, Henbit was arriving in the northern port city of Mortimer. She had tracked her sister Sugar and her friend O here, and she was trying to be as incognito as possible, moving with her hood up and her scarf around her mouth. It was just cold enough to get away with this, naturally, but she was still worried. Mortimer was mostly Snow Orcs and Sednaese humans, both of whom were very fair-skinned. Henbit, being a Vetian, stuck out with her dark skin and black-red hair. She had swiped an orange scarf while on the ship, and draped it around herself to appear more like the merchants from down south who regularly did business up here. Henbit was trying to find where they kept the slaves in the market. She saw two Treebrayers, wild, white-haired people just north of Veti, on shackles being dragged toward a traveling cart by some mercenaries, and set off opposite them to see where they had come from. The path winded a bit away from the open-air market pungent with fish and spices, and Henbit felt a cold wind at her back as she walked down the lonely stone path of the strange city. She passed two frosty-breathed men, one tall and skinny, one fat and short, passing a bottle back and forth at a street corner, and slowed down when she caught their conversation.

"Big motherfucker," the tall man said.

"Yeah?"

"Big as fuck," he continued, "the Myconid. Laeti. Bigger than they usually are, even. Maybe eight feet."

"They going to fight him?" asked the fat man.

"They should! It'd be a waste. They're drying him out now because they said he already broke his shackles once, so he ain't in fighting form now like he was."

Henbit pretended to tie her shoe about ten feet away from them. She peered over her shoulder as casually as possible to get a good look at the men. She could tell they were out-of-towners, merchants, most likely.

"Anyway, I got to get back to it," the tall man said.

"All right, all right. You got paid yet?"

"No, no, you know these fucking Orcs. They won't give you a scrap of silver until they check everything out. I'm sure they got their fingers up all their asses right now."

They shared a hearty laugh. Henbit walked ahead of the tall man and turned the corner in front of him. She ducked behind a cart until he passed, and poked her head around the corner to see what he did next. He turned into an alley, and Henbit slunk behind, following. She caught the tail end of a raised portcullis being lowered and hurried toward it. She looked through the lattice into the grounds and saw what appeared to be an empty auction block. Henbit jumped onto a pile of wood nearby and climbed an adjacent building and jumped down into the auction grounds. There was a large set of double doors just behind the auction block and a fenced-in alley leading around the sides. There were barred windows at ankle level, and she creeped her head down to look inside. People of many different species were chained to the wall, but she couldn't make out their faces. Henbit quickly got up and rounded the corner by the auction block and saw a small, open shed filled with groundskeeping supplies. She ducked in and closed the door. There was a moment of small respite where she began to formulate a plan. Even when it was all of them together, her, Sugar, Aisir, O, it was always her job to make the plan. She hated it, honestly. It was so much pressure, but she understood why it was always her. O wasn't clever, Aisir was too blunt, and Sugar was too impulsive. She thought about all of their faces and tucked herself into the corner of the shed.

And then she got mad. She got so mad thinking of everything that had happened, everything that went wrong. Stealing those fucking diamonds. Escaping to the swamp. Becoming the plaything of all these gods or spirits or extradimensional entities or whatever they were. A goat that kept telling her to ignore that her sister got captured by slavers and go west for some reason. She got so mad at all these events, and for the first time in her life, she really allowed herself to get mad. It's not that she lost control, but that she gave herself permission to get as mad as she wanted to get. And it didn't matter if it hurt her or was stupid or what, it was just that she decided that she would get as mad as she possibly could and see what happened. She sneered at nothing and tucked her lip in.

Henbit heard a door open outside and exhaled all of the heat in her body. She exhaled until her jaw shook. Two voices. She heard two voices. Henbit wrapped the orange scarf around her face like a bandit and hoisted her crossbow off her back. She calmly opened the door and saw two men holding clubs sharing a cigarette, and she shot one in the head. As the first one hit the ground, she grabbed a dagger from her side and flung it into the other one's head. He managed a short yelp, nothing too loud, but loud enough for her to worry someone heard it. She loaded her crossbow as fast as she could and pulled the dagger out of the man's head. She calmly walked through the double doors that the men had walked out of with her crossbow raised. There was a man writing something at a desk in the small entrance room of the building. He didn't even look up.

"Ahem," Henbit said.

The man finished his sentence and slowly looked up. He put the pen down calmly and placed his hands flat on the desk.

"Hello," he said, with the crossbow pointed at his face.

"I'm looking for two people. A Vetian girl, my age. And a Myconid. The big ones, a Laeti. Should have come in the last two days," Henbit said.

"Okay," the man said. "The Vetian is in the kitchen. She can't cook for shit so I don't know why. That's to your left."

"And the Myconid?"

"He was trying to escape every fifteen minutes so he's in the basement covered in salt. Dried him up pretty good. Still moving, last I heard. They're shipping him out tomorrow up north. Not sure why. Think he's a criminal," he said, "they won't tell us."

"Give me a key," she said.

"I don't have one," he said, "but I tell you what. I can make it easier for you, but you have to promise to let me live."

"Okay," Henbit said, "I promise."

"On what?" the man said. "You can't just promise. It needs to be on something, a pledge to a God, anything. Not a family member, because you could be a liar, or an orphan. I need your word."

"I don't like the Gods," Henbit said, "I don't trust them. The church. I don't get it. I will tell you that my father is a blacksmith. I will put my word on him."

"Really?" the man said, "Mine too. Say, if you let me die today, may all of your father's iron turn to dirt."

"If you die today," Henbit said, "may all my father's iron turn to dirt."

"Okay," the man said, standing up, "go wait right here."

The man pointed to a dark corner behind the door. Henbit obliged. The man walked to the door and leaned into Henbit's ear.

"Plug him when he comes in," he whispered.

Henbit nodded. The man opened the door.

"Duran! Come in here! There's something wrong with your numbers this month. You're not going to like your pay!" the man said.

"The hell," Henbit heard echoing from the other room. "I'm with someone right now. Can it wait?"

"Leave the slaves alone and get in here," the man said.

"For fuck's sake," Duran said, straightening his shirt.

Duran entered the room. As soon as he was in Henbit's line of sight, she shot him in the head with the crossbow, and he slid to the ground with a splat.

"He should have a key," the man said.

Henbit rifled through his pockets quickly, pulling out a few coins, finding a knife in his boots, but no key.

"There's no fucking key," Henbit said, eyes full of hate.

"Hold on, hold on, he has one, I swear, I swear," the man pleaded as Henbit leveled the crossbow at him.

"On my father, you said—"

"Henbit?" said a voice from the doorway.

Henbit whipped around and, from the sights of her crossbow, saw her sister Sugar, taking the shackles off of her wrist.

"See! She got it! I wasn't lying!" the man pleaded.

Henbit threw the crossbow down, and she and Sugar hugged.

"I'm sorry," Henbit said.

Sugar just laughed. "You were too late, dear, I already swiped the key from him. You know, for someone who always said I was impulsive, you're sure leaving a lot of blood in your wake lately. Don't go changing on me, sister."

Henbit held back the tears, then turned to face the man at the desk. He was already ready to speak.

"The basement entrance will be in the next room up. He's in the easternmost corner, shackled up. There should be a small hallway leading to supply store next to it, and in that room there is an entrance to the sewers that you should be able to escape into. Now, if I may ask a favor in addition to the favor of not killing me?"

Sugar looked at Henbit. Henbit nodded.

"Could one of you scratch me, or cut me superficially, or beat me up? So that I looked like I attempted to stop you in your rescue of your friends, and do not look like the accomplice that I am?" he asked.

By the time he finished his sentence, Sugar was already approaching him.

◆◆◆

HARPER AND AMELIA GOT lunch outdoors at a small, self-styled bistro on the cobblestone streets of St. Charles. The waiter had seated them underneath a Bradford pear tree all blooming white. It smelled like fish, but it was a pretty scene. When the waiter, a handsome college student from nearby, walked away, Amelia raised her eyebrows at Harper suggestively.

"Don't," Harper said.

"Just saying," Amelia said.

"I'm legally a child, dude," Harper said. "That's weird."

"You're not fun," Amelia said.

Lunch went uneventfully. They ate, soaked in the sights, and enjoyed the scene. It was mostly families or couples looking at the shops, but there were enough college kids around that the bars were already filling up already as well. It was still early, and Harper and Amelia made plans to split up and meet back at the car. Harper wanted to find some clothes to wear for when she went back to school, and Amelia wanted to look at marble figurines of baby angels for thirty minutes and not buy anything.

Amelia asked her if she had her cell phone and if it was charged five times. Harper just kept saying "yes, bye" until Amelia was satisfied and headed south down the cobblestone street.

Amelia walked as slowly as she possibly could, stopping whenever she could to look in windows, to look around. This is what she wished the Armin Main Street looked like.

There's just something nice about being here and walking and being alone. Nice in like how my grandma used to say it. It is nice. Just nice. Everything is just designed to look rustic and clean at the same time. Charm. It just feels fresh.

Amelia had some time to kill. She walked and smiled and left herself be alone with her thoughts.

There's a type of loneliness that I think people can only feel when they are with other people. Oh, not lonely in the bad way, I guess, but people I care for. Barrett and her and I guess my daughter, I always felt it. Same feeling I felt with my dad and my mom when I was a kid, I guess. And with those boyfriends I had before Barrett, yes, I guess I felt it then too. I don't know if I felt lonely because of them or because of me or maybe it's not one or both. I guess it doesn't really matter.

I guess I think maybe it's just impossible to not feel lonely because we are alone, aren't we, in here, when we think, and it's the opposite of the real world made of stuff and things, where we are always surrounded by people and in order to have the types of lives that we want to have people around and if you have people around it is because you rely on them and then if you rely on them they rely on you and you just find people and you press your borders into them and they press their borders into you and that can be very, very frustrating sometimes because we can never see or know the borders until they are already on us, in our armpits, in our brains, or clipping their toenails into the toilet. I hated when he did that, putting his bare foot on the toilet seat that we both sit on just clipping the toenails.

Oh, wow, he doesn't even care that I said that I hated that, he's a hundred miles away and I'm getting mad at him again, if I would have known that about him, oh, man, it is just very hard to be around people all the time and I think everyone feels that loneliness in companionship sometimes and sometimes I would make myself feel bad like is it okay for me to need a person so badly like I needed him but to also let a person like that make me raise my voice or defend myself or start a fight? And it is just like wow love is more desperate and complicated and hard to pull off then I ever thought it was when I was sixteen, listening to songs where it all seemed so fun and simple and you would get older and get married and then your husband would work eight hours a day at a factory then stop by the field to pick daisies for you.

Oh my goodness, look at that little dog. Oh wow, he's sniffing that flower. Wow, that is like a little greeting card. Wow, I think the woman walking him is drunk I think she just stumbled there what is she doing out like this with that dog.

And what do you do when the love fails anyway? And you know, I'm not sure it was the love that failed, it was something else with me and Barrett. I don't think it was about love it was like the resources ran out. There were no more trees left in the forest and his brain broke and mine did too and neither of us would be ever okay again after Edi and it's not like he wanted to remarry, I don't think. And I never even thought of remarrying ever again, how would I look at my age in a white dress, are you kidding me? Oh God, it would be so funny can you even imagine?

So what is love if not rarer than even I can give it credit for because I have seen so many marriages and so little love in my life. Not even in my own life but even in the lives of other people. And there is this narrative we are sold in our lives that everyone matches up and pairs off and there is a family and there is this big red cartoon heart that swells with love and love and love conquers all and I've seen people love their children and I'm not talking about loving children because that's different and more concrete than loving a person because romantic love, real, endurable romance that holds tight and never wanes is something I have seen less and less of. Even nowadays I wonder if kids know what it even is. They're on their phones so much and I don't think you can find it there.

And even as I am old, now, yes, I'm so old and my idea of love has never stopped growing or evolving and I think that love is the end all be all human emotion because you see how simple fear is, how simple anger is, how simple jealousy or even how embarrassingly simple happiness is sometimes, and you look at the idea of love and you think wow, it has depths beyond depths compared to anything else. Even people who have it can scarcely explain it, most humans even rely on other people's words to explain it, and there are no two loves the same, I think, I loved Edi and I love Barrett and I think I love this dumb little girl Harper, God bless her, and none of these feelings can even be compared to each other. They run threads all around your brain in different directions but the end all result is the swelling of your heart in your chest and the deep, deep want in your brain for the best of them at all times without even ever considering your own feelings.

Oh, look at me, doddering like all of those worried old women that I hated as a girl, sticking their noses in my business and telling me to get married and what type of husband to look for that's nothing like the current husband they have now and I am walking down a cobblestone street looking at knickknacks and watching people go by me and thinking about some girl I've known only two months and being worried that right now she is at some cool little teen store called Ho Flow or something buying a tube top or some little shorts that are a walking yeast infection they don't tell girls anything in school these days and I'm worrying about all this because I don't want anyone to ever say anything bad about her ever and yes I know they will I'm sure of it everyone will always say bad stuff about each other all the time and I absolutely know that bad stuff is inevitable in this world to all people and that no one gets out alive but still I worry despite the certainty of it happening because I have love for her and its irrational and you want to protect and ensure happiness for everyone because love is a feeling that inevitably lets you down constantly because it makes you make no sense.

Anyway, one thing I do know is that love and loneliness are not opposites and that you can feel none at the same time and both at the same time and each one separately and I know that people walk around the world their whole lives feeling like something is missing inside of them. And we say oh love is what is missing love is all you need to fill that little chip in your heart and that's not true that's the biggest lie I ever heard love lives with emptiness and nothing can fill that if you're missing it love is great and grand and all but at the end of the day ain't no one can save you, no one else, yes, you can't go around looking for saviors out of people or even God yes at the end of the day you have to save yourself whether you like it or not and I like that because it means I belong to myself even if I give myself to someone I love.

When Edi was alive, we came up here to visit my sister, who liked it up here when she was in the hospital with her back thing and I remember that her seventh grade teacher told me during the parent-teacher conference that Edi was really shy and not talking and I didn't know what to do you know I didn't know, I asked her, she said she's fine, well I didn't know so I made a big plan to take her up here and get some really nice clothes and I got her that tracksuit good lord I remember the one with the word on the butt and I said I will get you one that is twice as expensive as long as it doesn't have the letter on the butt and I had to do it because I said I'd do it and then after we went to the bookstore and she got that awful book with the elf on the front oh my God what was it even called with a purple looking elf on it with white hair and she read it the whole way home and I asked her if she was happy and she said yeah and she didn't hesitate or nothing and I asked her what she wanted for dinner tonight and she said she wanted Cornish game hen and I said stop messing with me and we both laughed.

Oh good lord, even I'm too young for the Hallmark store, they still have one of those here, oh wow, look they got the Beanie Babies right in the front do young people even know those were a thing?

I think it's a difficult or near impossible thing to sit and have a conversation with yourself and try to summarize up your whole life in terms of love or caring for other people or what you want and didn't get or anything. People get so wrapped up in the story and whatnot and it's not like this is making me change any of my decisions or anything but maybe it has made me think a little differently about love in ways I didn't before like I said I didn't love Barrett anymore but I was lying because I thought if I said it, it would make him try harder and he didn't and I told myself I believed it and I thought I did for a long, long time but the truth of it is that he left a big thumbprint on my soul. Not that I believe in souls you know but the metaphorical idea of one. He is right there in me, such a big and gentle and sad man and I think yes I really think just at the end of the day me and him would be completely different people and maybe happier people if Edi hadn't have died and yes I know that's true and I don't think that it makes me sad because she did die and we aren't those people but it makes me happy to think that all three of us we had hope together yes hope enough to smile plainly and be happy yes it could have been us yes I know it in my heart of hearts.

✦✦✦

Chapter 40 of *Pig Iron*
by Edi Markham

THE PEOPLE OF THE Pepper Coast gave a wide berth to the one-armed Red Elf. Aisir's face was covered in black stubble as he emerged down the path out of the pine forests of Western Veti and onto the calm coastlands of the ocean. It had been two weeks since he lost his arm and every night in his sleep, he had the same dream. He saw an inky outline of a person that clarified into Henbit. And then he heard the word. WEST. It echoed in his mind. For his first few seconds awake, he swore he could feel his head shaking, like his head was a drum still reverberating from the impact of the word. WEST. So he went west without aim, looking for her. He just wanted to find her again. He just wanted to look at her face again. When he reached the town of Pepper Coast, he rented a room, had an ale, and went to sleep. He was as far west as he knew to go. He awaited instructions, but the dream was the same. Henbit's face. Then WEST, ringing in his head as he awoke.

"No," Aisir said, "I don't know how."

Aisir threw some coins down on the counter and wordlessly ate breakfast at a corner table in the inn. When the barmaid came to grab his plate, he held onto the plate and looked up at her.

"What's west of here?" he asked.

"The ocean," she said, "there's been rumors otherwise, but I don't know."

"What rumors?"

"Slaves. During the war, about twenty years ago, a few came through here. They didn't say they was but you could tell by the look of them. Took a boat out and never came back."

"Okay," Aisir said.

The barmaid jerked the plate free and walked off. Aisir stood up and walked calmly out of the inn. He smelled the salt in the air and pictured her face. He didn't have much. He didn't have much at all. And even then, he didn't have her, but at least when he was with her, and traveled with her, Aisir had the idea of her. Them together and O and Sugar. Stability. Elves were considered bad luck on account that millions of them had been killed eons ago, but they didn't care. They treated him just fine anyway.

"Just fine," Aisir mumbled.

"What, buddy?"

Aisir snapped to and realized that he was standing on the dock. A man tying his small sailboat to the dock looked up at him fearfully.

"What's west of here?" Aisir asked.

"Fish," the man said.

"Past the fish," Aisir said.

"This about them slaves?" the man said.

"Yes and no," Aisir said.

"Look, I don't know what's out there, but that ain't no...It ain't no couple days sailing out if that's what it is. If there's an island out there, to the west, we're talking weeks or months of travel. We had a kid, a Wizard, come down here and say that a minute ago, but we don't know. I just don't know."

"Okay," Aisir said, turning around.

"That it?" the man called out.

Aisir kept walking. He wondered if Henbit would be able to look at him like he wasn't damaged goods because he lost his arm.

"What can I do for you, sir?"

Aisir came to in front of a supply store for sailors and fisherman. The shopkeeper was so tan he was crispy.

"You look nearly like a Red Elf yourself," Aisir said.

"That what you are? I was wondering," the man said.

"I'd like two barrels of water and a bag of dryshroom flour. A bag of boiled bread and a sack of dogapples."

"Okay," he said, "thirty silver sound fair?"

"Sounds fair."

"You want it delivered onto your boat?"

"No," Aisir said, "can you prepare it here and put it on a pallet for me? I only have one arm so I'll tie a rope to it and drag it."

"Okay," the man said. "When you need it by?"

"Anytime."

"Okay, give me a minute, I'll get it set out back."

Aisir thought about Henbit. He wondered if she would care about having a family. Elves could have children with humans, but because the offspring were sterile, most choose not to, because they want to have grandchildren. Half-elves have pretty hard lives and a lot of people don't want to be responsible for that.

Aisir shook his head and saw the pallet in front of him. He couldn't remember the man dropping it in front of him or how much time had passed. He took a deep breath and took a rope out of his bag and tied it to the cheap, driftwood pallet. He dragged the supplies all the way to the sailboat he had seen earlier. He rolled the two barrels of water into the bow of the boat and carried the dried food in on his back as he hopped in.

"That's not yours!" he heard a man yell at him. But the voice sounded faded, groggy. Like it was lost behind curtains or caught in a deep well. The sounds entered Aisir's head, but they didn't sound like anything to him. Just hollow voices.

He cut the rope with his sword as two men came running toward him.

"Thief! Thief! He stole my boat! The fucking Elf! The sneaky fucking fox ear! Fuck you! Fuck you!"

Aisir pointed his sword at the man and said nothing as the boat drifted away. He pulled the sails down and steadied the rudder.

"West," Aisir mumbled.

"What? Are you kidding me? What are you saying?"

"WEST," Aisir screamed with all his might.

Five hundred miles away, to the northeast, Henbit was meeting with the archaeologist, Rold, to give him the diamonds. He kept it quite cloak-and-dagger, which was particularly frustrating to Sugar, who kept ordering drink after drink to quell her agitation.

"Slow down," Henbit said.

"When's he getting here? What the fuck? Didn't he say sundown?" Sugar said.

"Sun's not down yet."

"It's close."

"Stop drinking," Henbit said. "After everything that went wrong, you think this will be easy? I mean, we were way in over our heads on this one—we lost Aisir, we almost lost O."

"Thank you, I didn't know what to do, so I kept breaking things. But then you came and—" O said.

"No sweat, no sweat, stop repeating it all, O, it's fine," Sugar said.

"Just slow down, and stop drinking, please."

"If it's a trap, then we're going to get got, okay, not much we can do about it now. Might as well be drunk if I go down," Sugar said, "and, by the way, if I pass out, O can just carry me. He's very strong."

"I could easily carry both of you if you choose to pass out at this time," O said.

The barmaid approached and placed three mugs of ale on the table.

"I didn't order anything," Henbit said.

"The man in the room with the red door upstairs got these for you," she said. "He said come up to pay your respects if you feel like it."

"Thank you," Henbit said.

The barmaid walked away.

"Well, it's either him or some pervert," Henbit said.

"Either is good," Sugar said. "I'm tired of waiting."

"I will pay my respects to the pervert," O said.

They all three stood and headed upstairs. The inn contained a single hallway on the second floor, about four doors on each side, all painted a different color. Henbit, holding her mug of ale but not drinking it, knocked on the door. It opened immediately, and a Snow Orc with a white mustache and a bald head waved them inside.

"I'm Rold," he said. "Let's be quiet, okay."

"Hello, Rold. I'm Henbit. This is my sister Sugar, and this is my friend O."

"I thought there was a fourth? I paid for four," Rold said.

Henbit looked at the floor and frowned.

"We don't—we don't know where Aisir is," Sugar said.

"Did he perish? Did you see him perish?" Rold said.

"No," O said.

"He went to a shrine, to help the River Orcs. He made an oath to them so that they would heal me," Henbit said, "then I left to look for these two after we all got separated. And that was the last I saw of him."

"This may sound blunt and uncaring, but may I see the diamonds?" Rold said, "Just follow me here, for a minute."

"O—okay," Henbit said, untying the bag from her belt and handing it to Rold.

He opened the bag enthusiastically. He tried to suppress his smile but it poked out of his mouth like his small, ivory tusks. He rolled a single diamond around in his hand.

"Marvelous, marvelous," Rold said. "Now, who was closest to Aisir, was it? I mean, emotionally?"

"Me," O said.

Sugar kicked him as Henbit looked sheepishly away.

"Her, then, I presume," Rold said. "Now, think about him. The last thing you remember."

Rold took the diamond and placed it into a small piece of silk. He flattened out the piece of silk on his dresser table and traced a pattern around it with his finger.

"Spit in my hand," Rold said, placing his palm toward Henbit.

"What?" she said, looking disgusted.

"Listen," Rold said, "magic never made any promises to us that it had to make sense. Just spit in my hand."

Henbit spit weakly into the pale, hairy hand of Rold, and he smeared it across both palms. His hands glowed blue for a moment as he held them directly above his hand in the air. Then he came down with both hands as hard as he could on the diamond, cutting into his hand, and a droplet of blood spurted out onto the silk and the diamond, and they all started to float an inch or two into the air.

"Oh, shit," Rold said.

"What? What is it?" Henbit said, worriedly.

"Smoke," Rold mumbled. "Anyone here smoke? I need some smoke to make this work. I forgot."

"I keep many different gases within various sacs in my body," O said.

"Exhale!"

O's crablike slit of a mouth parted and gray smoke flitted out onto the silk and the diamond. The smoke rested in the air above it, and a visage of Aisir started to form.

"No fucking way," Sugar said.

"He's alive," Henbit whispered.

"This is good news," O said, still emitting smoke.

"Look, though," Henbit said as the image started to clarify, "is that him? What happened to his arm?"

"It's gone," O said.

"But that's definitely him, sister, sorry. But he's alive. But where is he?"

"It appears he is on a boat," O said. "Look, you can still see the coast. Appears temperate. No swamp. Western Veti."

"He's sailing away," Henbit said. "Why?"

"Pahusk," Rold said.

"What?" Sugar said.

"Old land. Church isn't there, doesn't like to talk about it. Land of weird, scripted prophecies, written everywhere. Trees, hillsides, prophecies written in the dirt by the natives to be blown away by the wind and forgotten about and then come true anyway. Interesting, very interesting," Rold said, "some runaway slaves tried to settle it a few years ago, following a rumor. Made a little town. Some slave hunter burned it all to the ground, last I heard."

Henbit stood up.

"Thank you," she said, formally. "I would like my payment now."

"Of course," Rold said, scrounging around in his pockets, "seven hundred and fifty gold pieces."

It was the most money any of them had ever seen in their life. She took the sack of gold and tied it to her waistband and then tucked it into her pants. She nodded and left the room.

"Hold up, hold up," Sugar said, following.

"Let's go find him," Henbit said.

"Yeah, I mean—" Sugar said, frowning, "Let's go, okay, but don't storm off. Let me be the smart one this time, okay?"

Henbit pursed her lip and nodded. O lumbered out of the room with the red door and they all began walking downstairs.

Rold lay down in the bed with the pouch of diamonds resting on his belly. He exhaled, and closed his eyes for a few moments, thinking about how he would get back north from here and continue his experiments in solitude. He must have drifted to sleep, and the creaking of the door woke him up.

A man in a black-and-white outfit walked into the room. He had a black strip of cloth hanging down from his neck like a noose. Rold just stared, half awake.

"It's this one," the Company Man said.

A man in black leather rushed into the room and began to strangle the Snow Orc while The Company Man watched.

"Thank you, you did your part," The Company Man said as Rold's vision started to fill with blood.

The Company Man scooped the sack of diamonds off Rold's dead belly.

◆◆◆

EMERY WOKE UP SWEATING. Barrett's small trailer home couldn't really handle the heat of two human bodies inside of it, and the paltry window unit air conditioning lost to both the heat and the humidity. He groaned audibly and rotated himself into a sitting position on the couch.

"Jesus," Emery said, "I don't remember falling asleep."

"That's the point, right?" Barrett said, sitting at the small two-person table in front of the fridge. "Nobody remembers the moment they fell asleep."

"What time is it?"

"Almost sundown," Barrett said.

"What you been doing?" Emery said.

"Getting ready," Barrett said, "reading."

"Getting ready for what?"

Emery turned around and saw that Barrett's little kitchen table was covered in stuff. A shotgun; a rifle; a pistol; a large, matted tuft of hair; a big, disgusting yellow toenail; and about three empty cans of beer.

"What the heck is all this?" Emery said.

"These are guns. This is a chunk of hair I found behind my house. I think it belongs to the thing that killed your house," Barrett said. "Also, I got and drank some beers. You were out for a minute."

"Shit, I need to call the cops, call my insurance," Emery said, patting around the couch for his cell phone.

"You left it at the house, I think," Barrett said, "but wait, anyway. I'm going to go find the thing."

"Find what?"

"Bigfoot," Barrett said.

"What? You're pulling my leg," Emery said.

"No, sir," Barrett said.

"That stuff ain't real," Emery said.

"As real as your dead house," Barrett said.

"Well," Emery said.

"Yep," Barrett said.

"Got to be another explanation," Emery said.

"Maybe," Barrett said, "but this thing's been looking for me, I think, somehow. See, my daughter wrote about him. Or it. She died, a while ago, but I been reading her stuff and it's this thing and I keep seeing and I don't know how to make heads or tails of it so I'm going to take a bunch of guns to the woods and I'm going to find it and I'm going to see what's happening."

"I think, I think all my dogs are in the woods," Emery said.

"What?"

"My dogs," Emery said. "Lulu is the only one that came back. About two months or so ago, there was a storm, and they all ran away. And Lulu came back and she keeps trying to drag me in there. I've thought it was all so crazy, but I don't know. I been exercising to try to get my back healthy enough to go in there and—"

"I want to take your dog," Barrett interrupted. "I want her to smell the hair and find it. And you can come to, if you want, seeing as it is your property."

"So if it's been looking for you," Emery said, "is that why it destroyed my house?"

"Maybe," Barrett said. "It's been looking but it ain't. I've seen it, signs of it, and it came to my house once, I think. But it knows where I'm at. I think maybe it just wants my attention. I know it sounds crazy, but there's too many coincidences, all at once. And

I'm just too fucking stupid to parse it all out, I guess, but I figure, I'm tired, and whatever is about to happen to me will happen now if I just go in there and find out."

"All right," Emery said. "Let's just go then, before it's dark. Sun's going down now."

"Do me a favor," Barrett said.

"What is it?"

"Can you drive?" Barrett asked.

"Fine."

"I'm going to make a phone call," Barrett said, "then I'm ready."

◈ ◈ ◈

AMELIA HAD FOUND A nice bench in a small park on the banks of the Missouri River, which wound its way up from the southwest before the end of the line here, where it unloaded its silty waters into the Mississippi. She was too tired to think from thinking too much. She opened her daughter's book and read.

An excerpt from *The Riverside Ascetic*
by Edi Markham.

"I HAD A VERY specific idea of how I wanted this to go," Torbil said.

"How was it that you wanted it to go?" I asked.

"Not quite like this," Torbil said.

Torbil's black leather was matted red with blood. In all my weeks following Torbil I hadn't seen him injured once before. There were four members of a Vetian advance scout team at his feet. He had been caught off guard by trailers who had spotted us cross the Emerson Bridge. He kept a brisk pace and never expected an attack from behind.

"We're almost there," Torbil said. "I'll find someone on the way."

"Who?"

"It doesn't matter," Torbil said.

I remained quiet. I saw four dead men in the military purples of Veti dead at my feet.

"Did you see the fight?" Torbil asked.

"No," I answered, "I got thrown facedown when they rushed you."

Torbil grunted and dragged my chains. We marched for a few hours, not slowing. He stopped a few times at different intervals to pluck some leaves or flowers. He climbed and dragged me up a vertical sheet of rock at the border of Veti territory and made a small fire. He ground the flowers and leaves to a paste and matted his wounds with it.

"What's that?" I asked.

"Write it down. Whip leaves can clot your blood but only if you use the acid from Hagueflowers to draw out the mucus first. It works but no one believes me because I've killed too many people. Say you learned it from someone else," Torbil said.

"I can't do that," I said.

"Shut the fuck up," Torbil said.

He threw a clump of mud at my face and I remained still.

"Dumbass," he said.

He threw me some dried meat and I ate it wordlessly. He kept pulling a flask out and drinking it. I could smell the heat on his breath.

"You see that big slab of rock sticking out of that hillside? With the tents by it?" he asked.

I could only see a vague blur. My eyesight wasn't as sharp as his, I presumed.

"It's there," he said. "You know I'm going to kill the people guarding it, right?"

"I just watch," I said.

"You could warn them," he said. "I won't stop you."

I nodded.

"Dumbass," he sneered, "fucking nodding. Fucking mutilated piece of shit. You're still a man. You're still a fucking man like I am. Dumbass. Holy fucking idiot. You know, the Lake Boss told me a story that night. Before I killed him, when we were all hanging out, drinking. You know what he said?"

"No," I said.

"He said he was fucking a Recorder. Yeah, one of your order. Said that when it's just you and them they acted completely fucking different. Said the whole pretense dropped. So let's say that, hypothetically, you are the only motherfucker in your order actually following the fucking rules. And everyone else is lying, carrying on, being fucking NORMAL behind the curtain. Wouldn't you feel like the biggest fucking fraud in the fucking world? The fucking sucker who got sold a cart with no wheels? God, I mean, look at you. I was hoping for something interesting. You're the fucking biggest disappointment in the world. I mean, Lake Boss got to fuck his Recorder. That's crazy. That's what I said. I said, you're crazy, but he swore. He swore on his mom's grave. Which is a weird thing to swear on if you're talking about fucking, but still, damn. Fuck, what a disappointment you are. Surprise me!"

I remained silent. I tried to peer in the distance to see the slab.

"Come on," he said, abruptly standing up and swallowing, and slid down the hillside toward the camp.

We were onto it quicker than I expected. It was four leather tents positioned a few feet from the large, uniform slab of rock jetting out from the earth. The rock was adorned in writing, weird, archaic runes that crept from the very top to the very bottom. It must have been at least ten horses high.

"What does it say?" I whispered.

Torbil ignored me. He appeared to be setting some sort of trap in the underbrush, one with sharp metal teeth and a pressure plate. He set up another a few feet away immediately, and positioned himself right in between them. He pulled out a longbow and sat on one knee.

"Back away," he said.

I backed up about ten or fifteen feet. Torbil pulled a flask from his pocket and took a three-gulp pull.

"Warn them now or don't," he said.

I stood still, straight up. I wasn't hiding, so I was in full view of the camp. But I said nothing. Five seconds later, Torbil saw a man leave his tent. He walked a few feet away to a tree and began taking a piss. Torbil leveled an arrow into his ear and the man whipped around screaming. The blood shot out in a steady stream and the man spun around in circles unable to get his footing before collapsing into a tent. Torbil let out a scream in a strange language I hadn't heard before and loaded another arrow, but didn't move.

Four men came charging from a center campfire immediately. Torbil took down one with his bow and pulled out a shortsword. One man stepped into the trap, which activated and clamped down on his leg. As he screamed in pain the man next to him hesitated and Torbil stabbed him in the stomach. The last man got a small cut in on Torbil's arm. Torbil rolled backward and deftly jumped over the last trap, which the man barreled into. He fell to the ground as the bone spurted out of his caught leg. Torbil sneered and stomped the man's head in.

The last man was screaming in pain and begging Torbil for mercy.

"Please, please, please, please, please–" he said.

Torbil ignored him and looked straight at me.

"Do you want to know what it says?" Torbil screamed, "I've been fucking tracking this place down for fucking months, do you wanna know what it FUCKING says? Fuck! I'm the fucking reader! I read the language of the Gods! ME! The nastiest piece of shit you ever met; I'm blessed. I'm the blessed one, what a FUCKING joke of a universe. Fuck! I was hoping it wasn't this!

I was fucking hoping! But the world gets what it fucking wants, doesn't it! FUCK!"

"What's it say?" I asked.

"I'll only tell you, I'll only tell you the biggest fucking secret of the universe, the fucking prime cut of knowledge, if you fucking STOP ME FROM KILLING THIS GUY."

I gulped. I stared at him, mouth agape. I'm not sure for how long.

"SAY SOMETHING. Your code stands for acquiring knowledge. The farce is a means to an end. The code is a means to an end. Break it to get what you were meant for. Do something. Do anything, human."

"Tell me," I said.

"Say it," he said, patiently.

"I will," I said.

"So do it," he said.

"Spare his life," I said.

"Oh, my word," he said, putting the sword down. "I made you do it."

Torbil was blank faced. He looked around him in a wide berth before settling on the large rock covered in ancient symbols. He screamed in joy and started laughing.

> *"Now I'm down in this valley,*
> *Where the wheels turn so low*
> *At dawn I pray, to the Lord of my soul*
> *I say do Lord, do right by me*
> *You know I'm tired of being lonesome, ornery, and mean."*

"What does it mean?" I asked.

"It's wonderful," Torbil beamed, "I don't even care. I don't care. It could have said anything in the world. Absolutely anything. But the thing is, it's only for me. It's written just for me out of everyone in the whole world. That's why it's wonderful. Wow. Simply perfect. And you—you're just making this better. Good lord."

Torbil stomped through the camp, kicking over crates and peering inside the leather tents. He stopped at what appeared to be a trench dug into the side of the rock.

"Oh, looks like they've been digging," Torbil mumbled.

I trailed Torbil and looked through the remains of the camp. There were books everywhere—books that Torbil ignored. Books on metaphysics and divinity. Books on the Gods' crusade against the Elves. It looked more academic than militaristic.

"Boy, girl, whatever you are. Come here," Torbil yelled from down in the trench.

I hurried over to see Torbil lifting open a large, gilded gold treasure chest, bearing the symbol of the Kingdom of Veti. He removed from it a small, black case unlike anything I had ever seen before. He hopped out of the trench and sat down on the dirt above. The sound of the man I had spared struggling to escape from Torbil's trap was the only sound in the air. There was no hum of birds or bugs.

The small black case opened. Resting on some soft, alien material, was a metal object no bigger than a dagger. It was immaculately designed and smooth as a sword. There appeared to be some sort of tube, next to a handle and some mechanism at the bottom.

"What is it?" I asked.

"Says here—it is a Glock 17 Gen4 Semi-Automatic Pistol," Torbil said, reading the markings on the side of the case.

"What does it do?" I asked.

"Hold on—just…shut the fuck up for a second. Shut the fuck up, hold on," Torbil said.

He had grabbed a small scroll that was tucked into the top of the case and was reading through it greedily. Every time I made the slightest movement he turned to scowl at me, and I tried to remain as still as possible for the duration of his research.

"I take this, and I put—here they are—I put this in there, I pull this, and..."

Torbil made a myriad of movements decoding the metal object. He flipped switches and pulled on it strategically in an apparent unlocking of the mechanism in order to work. I still had no clue how it was done, but he appeared to know something I didn't. After a minute, he seemed satisfied, and turned smiling toward me.

"Go sit over there, codebreaker, betrayer of the Recorders," he said to me.

I stood up and walked to the center of camp, trying not to be sullen. He was right. I had violated my oath. I was not just a watcher. I was a player in the scenario. I had let myself be manipulated. I began to think of heading home to meet with the rest of the Recorders, reporting in, and letting them decide my punishment. I had no recourse to survive on my own, no skills, if they removed me from the order. The best I could hope for was to pledge myself to a local lord as a scribe, if they would even have me. By all means, my life had begun to feel muggy and clouded. I sat in the dirt as Torbil commanded.

He stood up with the metal mechanism in hand. He held it like a small crossbow, with one hand, and pointed the open end of the tube at me.

"Write down everything I am doing," he said.

I nodded. I opened my journal and wrote everything that had happened since we ambushed the camp. I wrote for a minute or two.

"Are you done yet?" he kept asking.

"Not yet," I said.

"Did you remember what the rock said?"

"I remember," I said.

"Good," he said. "I tell you what, I am just in a stupendous mood."

I wrote about the black case and the tube mechanism within. I wrote about sitting down. And I am writing this part right now.

"Okay," I said, "I'm caught up."

"Describe me," he said.

Torbil faced me with his back toward the gargantuan rock covered in an ancient, dead language. He called it the language of the Gods. He was wearing black leather that had been stained a bit with the blood of him and others. A few holes were clogged with matted plant matter. He had long, coarse black hair and steely brown eyes. He had a short mustache and a long goatee with the rest of his face covered in a short stubble. He wore a black rancher's hat and had a long, side-slung belt that was adorned in different types of short blades.

The skin of his face was cracked and red. One could see little flakes of dead skin on it. The harsh lines of age were starting to show under his eyes. He kept the tube level toward me and did not move, holding his pose with the outstretched arm aiming at me and his other arm resting on his belt.

"Okay," I said, "I described you."

"You sure? You done?" he said.

"Yes."

"Do you remember what I told you when I first met you?" Torbil said.

"Yes," I said.

"Write that down," he said.

When I first met the mercenary known as Ignatius Torbil, he told me that

⚫⚫⚫

THAT WAS IT. THAT was the end of the book. Amelia turned the page to see if there was an epilogue, a wrap-up, anything. Nope. That was the end of the book.

"Not bad," Amelia said.

Amelia breathed. She loved to have quiet moments to herself after finishing a book, to go on a walk or a drive, and just think. She looked at the river and watched the water flow by. Her lips pursed together, and she put her face in her hands.

"I'm very proud of you, wherever you are," Amelia said, "and I'll always love you very much. I love you so much, and I miss you more than anything. Oh, fuss, look at me."

Amelia wiped her eyes dry and got up. She shook off the emotions and grabbed her purse to walk away. She wondered what time it was, if she was late to meet Harper, and she checked her cell phone. She had a missed call and a voicemail from Barrett. She opened it.

"Hey, um, so, you were right about everything. I never really, well, could handle much, and I didn't try my best, I was just, I was just too hurt and I let everything go. Like, the sky fell, and I relished in it. Not out of enjoyment, but out of like, wallowing in my own hurt. It's a…it's addictive to just be that sad when everything feels that bad. And I know we went through the same thing and I figured we were done and I lost her and you and I wasn't the type of man that could like, I could love I mean, I know how to love, and I loved you and her with everything in me, I just…I'm just too flawed, too unable to help others, too much of a baby, and I just…let my life be over. Because, I mean, it was. It is. I've just been like…watching baseball and drinking for years now. That's just it. The years got away from me and I hid from the memories of you, too, and you were right, in a way, I was killing myself the boring way, just…choosing not to be alive. Not to be a person. And I just wanted to say you're right. And I love you. And the last few weeks have been hard as a whip. And I poked my head out of my bubble and started to try and feel stuff again and I really feel like I've completely lost my mind. I haven't been telling ya because I didn't want you to worry but

I want you to know what happened if something unusual happens. Because I been reading Edi's book and everything seems like a sign and I told nobody. I seen roadkill throw itself under my wheels, I seen a fucking bigfoot, can you fucking believe it. Seen her all through in that book she wrote. Henbit. That's her, and she loved an elf, and remember when we went mushroom hunting down in Iron County? And she, um, she came back with ice cream on her face and you yelled at me for spoiling the dinner you had been cooking? Well, I bribed her with that, because we found a shack, and there was a guy making meth and, he had a, well and I had to fight him, and I just hit—I knocked him out, and we just ran, I ran, I got her out of there, and I thought, you know, if you knew that, you'd kill me, and, that was the only real thing we did together, and if not that, I don't know, it's so stupid now, but she wrote about it, she wrote about a lot of places we were, and I always worried that like, she wasn't my daughter, not in that sense but in like, she was your daughter and I was just there, just the dad, and that we weren't as close and I read this book and I feel so close to her it hurts like I was there the whole time and I can feel my heart like this thermometer about to boil over in the heat and I don't know what to do, Amelia, I really don't, I fucking don't, I just see all this stuff everywhere, all this stuff that she wrote, in the book, and it's here, in my life, it's here and I'm seeing it with my own two eyes, and I think I know exactly where it is, the bigfoot thing she wrote about, it's here, and I'm sorry, but I got to know what it's all about, if she's the one doing this, sending this all to me, talking to me, or maybe if she just unplugged something in the earth that's more surreal and shouldn't exist but does and I got to look, I got to look, for her. I love you. I love you hard. And I never—I just hope that I was the one you wanted. Because if I ever deserved even an inch of your love I'm grateful. I love you, Amelia. I'm sorry."

Amelia was running north with pale, wide eyes. She had to find Harper and go home.

✣✣✣

Pig Iron (the Final Chapter)

"It's been two days since we landed on this island," Sugar said. "What if he isn't here?"

"It is very dry here," O complained. "I will need water soon."

"Just keep your eyes peeled," Henbit said. "he'll be here."

The three of them walked through the savannahs of Pahusk with the long, tan grasses brushing against their hips.

It was a strange island with thick air that felt rich with doom. There was writing everywhere, on the trees, in the dirt, on rocks, in so many different languages. It seemed like a nexus point for madmen everywhere, but the party had seen no people so far. They had only heard unseen scurrying around them at night, but no one ever emerged.

The midday sky grew dark, and Henbit felt the wind pick up.

"You're in luck, O," Henbit said. "It's going to rain."

O's little crab mouth flitted out a joyful noise like the shrillest note of a pan flute. Sugar drew her cloak over her head as Henbit stopped and peered around. Henbit heard the faintest sound on the wind, and turned to see a distant figure on a small hill about a mile away.

"What's that?" Henbit said, pointing to it.

"I cannot tell," O said.

"Is it Aisir?" Sugar asked.

"No...it's a goat," Henbit said.

"What?" Sugar asked.

"It's a sign," Henbit said, and confidently marched in its direction.

The goat slunk out of view. After a few minutes the rain started to fall hard on the savannah. The cracked earth drank it greedily and the tall grass was bowled over by the little shallow pools and streams that started to form from the excess. O's visibly desiccated body began to get full and unwrinkled itself in the summer shower. He emitted a small whistle of delight.

Henbit marched ahead. She crested the hill in eager anticipation. Sugar ran to catch up.

"You sure you know what you are doing?" Sugar asked.

"Yes," Henbit said.

"You didn't even seem to like the guy when we traveled together. You guys didn't say much. And now we're here, right? Like, now you love him or whatever? Is that it?" Sugar said.

Henbit said nothing.

"I didn't say anything, early on, you know, because I thought it wasn't my place. But you really don't have much experience with men, girl, and I feel like you might be going a little too all in just because, what? You both fought together? You survived together? He saved your life? That's good and all, but this...we're in uncharted territory, girl, and that's risky. Just...I don't want to see you get hurt. I'm supposed to be the impulsive, dumb, emotional one, right? I just don't want you to get hurt. I mean, what do you expect from this guy, anyway? Aisir is an elf, how would that even work?"

As the two sisters crested the hill they looked down on a low, unexpected grove. The hill dipped down into a shallow bowl of land that was beginning to flood. The tan grass that had adorned this island was now colored purple, and in the center of the clearing, ankle deep in water, were three figures.

It was Aisir, The Company Man, and Bigfoot, standing about fifteen feet away from each other in a triangle formation. They were about a quarter mile away from the party.

"Aisir!" Henbit yelled, and they all turned to look.

No one moved. The rain fell hard. Aisir had his sword in his hand. He yelled something, but Henbit couldn't hear it. He was too far away now.

"Aisir! Aisir! I'm here!" Henbit yelled, and started running forward.

As she ran, she saw Bigfoot reveal something from behind his back and throw it on the ground in front of Aisir. It was his severed arm. Aisir turned to Henbit, running toward him, still quite a distance away.

"I AM SORRY," Aisir screamed, "MAYBE IN ANOTHER LIFE, IT COULD HAVE BEEN NICE AND EASY."

Aisir turned away and took three steps toward Bigfoot. Bigfoot came forward and tried to grab Aisir, who darted to the side and went and took two low slashes at Bigfoot's ankles. The matted hair flew in the air as he doubled back around. The Company Man stayed still and started laughing. Bigfoot spun around and kicked Aisir, who went ass-over-elbows falling into the shallow water. He stood back up to see Bigfoot charging him again. Aisir slid between Bigfoot's legs as he came forward with his fists balled. Aisir doubled back, and Bigfoot raised his hand in the air and opened it. A purple mist formed in his palm and dissipated as birds started to coalesce in the sky above him. One by one, they started to dive-bomb at Aisir as he tried to deflect them with his sword, but they started to batter him as they fell lifeless into the water nearby. Bigfoot slowly walked up to Aisir as he caught his breath. His face was battered and misshapen as he attempted to stand.

Henbit was still running, but the water had slowed her. She steadied her crossbow from about three hundred yards. She breathed hard and wished. Wished for anything. It didn't even have to be a happy ending. Just close. Just close enough to him.

She pulled the trigger on the crossbow.

Aisir watched as the beast lumbered above him. Bigfoot raised his hand for the deathblow.

He mumbled, *I'm sorry*, while his yellow eyes looked right at Aisir. There was a true expression of agony there, behind all the hair, behind the violence. Aisir heard the slit of the air as the bolt flew, and Bigfoot's arm stopped as the bolt slid into the side of his neck. Aisir leapt up as he hesitated and buried his sword directly into his chest.

Bigfoot serenely crumpled to the ground, black blood dripping into the water. The Company Man laughed, his black-and-white suit sopping wet. And as Henbit ran forward, she saw The Company Man approach Aisir, pat him on the shoulder, and, in an instance of superhuman quickness, twist his neck around backward, killing him instantly. He turned around to face the party approaching.

"Everyone is right on time; everyone is right on time!" The Company Man screamed.

Henbit screamed. She shot bolt after bolt at the Company Man. He seemed to be able to easily catch them or sidestep them. O ran at him with his sword, swinging with futility. Sugar's magic didn't seem to be much help either; her eyes glowed green as she cast bolt after bolt at him.

"You're here! How do I do it! Everyone's here!" The Company Man screamed.

"Fight back! You demon! You murderer!" Henbit screamed.

"I didn't plan on anyone else having to die here today," The Company Man said, "and trust me on one thing, I only do what is necessary. For me and this world to survive. Oh, and look what I have here!"

Henbit, O, and Sugar paused as The Company Man pulled out the bag of diamonds. He stepped over to where Aisir and Bigfoot lay dead. He turned the bag upside down and poured them all over their dead bodies.

"I only needed one of you," The Company Man said, looking directly at Henbit. "It is nothing personal. Thank your boy for me when he wakes up."

"Wakes up?"

The sky cracked with lightning. The water was over their knees now, and moving was difficult. And the visage of the Company Man became hazy, partial. It moved uneasily but seemed to remain perfectly still. The sky cracked again with lightning, lightning that seemed like it never stopped. And each bolt came down from the sky over and over until it seemed like all the sky was nothing but lightning. And The Company Man took a step forward, and she blacked out.

Henbit woke up to the tranquil sounds of the ocean, all of her clothing filled with sand, lying down on the beach. And she turned to see the rough red skin of Aisir next to her, and she put her finger next to his nostrils.

He was breathing. And she, worriedly, turned to the ocean, and immediately decided that she didn't care about why or what. She didn't care at all. She laid back down and waited for him to wake up. Happiness is fragile. Henbit does not think. Just lie down. Just lie down.

THE END

◈◈◈

HARPER WAS WAITING BY the car with a few bags when Amelia came running toward her like a crazy person.

"What's wrong?" Harper asked, registering the mania immediately.

"Get in the car!" Amelia screamed.

"What?" Harper said, climbing in.

"Just—oh, my God. Oh, my God, Barrett's going to die! He's going to die!" Amelia screamed, climbing into the driver's seat.

"Wait—hold on, breathe, he's not going to die, okay, he's not, why do you think—"

"Crazy fucking voicemail, oh, my God, if you could even hear it, oh, my God, said he saw Bigfoot, roadkill killing itself, oh my God, if you could even hear it—" Amelia started, whipping the car into traffic.

"Hold up, you're going right past—the hotel! All my shit is in there! All your shit is in there! Okay, it can't be that serious, can it? Amelia? Amelia, talk to me," Harper pleaded.

"We lose our FUCKING daughter and he goes and gets all— all—whatever the fuck it is he is and now he thinks he can go and lose himself too? Like I'm not the one that has to go and fucking scoop up all the pieces? Like he thinks he can do this to me? He thinks this? I'm so mad right now oh my GOD I'm so mad," Amelia screamed.

"Okay, okay," Harper said.

"You want your stuff? Do you? You want your stuff, right?" Amelia said, sneering, turning the car around.

"No, no, it's okay, Amelia, I get it, it's scary—"

Amelia pulled into the motel parking lot. It was getting late and the orange sun cast it in a different light. The motel looked soft and comfortable, and Amelia pulled into a parking spot and slammed it into park. She dialed Barrett. No answer.

"Let's go, I'm sorry, I know, I'm being mean, ridiculous, I'm just worried, grab your stuff, I'll grab mine, did you get the clothes you wanted? You know, for school?" Amelia asked.

"Yeah, I did, thank you for driving," Harper said.

"Good, good, okay, okay," Amelia said, unlocking the door and grabbing her bag.

They were in and out of the hotel room in a few minutes. They scurried back to the car, Amelia breathing steadily and attempting to look as calm as possible. Harper worried and cast side glances toward Amelia as she drove in silence back to Armin. She kept waiting for Amelia to talk, and she didn't. Harper was usually uncomfortable with silence. Amelia, on the other hand, couldn't stop thinking about everyone she ever really cared about being dead, and just being left in the world after.

"I want to say something, and I'm worried, and I'm freaking out, and, I don't know if it is even fair to say it," Amelia said after a half hour of silence.

"You can say anything you want right now as long as it makes you feel better," Harper said.

"I—I don't know if it will make me feel better but I want to say it anyway," Amelia said.

"Okay," Harper said.

"So, if it's mean—"

"You're going to say it so just say it," Harper interrupted. "It's okay, I promise."

"But it'll make you sad," Amelia said.

"You don't need to preface everything, frontload it, just say it, okay?" Harper said.

"But it's not fair for me to say to a young girl with her life ahead of her and—"

"For fuck's sake, just say it!"

"Oh, my God, don't talk like that," Amelia said, aghast.

"Just say it. Please," Harper said.

"Okay. Okay," Amelia said.

"Just say it," Harper said. "The longer you wait the more I get worried."

"It's just not fucking fair," Amelia blurted. "It's not. The people you love, they get to grow with you, you get to see them, you get to love them, and they just die on you. They die because they are stupid or arrogant or unlucky and you are the real unlucky one because you just have to keep on living and the more that you live and others die you have to get stronger and stronger to keep helping everyone else. And you're never, ever allowed the luxury of being weak, because everyone is falling down around you. And you're young, Harper, girl. You're just a baby. And you've already tasted that salt and it makes me sick. And Barrett, God, dear God, don't let him die, I ain't been there but please, he's off his fucking rocker, he's in outer space, and you need to drag him down, because I can't, because I didn't see it, and I'm so stupid. I didn't see it and I knew it and I gave him those guns back because I was scared. I was scared. And what do you do? What do you do about the fucking worst, fucking darkest most evil things in the universe? You just watch them and drool? Oh, God, please. Please. If I was happy, if they were alive, I'd never have to ask. I'd never have to ask. I'd just be me."

"Pull over. You can't drive like this, you're crying, pull over, for a second, I'll give you a hug," Harper said, tears welling.

"I can't! I fucking can't! I got to drive!" Amelia said, crying.

And they both cried, driving down Interstate 70, crying as McDonald's after McDonald's passed them.

◆◆◆

EMERY PULLED ONTO SUPPLEMENTAL Highway QQ. He drove slow and clear and looked to the left up the hill to the woods where the sun started to change colors and crept down the foliage to the blacktop below. He envisioned his house, crumpled by timber. He felt neither sadness nor anger. He felt the order of things. Barrett sat in the passenger seat holding two guns.

Emery thought, *Nothing is that bad that ain't done by people.*

Emery pulled into his gravel driveway and saw his wrecked house.

"Lulu, come here," Emery said, sliding her belt on, "you either doing us a favor or you ain't. Been doing all that barking and fussing anyway, might as well smell out the big baddie."

Lulu whined. Emery opened the door as he put the truck into park, and Lulu nearly took his arm off darting out.

"Ah, fuck, ah, shit," Barrett whined, cheeks pursed, "we're here. Oh, God. Time to figure it all out or don't."

You got an idea of your life in the world and how it works and how people intersect with that and then you live it and figure out all the ways you were wrong. And when I got old enough I thought it wasn't about being wrong, but how you act when you were wrong because you were always wrong, right? With Amelia with Edi and with everything involved and then you think the only way not to be wrong is to lie down and lie down and lie your ass on down. And guess what? You were right, but you were fucking shitty and you sucked and hated your Goddamn life so hard and so palpably that you fucking dedicated it to beer and baseball. You were too late, weren't you? For her. You could have had something RARE don't you get it with all the fake fucking love in the world? WHAT IF YOU HAD IT WITH HER? REAL, RARE LOVE. AND YOU RUINED IT, BECAUSE GUESS WHAT?

THE WHOLE WORLD CONVERGED TO KILL YOUR LIFE WHEN EDI DIED AND NO ONE WILL EVER FORGIVE YOU FOR IT. AMELIA LEAST OF ALL BECAUSE YOU LEFT HER ALONE AND DRIED UP LIKE A WORM ON THE CONCRETE.

"Let me and the dog lead," Barrett said.

"Oh, I don't know, I don't know, the dog likes me and all, Lulu—" Emery started.

"Emery, you can just go home," Barrett said. "I got a bad feeling."

"There's nine more dogs in there," Emery said. "And I owe something to them."

"Dogs," Barrett said.

"Yeah," Emery yelled. "And so what?"

Barrett started walking into the tree line. The twilight had started to creep. From the west, beams of light bled into the woods and the thick overgrowth below. Yellow, orange, and red light eased through the foliage and cast a pale, warm glow on the woods. Emery and Barrett crept up with their old-ass bodies, being dragged all the while by Lulu, aware, barking her head off. Barrett climbed quicker than Emery, and Lulu, making such a fuss, broke free from Emery, rushing forward to the top of the hill.

Barrett tried to snag Lulu's leash as she ran by but she crested to the top of the hill, dodging his hand.

"Leave me," Emery said. "Just get the dog."

"Aw, shit," Barrett said. "Toughen up, you're being dramatic."

Barrett kept walking forward. It got a little steep at the end, and Barrett dug his knees and fists into the mud to force his way up the last part of the hill. He saw a small grave of rocks and stumps, surrounded by mushrooms, and he saw Lulu sitting patiently at the edge of the mountain down. He slowly crept over to pet Lulu, and heard a voice behind him the exact second he touched her head.

"Don't let him get up this hill," a man said calmly behind him.

Barrett fumbled for his gun and turned to point it at a man in a clean-pressed suit. Black and white, no wrinkles, as sharp—if not outdated—as could be.

"How am I supposed to do that?" Barrett asked.

"You're resourceful," he said.

"Who are you?"

"You remember me. On the road. 'Mr. Mann,' you said," he said.

"What are you doing up here? Do you—do you know—"

"Aren't you tired of metaphors?" The Company Man said, "keep looking. It isn't personal. Nothing that has happened is."

Barrett approached the man with the pistol, and he leveled it right in the center of his forehead. He stared at the man hoping for a response. He felt the saliva roll around in his mouth. He held the gun there, pressed against the skin of the man's head, for a very long time.

The smell hit. Barrett looked downward as his nose curled. He was surrounded by the long desiccated smell of nine dead dogs, ripped open, torn asunder, by forces beyond understanding.

"Your man gets here," The Company Man said, "Barrett, lights out, for a very long time."

"Gimme a minute," Barrett mumbled, withdrawing the gun.

"Lulu is gone! Think! Think!" The Company Man said, unsmiling.

Barrett looked over to the edge of the hill. He saw Emery creeping forward very slowly, nearly falling.

"Emery," Barrett said.

"What?"

"You just...you gotta go. You gotta go home," Barrett said.

"Where's Lulu?" Emery said.

"Say something he will actually believe," The Company Man said. "The thing I've learned, in this desperately short amount of time, is that the thing that people want to hear is exactly what they want to hear. And then they'll do whatever you say."

"Emery. Lulu went down the other side of the hill, east. She collapsed. You can get to her bud. Just get her and save her. I got something up here. I'll find your dogs, I promise. I swear to God. Get her and go home. I got this," Barrett yelled down the hill, soaked in twilight.

"Attaboy," the Company Man said.

"All right, all right, I got you. Get my boys home!" Emery said, clambering across the hill, looking for Lulu.

"Nothing but time now," The Company Man said.

"What are ya?"

"If I tell you what you want is down there and it won't be later, does it matter?" The Company Man said.

Barrett turned to hear Lulu bark in the distance. The base of the hill was covered in water, which meant that the river had swept over Highway Q.

"So I ain't smart, I ain't wise, I'm not too good at this stuff, right? But I pay attention. And I been around and paid attention and looked around and thought about what was and wasn't and I'm smart enough to what is and what isn't and you are what isn't and I just want to know what you have to say about that?" Barrett asked the Company Man.

"You're the first person around here to get it," The Company Man said, smiling. "You're right. I'm what isn't. So is what is down there."

"So, what are you doing? I mean, really?" Barrett asked.

The Company Man's face twitched. His eyes widened and he did not blink.

"I'm dragging the deer off of the side of the road so that nobody gets hurt," he said.

Lulu barked again, and the bark turned into a squeal. Barrett turned from there to The Company Man who cast his eyes wide in the direction of the suffering.

Barrett started marching down the hill, heel first, trying his damnedest not to fall.

"Thank you for getting me out of here," The Company Man shouted down the hill.

᛫᛫᛫

"FUCK! WHERE'S HIS TRUCK!" Amelia cried, pulling into the gravel of Barrett's driveway.

"Did he say anything?" Harper said.

Amelia buried her hands in her face. She was too tired. She exhaled and inhaled the appropriate amount of times and started to put the car in reverse. She moved backward and whipped the car around to face the highway.

"I'm taking you home," Amelia said.

"You shouldn't be alone," Harper said.

"I shouldn't be putting this on you," Amelia said.

"I want to be here," Harper said.

"I'm old," Amelia muttered. "I'm the responsible one."

Harper said nothing. She stared at the bridge that stretched from Howe County to Duden County. It was a big fancy thing built from government money. It lit up pretty at night, and just as the sun turned sour, it lit up in big pretty white lights.

"Would you look at that," Amelia said.

"It looks nice," Harper said.

"You'll remember stuff like that bridge. I remember it being built. We all thought it was a metaphor," Amelia said, laughing, "and the next day, everything was the same."

"Maybe that's your fault," Harper said. "Seems silly to blame a thing like that on a bridge."

"Let's get you home to Rose," Amelia said, "she owes me some gift cards."

"Can I stay with you?" Harper said, "I'm worried."

"I'm worried…what would happen if something did happen?" Amelia said.

"Okay," Harper said. "Okay. I can't convince you. Just be okay."

She drove Harper back to her old house and dropped her off. Harper knocked on her door. Amelia did not stop to see if she got inside. Amelia drove to the Tin Nickel to look for his car. When she saw it, she wanted to cry. She went to tear the hinges off of the doors of the Tin Nickel until she saw it was closed. She looked around in desperate circles. She heard a moan from the west, and saw that the river flooding had crept in over the airport and over the Q. And she just looked in the direction of the moan and knew she was too late. She swallowed the perdition-like prophecy and watched the ichor of that brown river spill slowly over the road.

Amelia looked into the woods and tried to stay strong until she didn't see the point.

A mile away, Harper was sitting on her family's couch, clutching her knees to her chest, thinking.

Amelia is the strongest woman I've ever met, I think, she thought.

⸭⸭⸭

Barrett walked down the hill with his hands in his pockets. He was unconcerned for a dog. He wasn't worried about a man. He bore the whole weight of prophecy upon his head as a gift to himself. God, was it heavy. What a world. When things like this make the fabric so wrinkled. Everything got fuzzier and fuzzier. The world felt like some eye contacts on backward. He couldn't trust his vision. He trusted feelings and smells.

Barrett didn't feel at home until his ankles hit the water. Wow! How they made sense. Everything unsaid, right?

Just like Aisir at the end of the book. Honey, he killed him. He did it and you lived happily ever after? And Bigfoot died and he was sad and enviable in many ways, right, but guess what he was destructive and mean and awful and he carried around dread with him like it was a fucking boombox and guess what it was him right it was him it was him? Same guy? Same guy as now?

As Barrett hit the water he drew out his shotgun from the satchel hoisted on his shoulder. It felt good. It felt like a smell, moving slow, ending in a gratifying ah! Guess what, buddy, you got a life in your hands.

Guess what, buddy? You got a life in your hands, you just don't know whose yet. Holy shit, you're God, ain't you? Just like your little girl was?

Huh, yes, you cast light onto the world just like she did and your thoughts are more powerful than anything because it turns out we all had the power to just change things around us, huh? You showed me the initiative, huh, and now I'm gonna figure it out for you! All for you! I miss you so much, you know that! You'll always be my baby girl and it's time to figure out why you left so much behind to find me.

A picture: a fracture. The water was about a foot high cresting over what foliage it could with the only thing escaping the dirty water were the tree trunks, necks outstretched, metaphorical teeth clenched. Barrett didn't hear any dogs. He only smelled the low dank stench of complete dog shit that he knew from the first encounter with the thing his daughter wrote for him to find. He kept his shotgun close to the chest, not necessarily desperate to stay alive but with a hard heart wanting to keep his daughter relevant. Wanting to unwrap the gift she lay before him.

IT WAS ONE STEP!

That was the one. It appeared.

It was a man that was nine feet tall and covered in hair. It was close, close enough to smell instantly. The speed of smell was slow so that meant it was close. The light was fading. It went from orange to red to purple and bounced right off the water straight into your eyeballs. The color of creamsicles and raspberry sorbet in the sky, bouncing mockingly off the rancid water below. And there, casting a shadow from the backdrop like a wild west hat, was the thing. Bigfoot. The large, bipedal North American Forest Ape. Either born from or witnessed by Edi Markham.

The yellow teeth and the benign cysts hidden behind the coarse brown hair. The beast stood in place, wavering slightly. Barrett imagined music as he looked at Bigfoot. It was sporadic, unsettling banjo music. He heard some crickets flaring up around him.

Good lord, you go out of your very mind for life, right? Everything you ever wanted or planned for another person, and then what, it's gone, and there's something else, just dread, bitterness, flinching at the world, mad at other people for their dreams, for their happiness, for their satisfaction. It's worse and more putrid and vile than you could ever imagine because you got that taste of satisfaction years ago. It warmed your tongue and plunged it into eternal ice. Don't you hope to smell death when you flinch? Wouldn't that make it mean something?

"Hey, buddy," Barrett yelled. "Don't you hope to smell death when you flinch? Wouldn't that make it mean something?"

A large, bipedal ape that was about nine feet tall squared up to face him about twenty feet in front of Barrett.

"I'm sorry," Barrett said. "It's been hard."

Bigfoot stared at his feet and grunted. Barrett stared at the ground. He whimpered at his question with his chin down and his eyes crested upward.

Barrett asked, "Listen, did you know Edi? Did you know how much she wrote about you? What she...I don't know, thought about? That you might, shit, that you might be like, beyond most peoples' understanding? Fuck, fucking hell, fuck, does it ever worry you that everyone is beyond your understanding, and that just, well shit, maybe happy people are better at faking it better? Or maybe they just don't care? God, if I could go to school to understand everything, be kind, be decent, I'd know some shit, I hope, and I wouldn't lie. I wouldn't. I promise if I knew it that I wouldn't lie or be mysterious about it. I don't know. I don't know why I'm saying this. I saw you that night. You were by my home, in the back, by the cliff. I don't know if you sent for me, or if you was just peering off my cliff looking at the river. Do you know Edi? Did you ever know of her?"

Bigfoot let out a groan. Barrett didn't know how to interpret it.

"Well," Barrett yelled, "you have to give me something. You gotta. I found you. You looked for me and I found you. And this can't just be it. I heard you were the one and only, right? That's not okay. You can't leave me high and dry. That's not. That's not okay. Tell me now, what did Edi tell you? I know she knew you. You had to sense something. This can't be the end of the road."

There was thirty seconds of silence. Bigfoot let out a slow, cool moan.

"You gotta tell me, Bigfoot, this isn't a thing, this, okay, this isn't a deal. This isn't a deal. This isn't a deal. You are not—okay. This isn't a deal."

Bigfoot stared right at Barrett with its yellow eyes.

"You gonna make me beg you like a dog," Barrett said.

Bigfoot's eyes got big as eggs, and he stared off into the distance, at the western sun.

"That ain't good enough," Barrett said.

Bigfoot moaned.

"You took her," Barrett said.

Bigfoot moaned.

"You just think you take, take, take, and then, guess what, you got to tell a person why you take, take, take," Barrett said.

"No," Bigfoot said.

Barrett took the shotgun and aimed it at Bigfoot. Bigfoot remained still, unaware of the context. He watched the tube until he was sure it wasn't food, after about four seconds. Barrett pushed it closer.

"Could I even kill you right now?" Barrett asked.

Bigfoot grunted.

"I wish you could kill me," Barrett begged Bigfoot.

Bigfoot said nothing.

"Do you remember Edi?" Barrett asked.

"Edi," Bigfoot moaned.

"What do you know?"

Bigfoot turned.

"Don't you dare," Barrett said.

Bigfoot turned to walk away.

"You can't," Barrett said.

Bigfoot sloshed through to head to dry land.

"Say something," Barrett pleaded.

"Aughhh. Eughhhhhh," Bigfoot said.

"I ain't gonna find you for nothing! You understand, you big fucker! I didn't go through all this for nothing! I got you! I got your ass! I got a bead on your ass, and I'll fucking bury you! It can't be just this, right! It can't! Tell me it can't!" Barrett yelled.

Barrett marched behind the large, bipedal North American forest ape, teeth gritted. The backdrop of the pretty sky faded as he marched out of the water onto the land. Bigfoot walked with an incredibly slouched posture, the back of his hairy hands nearly scraping the ground, head held low.

"I thought this is like, the one thing that couldn't happen. I...I lost it all. I lost my daughter and my wife and that's all I ever really had that I wanted. I'm not going out like this. You have to give me something, anything. She didn't tell you to say nothing? No message? No note? Nothing? I got nothing, you get it? I can't walk out of these woods, you hear, and go back to the black-and-white version of my life. I can't," Barrett pleaded.

The large, bipedal forest creature whined lowly and kept walking.

"I can't. I can't. I can't go back with nothing," Barrett said, quietly.

Barrett pointed the shotgun at Bigfoot's head and pulled the trigger. His hair, skull, and brain painted the tree trunks and dead leaves of the forest floor. Whatever purple convalescence was around him died instantly and Barrett remained holding the smoking shotgun as the remnants of Bigfoot fell onto the wet forest floor like piles of dog shit. And as Barrett began to register his actions, he thought of Edi, he thought of Amelia, and his lips turned fragile. There was an enormous, hairy body lying in front of him, mostly without a head, and Barrett kept staring at it, waiting for it to say something.

The brown river, in the black of the night, swallowed up all of the stars out of the sky.

THE END